ABOUT THE AUTHOR

Sam Youd was born in Lancashire in April 1922, during an unseasonable snowstorm.

As a boy, he was devoted to the newly emergent genre of science-fiction: 'In the early thirties,' he later wrote, 'we knew just enough about the solar system for its possibilities to be a magnet to the imagination.'

Over the following decades, his imagination flowed from science-fiction into general novels, cricket novels, medical novels, gothic romances, detective thrillers, light comedies... In all he published fifty-six novels and a myriad of short stories, under his own name as well as eight different pen-names.

He is perhaps best known as John Christopher, author of the seminal work of speculative fiction, *The Death of Grass* (today available as a Penguin Classic), and a stream of novels in the genre he pioneered, young adult dystopian fiction, beginning with *The Tripods Trilogy*.

'I read somewhere,' Sam once said, 'that I have been cited as the greatest serial killer in fictional history, having destroyed civilisation in so many different ways – through famine, freezing, earthquakes, feral youth combined with religious fanaticism, and progeria.'

In an interview towards the end of his life, conversation turned to a recent spate of novels set on Mars and a possible setting for a John Christopher story: strand a group of people in a remote Martian enclave and see what happens. The Mars aspect, he felt, was irrelevant. 'What happens between the people,' he said, 'that's the thing I'm interested in.'

ALSO PUBLISHED BY THE SYLE PRESS

Hilary Ford

Sarnia

A Bride for Bedivere

John Christopher

The White Voyage

SAM YOUD *as*
JOHN CHRISTOPHER

CLOUD
ON
SILVER

THE SYLE PRESS

Published by The SYLE Press 2018

First published in Great Britain in 1964
by Eyre & Spottiswoode

Cover design by David Drummond

ISBN: 978-0-9927686-6-9

www.thesylepress.com

1

IT WAS A BIG PARTY, in a big room, but Sweeney was very much in evidence, towering above his guests. He was four inches over six feet in height and broad with it, massive in shoulders and chest and, in the last few years, increasingly so in girth. His head was in proportion, the neck jowling, large grey eyes contemplative under heavy black brows flecked with white. His hair was thick, wiry, curling a little, black on the crown and white-winged. His nose was slightly kinked: he had broken it boxing as a schoolboy, twenty-five years before, and although no expense had been spared in the setting, the mark remained.

The party was being held in his house in Bishop's Avenue, a modern Georgian-style mansion built in the thirties by his father, from whom, as the only son, the solitary child of a late and unhappy marriage, he had also inherited the shipping millions, and the minor, though still considerable, oil interests. It was a mixed bag, such as he enjoyed having around him. There were senior civil servants, a junior Cabinet Minister and a couple of Private Secretaries, directors of major industrial concerns, a senior executive in commercial television: members of the Establishment of power and wealth. But, in addition to those, there were others – an American television star currently appearing at the Palladium, a middle-weight boxer shortly to be a contender for the world title, two lady novelists in high critical favour, a painter of note, a duchess of notoriety, a comic actor who was a household word. And there was a third group of people not particularly powerful nor influential, not particularly rich nor famous; in many cases the reverse. It was among this group that Sweeney moved, towards the end of the party, bending down courteously from his great height and speaking to them quietly. One of these was Joe Willeway, a soft-looking man in his middle thirties, himself about six feet tall. He looked up at Sweeney, smiled and nodded.

Roger Candie, undeniably belonging to the third group, watched this over the shoulder of the wife of one of the Parliamentary Private Secretaries, a short, plump woman who was a tribute to her husband's ability in having gone so far despite her. She talked quickly and continuously, needing only the occasional affirmation of a smile or a nod. Candie had attracted such women before and was skilled in getting rid of them, but at the moment depression unnerved him. His hopes for the evening had been high: Sweeney had told him the television executive producer would be there, and had hinted that he might be able to influence him on the casting of an important new drama series. They were looking for a male lead, and Candie might be the type. Candie most certainly needed the job, any job. He had done his little tricks for the executive producer, and the producer had smiled coldly and nodded and turned away.

Thinking of this, he considered Sweeney and his own feelings about him. Did he hate him, admire him – what? Sweeney was too big, in various ways, for feelings to be negative, but neither were they positive in any ordinary sense. Sweeney was one of a number of people who, in the past, had provided Candie with free drinks and food, occasional accommodation, but he was different from the others. There was no need, with Sweeney, to pay back in forced charm, sycophancy. It was not possible, even. Sweeney gave, asking nothing, not seeming to recognize the existence of the gifts. And therefore it was not possible to despise him, as one despised the others one exploited. Resentment, of course, was another thing. He wondered if he resented Sweeney, and decided that he did. Some of the time.

Sweeney moved towards a tall angular blonde, whom Candie had seen before at the house, but whose name he had forgotten. With careful ease he detached her from her group, spoke briefly, received an affirmation and went smiling on his way. The wife of the P.P.S. chattered on, waving her gin and tonic and spilling some of it. Candie offered her a handkerchief and she mopped her arm without stopping talking. Sweeney had let him down, Candie decided. There had been a distinct implication that he would go to work on the executive producer; and he had done nothing beyond the bare minimum of introduction.

The small plump woman returned his handkerchief, and he pushed it back into his breast pocket.

'Thank you, Roger,' she said. She had gone to first names without batting an eyelid and kept on using his as though afraid of forgetting it. 'Have you known Sweeney long?'

It was a question, not a resumption of the monologue, and, as a constitutionally polite young man, he was obliged to make some response.

'A year or two.'

'He knows so many people, doesn't he?'

'Yes.'

'And so many *important* people.'

'I suppose.'

'Henry was telling me that he mentioned something about a rather hush-hush thing at the Ministry – very obliquely, you know, no details – and it was quite obvious that Sweeney knew all about it. Really all.'

Henry would be the husband, the slim nervous chap, Candie thought, talking earnestly to Gwen Bailey, whom he had once known in his own kind of poverty in Notting Hill, but who was now a lady announcer and married to someone in toffee. He nodded, in reflection on the fates of man and woman.

'And Growton – he's with the Mirror group – was saying much the same thing. The best-informed dilettante in Europe, he called him – if not the world. It's strange, isn't it, that he's never gone into politics or anything?'

Candie said, forgetting about her husband for a moment: 'He would probably find it boring.' Remembering, he added:

'He would find anything boring he had to stick to. Isn't that what dilettante means, anyway? Sweeney's good at amusing himself, but then he rings the changes.'

He saw Sweeney approach Tony Marriott, and go from him to a small, auburn-haired, cosy-looking girl whom he did not remember seeing before. It was plain that some kind of selection was taking place, that from the milling members of this cocktail party Sweeney was picking a handful, discreetly, for something else. To go on, perhaps, to a supper party with him. Inescapably, Candie brooded on his own chances, concluded that they were small, and returned the major part of his attention to the woman who was chattering in front of him. She was speculating now on why Sweeney had never married. There were rumours, of course ...

'There always are,' Candie said. He spoke curtly, more so than he had intended. 'And people to invent them, and more to pass them on.'

He spoke not particularly to defend Sweeney – it was difficult to think of Sweeney as being in need of defence – but because, despite the years he had spent on the unsuccessful fringe of the acting profession, malicious gossip always upset him. A relic, perhaps, of Aunt Lilian in Cheltenham, of those past and dead but not forgotten afternoons of tea parties and imprisonment. He saw her again now, and hated her again.

'Oh, yes,' the wife of the P.P.S. said hastily, 'I do so agree with you, Roger. Personally ...'

She flowed on and Candie gazed, past her right ear, at a distant group, among whom the executive producer was plainly enjoying himself. It might be possible to ring him, of course. 'Probably you don't remember me – we met at Sweeney's the other night – yes, great chap, Sweeney – I was wondering whether ...?' The imagined talk faded away in improbability. Just another of Sweeney's hangers-on: it fitted without a wrinkle. But Sweeney himself could have done something. That would have been easy enough.

Candie felt pressure on his shoulder, a familiar pressure, and half turned to look up at Sweeney, who smiled across him at his companion.

'Madge,' Sweeney said, 'I'm taking you away from this chap. Colonel Bleeker here wants to meet you.' He had a voice that was deep but without resonance; the words came out flat, emphatic through lack of emphasis. 'A member of the constituency, so you need to be nice to him.'

Candie watched the introduction, relieved to be rid of her. Presumably, he should move on, but there had been a brief look from Sweeney which now kept him in his place. He sipped his brandy and ginger ale, and thought gloomily about his financial position. Six weeks' rent due on the room, and an overdraft at the bank at least fifty pounds above the level old Wilkinson had stipulated. It might not be a bad idea, before he got landed with someone else, to go foraging for canapés. He liked to show moderation in company, but it ought to be possible to find an unattended tray and fill up quickly. The alternative was buying something on the way home – drinking always sharpened his appetite.

Sweeney, the introduction completed, stood in front of him, his face calm with a trace of a smile. 'Roger,' he said, 'I've been looking for you.'

'I'm here, Sweeney.'

Another stab at the producer? It was depressing how swiftly, as well as eternally, hope sprang in the human breast.

'Can you stay on after?' Sweeney asked. 'Nothing elaborate. Just a cold snack.'

Not what one wanted, but better than it might have been. That was the prescription, Candie felt, for his life. At any rate, no need for surreptitious grabs at the tray of canapés, bolting things down with one eye alert for who was watching. And the cold snack might well be game pie, Scotch salmon, pheasant ...

He said warmly: 'Thank you, Sweeney. I'll be glad to stay on.'

2

Toni Marriott came over to her husband, Tony Marriott, and looked up at him in a way that still excited him more than a little. Though perhaps that had something to do with the drinks which, as usual, had been generous. She said:

'Time we got on the road, darling?'

Slim, dark, certainly the best-looking woman in sight; and bedroom-eyed with it. No, not merely the gin. Whatever his other failures, he had done well in the matrimonial stakes: there was no denying that. He felt like taking her off to one of the many empty upstairs rooms in Sweeney's mausoleum. Perhaps he would do, later. Sweeney wouldn't mind.

'We're to stay on, honey,' he said. 'A spot of supper in prospect.'

She nodded. 'Who else, do you know? Anyone O.K.?'

By 'O.K', she meant useful. Marriott said:

'I rather doubt it. I saw him asking Roger Candie.'

Toni shrugged. 'Ah, well. I think I'll go and powder my nose. Things seem to be thinning out.'

As things continued to thin out, to a point where the ones remaining were clearly the members of Sweeney's impromptu supper party, Marriott found himself confirmed in his pessimism. The Willeways, like Candie, he had met here before. Joe Willeway, it was true, was well off – rich, even, by other than Sweeney standards. That aunt of his had left him upwards of seventy thousand the year after he qualified as an architect. Since then he had put up a pretence of practising, but his chief interest lay in looking after his capital. The meanest men in the world, Marriott decided, were the ineffectual men of independent means. Willeway was no more use to him than Candie, and Candie was no use at all. A dead-beat and a sponger. He made his own relationship with Sweeney look good. Admittedly, when he had engineered the Brixton property deal he had thought Sweeney might be going to take a beating on it. But Sweeney had known more than he had, and Sweeney had come out on top with a fat profit – probably ten times the commission he himself had made. He wondered whether it was worth while putting Arrowsmith's proposition up to Sweeney, if he could get him on his own later. He decided, regretfully, that it wasn't. Sweeney, he knew now, was too fly a bird, and anyway the deal was too small to be worth jeopardizing a link that, somehow, some day, was going to pay off.

He considered the remainder of the party with quite a different eye. Katey Willeway, for instance. She was beginning to put on weight, and he had never cared for women with blue eyes and hard mouths, but it was fairly obvious that there was nothing much left between her and Willeway, and that she might, under the right circumstances, be amenable. File that for reference and opportunity. Of the other two women, there was one he had met before: the tall, somewhat angular blonde, Lydia Petrie. Father Sir Graham Petrie, second or third baronet, late Victorian creation following heavy contributions to Tory Party funds, following some kind of carve-up in India. Thought a hell of a lot of herself, rude as hell when she felt like it, but one never knew … No, he decided, too much trouble, and you could never be certain what was going to happen when she opened her mouth.

The other girl was quite new to him: rather small, hair a deeply rich auburn, a general look of homeliness in the nice sense. Blue eyes, but a warmer blue and nothing at all hard about her mouth. Candie was talking to her, and she was listening well. Not beautiful. Pleasant looking, and clearly there would be a modesty which it would be sheer delight to overcome. Not to live with – he thought of Toni with appreciation

– but on a short-term basis … distinctly rewarding, he would say. He moved across the room, and ranged himself beside Candie.

'Hello, Roger,' he said. He smiled at the girl, with a nod, almost a small bow. 'I don't think we managed to meet, in all that throng. I'm Tony Marriott.'

'Susan Malone.'

Her voice was small and husky, the accent a touch provincial – north Midlands? He said:

'I take it you're staying for scoff, as well?' She nodded. 'How do you come to know Sweeney? Stage? Television?'

She could not possibly be either, but most girls found the suggestion flattering. She shook her head, and he thought she blushed a little.

'Nothing like that. I'm just a technical journalist.'

'Technical journalist? Has Sweeney got a finger in that pie as well?'

'He's interested in science and technology. And he knows my boss very well. We met at a party given by the magazine. I can't think why he asked me here.'

Marriott smiled, looking into her eyes. 'Sweeney has an eye for interesting people. Let me organize another drink for you.'

She shook her head again, very firmly this time. 'No more, thank you. The barman pours such strong ones, doesn't he?'

'I could organize a very weak one. I have some influence.'

'No, not even that.'

Candie said: 'I was putting the same notion up to her just before you arrived, Tony.'

'Yes,' Marriott said, nodding. 'She looks like a girl whose mind stays made up. Well, my nature is weaker altogether.' He made a waving gesture at one of the waiters. 'Ah, that's my wife bearing down. You must meet her, Susan. Toni, this is Susan Malone.'

It was even more pleasant, he thought, watching the female reactions to Toni than the male ones. And, undeniably, it helped. To attract a man over the competition of a wife like that … it was something that really brought out the competitive instinct. Good old Toni.

Sweeney appeared, made a gesture of negation to the approaching waiter, and the waiter turned away. Sweeney said to his guests:

'I think we can go in now.' He looked them over, his glance tracking but taking in each face. 'We seem to be all here.'

An elaborate cold buffet had been laid out in the dining-room. Marriott waited until the ladies had been served, and then made his own selection. The choice was wide and many of the items exotic: the caviare was Caspian and heaped in gleaming black piles, the Scotch salmon elaborately decorated in aspic. Marriott contented himself with cold ham and beef. Food did not interest him very much. He refused champagne, and took a lager. He went with his plate to where the girl Susan was already sitting in one of the large window seats, and sat beside her. It looked like a cold blowy evening outside, but Sweeney's air-conditioned central heating lapped them round.

It was not as easy as he had hoped to engender the same snugness between them. She was not unfriendly, but not at all welcoming either. Her replies tended to be short, offering small purchase to his efforts. None of this, however, deterred him. Shyness, he had always felt, offered great rewards to someone applying courtesy and warmth and, above all, persistence. He went on talking to her, ignoring the lack of response.

There was some kind of ice-cream pudding which Marriott did not have, but he brought Susan's to her. He watched her take a mouthful and asked:

'Is it good?'

'Very good.'

'Feed me a little.'

She hesitated. 'You could get some.'

'I'd like to try it first.'

The hesitation was still evident, but she spooned some up

9

and offered it to him. He took the spoon between his lips with lingering deliberation.

'Not bad,' he said. 'But I haven't really got a sweet tooth.'

She looked at the spoon, and he wondered if she would have the courage to do as she so plainly wanted – put it down and leave the rest of the pudding untasted. He made a small bet with himself, and won. She dipped the spoon in, and ate a few more mouthfuls before she laid it down.

'Not quite as good as it seemed at first?' Marriott suggested.

'No.' She shook her head. 'Would you excuse me a moment?'

He watched her go with appreciation, and not without satisfaction. It would be easy enough to find out from Sweeney what magazine she worked on. After that – well, it would be interesting at least.

The waiters left after they had brought coffee to the drawing-room, which looked out on to a lawn whose shrubs were lit in various ways. From the Wharfedale speakers, bedded in concrete in the corners of the room, stereophonic Mozart issued with sweet clarity. Susan had found herself a seat away from Marriott, between Candie and Katey Willeway. Her shoes were off, her legs curled up beneath her. She looked very pleasant, he thought.

Sweeney said: 'Black coffee and pleasant company: the best way to round off an evening.' He glanced over them again, his gaze going from one face to the next. 'I'm glad you were all able to stay for supper. There is more to it than that, though.'

Willeway said: 'We can't stay much longer, Sweeney. It's a long drive back, and we've had a few late nights lately.'

'I won't keep you,' Sweeney said. 'Not at the moment. But I have a suggestion to make. I am thinking of doing a little cruising, in sunnier waters. I hope you will all find it possible to join me.'

'Next year?' Willeway asked. 'It's a bit early to start making plans, surely?'

Sweeney said pleasantly: 'Not next year. Next week.'

Marriott said: 'Count us out, I'm afraid. Can't spare the time for holidays until the exchequer builds up a bit.'

'Now, consider,' Sweeney said. He ignored Marriott and turned to Candie. 'I believe you are what is known as resting, Roger. Is that right?'

'At the moment, yes, but I'm hoping …'

'Deferring hope three or four weeks does not mean abandoning it. You can rest more comfortably on the sun-deck of a boat.'

Candie shrugged and smiled. It would never take much, Marriott reflected, to convince that lazy bastard that it was a good time to take a holiday, especially a free one. He watched Sweeney turn to Lydia Petrie.

'And you, my dear Lydia, told me only this evening that you were bored, at a loose end, with nothing much in prospect until the winter sports season gets under way. Will you come with us? You might get a little under-water swimming.'

'Yes,' she said, 'I'll come, Sweeney. As long as it doesn't involve spending money. I'm through next month's allowance.'

He raised his broad right hand. 'The proviso is unnecessary. As a lonely man, I am in the market for your company.'

He neither sounded nor looked lonely: complacent, inscrutable fitted him better. Overlooking Susan, he said to Joe Willeway:

'I am sure, Joe, that there is nothing in your own immediate programme which cannot be put off for a while.'

'I'm doing a house for Henry Bresslaw.'

Sweeney nodded. 'Of which I know. Bresslaw is in no hurry. I will have a word with him, if you like.'

Willeway looked startled. Marriott, too, was surprised. There was a hint of pressure there, and Sweeney did not apply pressure lightly. But, of course, he did not brook opposition easily, either. Sweeney went on:

'And now that both of the children are away at school, there is nothing to hold Katey here. What do you say, Katey? Will you walk through grey cold English streets, or come with us down to the warm south?'

She said: 'It sounds like fun.'

'Good, then.' Sweeney turned, with the disconcerting swiftness that sometimes marked his physical actions, to Marriott. 'How about you, Tony?'

Marriott shook his head. 'I do have things to attend to, I'm afraid, Sweeney. Otherwise we would have loved it.'

He spoke with real regret. A cruise involving Katey Willeway and, it seemed, Susan Malone, offered attractive possibilities. Even Lydia might be worth something under warm blue skies.

'Nothing very much, surely,' Sweeney said. 'Nothing of overwhelming importance. As a matter of fact, the trip would have an element of business as far as you are concerned. There is something I have been meaning to discuss with you for a long time. What one might call a long-term project.'

This was pressure again. Marriott thought swiftly, and decided he could not afford to turn it down. Of all the contacts he had made in ten years of dubious dealings since coming down from Oxford, Sweeney was incontestably the biggest and most important, the whale among the minnows. He laughed easily.

'Well, if we can find a way of justifying it … I'm as keen on the idea as anyone.'

Toni, watching him and smoking a cigarette, nodded slightly. Without having a business head, she had a shrewdness with regard to people and events which had helped him in the past, and on which he increasingly relied.

'So that leaves only you, Susan,' Sweeney said, turning to stare at her.

She laughed nervously. 'And I, unfortunately, am a working girl, who has already had her three weeks' holiday for this year.'

'But one, I believe, with a letter of resignation in her handbag or, at least, plotted out behind those smooth young brows.'

Her look was startled and a little angry. 'Who told you that, Sweeney?'

'No one. I had a feeling about it. I'm right, am I not?'

'Even if you were right, I should need to look for something else. I could hardly throw things up and go on a cruise. And I have to give a month's notice to the magazine, anyway.'

'Let us dispose of these points seriatim.' Sweeney held a hand up, with two fingers outstretched. Touching one, he said: 'An Assistant Editor is wanted on New Science Review published by a company on whose board I have the honour to serve. The salary will be three hundred more than you are now getting, and the position will be kept open for you. Secondly, you need a rest. I have already spoken of this to John Hiscock, your present chief, and he agrees; and agrees to release you immediately and without prejudice. Well, my dear?'

She had coloured during the latter part of Sweeney's little speech, and the flush became her. Marriott looked at her with sympathy and interest, and admiration for the way Sweeney went about getting what he wanted. For whatever reason he wanted it. He had never given the impression of wanting women sexually; or, for that matter, men.

She said in a low voice: 'If Mr Hiscock is willing to release me, I suppose I could come.'

'That's settled, then,' Sweeney said. 'We shall make a pleasant and happy company, I am quite sure. Today is Thursday. We reassemble here next Tuesday. We will spend the night here, and the following morning motor to the airport. I suggest that you travel lightly. There will be no formality on our cruise, and only two nights in hotels. Once on board we shall not need much in the way of clothes.'

'What kind of a boat is it?' Susan asked.

'The *Alethea*,' Lydia said. 'Fifty-five footer. Sweeney keeps her at Cannes.'

'No,' Sweeney said, 'not the *Alethea*.'

'Then what?'

'In good time.'

Marriott said: 'In that case, perhaps not Cannes?'

Sweeney nodded. 'Not Cannes.'

Katey said: 'Where? Athens? I've always wanted to see the Greek islands.'

'You will have to wait a little longer, Katey,' Sweeney said. 'The boat I have in mind is rather further away. We shall be boarding her at Honolulu.'

Despite his own amazement, Marriott was able to observe the incredulity in the faces of the others. Lydia said:

'Honolulu? Are you serious, Sweeney?'

He nodded. 'Quite serious.'

'But why?'

'An old urge, to sail the southern seas. I have intended to do it from the time, as a boy, I read *Coral Island*. Other things got in the way.'

'We can't possibly go,' Katey said. 'It's the other side of the world.'

'The world is smaller than it was. Five hours to New York. Another hop across the continent. A night in a hotel in Los Angeles, and the next day on to Honolulu.'

Sweeney spoke with a measure and precision that made it all sound simple. As the idea took hold, Marriott, despite himself, felt excited. The gesture was a grand one, even for Sweeney. He looked at the others and saw that it had excited them, too. The little Malone girl looked stunned, but fascinated.

'Well,' Sweeney said. 'I take it we are all agreed?'

3

Watching the sun settle towards the western peaks of Oahu, Susan Malone was acutely aware of a sense of detachment, of dislocation in time and space, of loss and at the same time of alleviation. She was sitting, in a steel and green plastic deck-chair, near the taffrail, where a raised section behind the wheel formed a small sun-deck. She could see two of the hands scrubbing decks forward and Sweeney, she knew, was in the charthouse discussing things with Cranach, the owner and skipper of the *Diana*. The rest of the party, together with the steward, were ashore in Honolulu. She had chosen to remain on board because she did not feel like sight-seeing or merry-making, and because Marriott had been so persistent in pressing her to come with them. She considered how much she disliked Marriott: she had always disliked short, dark, dapper men, and the brown, silky, well-groomed beard was a final affront. Remembering the incident of the pudding spoon, she shivered a little with nausea.

Smells came over the still waters of the harbour, unidentifiable, disturbing in a way that she was not sure if she liked or disliked. And distant cries, in a language she did not know. A large catamaran, with twin red sails, was cutting across the bows of a motor-launch which was chugging out on one revved-down engine. Across the harbour the town glittered white under blue skies lightly strewn with cirrus. She thought suddenly of London, and so of John. He would be leaving the office about this time, joining the crowd that surged towards Holborn Viaduct station. Or perhaps calling in at the Printer's Devil for a drink. She smiled; that was, on the whole, more likely. Standing with one elbow on the bar, a pint of light ale in front of him, talking boisterously, laughing from time to time that deep reverberating laugh which, she so well remembered, drew people's attention to him from the furthest corner of the most crowded bar. He would not think of her until later – in the compartment crowded with strangers, walking alone along the road from the station to the neat detached house with the garden he was so proud of, and the three boys he was so proud of, and the wife with whom he spent his evenings and week-ends bickering.

At the beginning she had not minded about the wife: his life at home had been something remote from the excitement and confidence of their shared intimacy. Then, a year or two later, she had minded very much. Later still she had stopped minding again, resigned to the fact that she would get no more of him than the office day, an occasional evening, far more rarely a week-end. It was the Paris conference that had shattered the resignation – ten days together, the chestnuts in blossom under hot skies, anonymity in the laughing, sauntering crowds. At the end of it she had known two things: that, whatever his feelings about his wife, he was looking forward to his home and his boys again; and that she could not go back to the old scrappiness and wretchedness. Sweeney had been right. She had made up her mind to leave before he had asked her to come out here.

But how had he known? It had all been discreet. One or two in the office might have had suspicions – some of the things Jane Ashton had said had been barbed – but none could have been sure. And even if they had known that, they could not have known of her resolution to break and run. Yet Sweeney had guessed it. And Sweeney had fixed things with John; she had not even had to ask permission to leave without serving her month's notice. He had called her in, and said he'd heard the news, and of course the job was so much better and the cruise would do her good. All that will-power summoned up to refuse a plea had been unnecessary. He had asked her to have lunch with him, and she had shaken her head, and he had said he understood. They had not even kissed goodbye.

That was the way it had ended, more sharply and easily and hopelessly than she could have dreamed it would. Was Sweeney a magician, a sorcerer? The world of magic was a child's world, and one grew out of it. The real world was always clearer and always darker. John knew Sweeney well and John, she knew, was indiscreet about others; perhaps he had been less discreet about himself than she had thought, than she had been. Might it not even be that Sweeney had been asked to help, to bring the easy end to a situation which had gone on too long? For a moment she disliked herself for the cynicism and lack of trust, for the betrayal. But the separate world was as different from the shared one as the adult's world from the child's. And it would help to dislike him. So far things had moved too fast for feelings to catch up, but they would catch up in the lazy days ahead. And then, perhaps, resentment would be a prop.

She thought of the bar in the Printer's Devil, the chatter and cigarette smoke and John, rubbing his forehead and laughing, and felt the sudden constriction inside her. She got quickly to her feet and began making her way forward to the cabins. She could shower, perhaps, or find a book to read. But as she passed the charthouse the door opened. Cranach came out, Sweeney stooping behind him.

He said: 'Miss Malone, isn't it? You didn't go ashore with the rest?'

Cranach was a tall, handsome, black-moustached American, with a bland manner and a soft, probably Southern accent. He would be about forty. His manner showed an easy deference, but in his eyes, she thought, there was contempt. He had converted the *Diana* from copra-carrying into a cruise ship five years earlier, and he looked as though the five years had softened and angered him.

Susan said: 'No. I didn't feel like it.'

Sweeney followed the skipper out on deck. He said:

'Al is proposing to show me over the boat. Would you like to come along?'

She was confused. 'If you like. I mean, yes, I would love to.'

Sweeney put a hand on her arm, and the touch warmed her. It had nothing of sexual approach, but there was something in it which was reassuring and to which she responded.

Cranach said: 'Always a pleasure to entertain a lady.' He showed white teeth in a grin. 'We'll go right up to the sharp end and start from there.'

He led the way past the skylight over the saloon and past a second companionway to the bow of the ship. A wooden figurehead rested on the stem under the bowsprit, a large-busted young woman in flowing robes who clutched a bow.

'There she is,' Cranach said, 'the moon goddess herself.'

'It looks quite new,' Sweeney observed.

'Had it carved when I refitted her,' Cranach said. 'An ordinary workaday copra schooner doesn't bother with fancy items, but she's in the romance business now.' He patted the statue's head. 'An old guy in 'Frisco cut her for me. He carved wood in Nantucket back in the whaling days. She looks good, wouldn't you say?'

'Did she have the same name before?' Sweeney asked.

'No.' Cranach shook his head. 'Santa something – Spanish name. Anyway, I didn't like it.' He looked at Sweeney. 'It doesn't have to be *Diana* if there's something else you fancy.'

'No,' Sweeney said. 'I like *Diana*. Apollo's twin, the great Mother.'

Could one, Susan wondered, change a ship's name for the purpose of a charter cruise? Didn't there have to be registrations and things? But probably it was the kind of large gesture Cranach thought would appeal to Sweeney, but which he was fairly confident would not be taken up. Leaning over the rail, she said:

'Is it all metal further down?'

'Copper sheathing,' Cranach said. He glanced towards Sweeney. 'In good condition, I assure you.'

'To keep the teredo at bay, I presume,' Sweeney said.

'Teredo?' Susan asked.

'A sea-worm, ma'am,' Cranach said, 'that's remarkably fond of timbers. When our boys moved down into the Pacific after Pearl Harbor, they had to build a lot of wharves fast and they underpinned them with Oregon elm. The old teredo never had it so good. He didn't believe that kind of living existed.'

Cranach stared up at the masts, at present empty of sail. 'She runs a couple of jibs here forward, and then she's gaff-rigged on the masts. But all that can be left to the boys. They're a good crew, and my Number One can handle her on his own.' He led the way back to a covered companionway. 'These are their quarters.'

They followed him down the steps into a cabin that curved to the bow of the ship. There were three-tier bunks on each of the converging bulkheads and a table with fixed benches in the space between. Everything was clean and tidy.

'If the crew's quarters are shipshape,' Cranach said, 'there's a good chance the ship herself will stay in trim. You have to bear down on them from time to time. But not too much – they're good boys, as I said.'

To one side a steel ladder led into unlit depths. Susan said: 'What's down there, Captain?'

'Chain locker.' He pointed to a pair of metal pipes that ran vertically down beside the bunks. 'The anchor chain runs down there and coils up below. And we store sails, rope and so on down there, too.' He looked at Sweeney. 'Care to inspect that side of things?'

Sweeney shook his head gravely. 'No, thank you. I'm sure it's all in order.'

'Then we'll go up again.'

The skylight rested on a coaming that covered a good part of the deck between the masts. The companionway leading to the saloon was aft of this. Descending, one saw the long table of polished red wood in the centre of the saloon, and beyond it the bar, of the same wood tricked out with chrome and plastic.

Both the table and the bucket-shaped wood and leather seats surrounding it were anchored to the deck. Cabin doors ran off on either side; the cabin Susan was sharing with Lydia Petrie was at the end of the left.

'You've seen this already,' Cranach said. 'This used to be the hold, of course. If you take a deep breath you can still smell copra.' There was a strange lingering scent in the air; she remembered something like it as a child, from a visit to the docks on Merseyside. Cranach kicked the deck. 'Mostly fresh-water tanks below. Amazing how much fresh water civilized people get through.' He gestured towards the doors directly on either side of the companionway. 'Ladies' bathroom on the port side, gents' to starboard. Showers, of course, not bath tubs, but a certain amount of discipline is advisable, even so. The toilets are salt-water flushed, of course.' He grinned. 'So no restrictions on their use.'

Sweeney pointed to a door leading into the space below the companionway itself.

'And that one?'

'Cold store. Over two hundred cubic feet at zero temperature.'

'That's quite a lot of refrigeration.'

Cranach shrugged. 'The American tourist likes his steak large and his lettuce crisp. Do you want to check food stores, by the way?'

'I don't think so. The steward knows what's there, and what's needed?'

'He knows what's there. I would say there isn't a thing needed.'

They went back on deck and then down a ladder to one side of the charthouse. Below decks there were the dry food stores and the galley; the latter was spotless and electrically equipped throughout.

'Cookie's little preserve,' Cranach said. 'He bunks next door. Steward and Engineer live in the cabin opposite. Billy's in town with your party, of course. I don't think you've met Yasha.'

He knocked on the cabin door and, after a moment, opened it. There were two bunks with a small table between them. A man was sitting at the far end; he looked up slowly. He had a square, jagged face and wispy greying hair above a high forehead. His hands, which rested on the table, were large and bony and very white.

When Cranach introduced them, he made perfunctory but courteous replies, rising to his feet and bowing to Susan. He remained standing as they went out, blue eyes fixed on them in a grave, reflective stare.

Outside, Cranach said: 'He's a good engineer. Maybe a little kooky, but I've never met an engineer who wasn't. And he can navigate if he's needed.'

'Russian?' Sweeney asked.

'White Russian. His folks came out in '17. They went east, not west – wound up in Hong Kong. He's been kicking around the islands the last twenty-five years. I'll go first down this ladder.'

The ladder took them into the engine-room. Cranach led the way to the engine itself and Sweeney examined it with what looked like a practised eye. He said:

'That will be your feed tank up there, I suppose? And do you generate all your electrical power off this?'

Cranach said: 'No. She's not always in use, of course. That's the stand-by generator over there. You won't run short of power.'

'And oil storage?' Sweeney asked.

'Below deck. Tanks all full. Enough for three months' cruising.'

Susan laughed. 'That's longer than we need!'

'Yes?' Cranach glanced at her, smiling. 'Shall we go back up on deck?'

He stood aside for her to go into the charthouse. It was a small, barely furnished, wooden room, with a table and two chairs, a book-case, and a door leading off at the back. The door was open and she could see through to a second compartment which had a bunk in it. Cranach nodded in that direction:

'Will you bunk there, or with the others?'

'There, I think,' Sweeney said.

It brought the vague bewilderment she had felt into focus.

'You, Captain,' she said, 'where will you sleep?'

'Tonight,' Cranach said, 'in Honolulu. Tomorrow night in 'Frisco.' He nodded at Sweeney. 'I'll see you clear the harbour.'

'You aren't staying with the ship?'

'Why no,' Cranach said.

Sweeney said: 'Captain Cranach has sold me the *Diana*. I shall be running her myself.'

'But you can't,' Susan said, 'can you?'

'I was at sea,' Sweeney said, 'as a younger man. My ticket is still valid.'

He spoke with a simple yet majestic confidence. Cranach said:

'A little surprise for your guests, eh? No need to worry, Miss Malone. A boat like this, with a crew like she has, runs herself. The skipper's not a lot more use than that wooden painted lady under the bowsprit.'

'The others don't know, either?' Susan asked Sweeney. 'None of them?'

'No,' Sweeney said. 'The point did not seem worth mentioning.'

Apprehension was succeeded by a feeling of strangeness, of excitement almost. She looked at Sweeney and thought: we are in his hands, denizens of his small world. He had not told her, or any of them, of this, but had been willing that she should find out. It was part of a monumental indifference. And yet she did not feel that he was indifferent to the party he had brought with him. She wondered, should she tell the others? Sweeney looked at her.

'Do you regard it as a point worth mentioning, Susan?' he asked.

'No,' she said. 'I don't think so, Sweeney.'

4

DURING THE NIGHT LYDIA PETRIE WAS WOKEN by a harsh rhythmic grating sound which she recognized as that of the anchor chain being taken up. She snapped awake and, as readily, dropped back into sleep; she was a person to whom sleep came easily and, for the most part, dreamlessly. In the morning she awoke to the motion of the sea: the *Diana* was rolling and through the scuttle between her bunk and that of the Malone girl sky and sea alternated in regular dizzying sequence. She climbed out of her bunk, pulled a wrap over her pyjamas and went in search of the bathroom.

She had a quick shower and came back to dress. The Malone girl was awake now, but looking as though she regretted it.

'Feeling sick?' Lydia asked her. The Malone girl nodded silently. 'There's a bowl thing in the part that pulls out below your head.'

'I know.' She grimaced. 'I don't feel as sick as that just yet.'

Lydia finished dressing, and slammed on a face at the built-in dressing-table between the bunks.

'Well, I'm off,' she said finally. 'A breath of fresh air would probably do you good, too.'

'Not just yet.'

She shrugged. 'You know best. Breakfast?' The Malone girl closed her eyes. 'O.K. I'll tell Billy you'd rather be left alone.'

There was no one in the saloon, but she heard the sound of movements from some of the cabins as she went up the companionway and out on deck. The day was bright, the sun well clear of the eastern horizon and the sea calm except for the long swell in which the ship rolled. White sails billowed overhead; one of the deck-hands was up aloft doing something at the gooseneck. On the starboard quarter, where she had come out, there was no sign of land, nothing but the wide blue steppe and the sun hanging over it. She walked round the deck, passing one of the Hawaiians, who smiled and ducked his head. From the port side, land was visible, hazy and diminishing. She could make out two islands. She was staring out over the rail at them when there were footsteps on the deck behind her. She wheeled round to see who it was.

The steward, Billy Railer, approached her. He was in his uniform – a white jacket over royal blue trousers – and he had the slight, somewhat ingratiating smile on his face with which she had become familiar the previous afternoon on the tour of Honolulu. He said:

'You're up early, Miss Petrie. The arrangement was for morning tea at eight, and breakfast from eight-thirty on. I could arrange to bring yours earlier, if you prefer that.'

She shook her head. 'I never touch tea, thank you.'

'Coffee, then.'

'I don't want anything until I'm up and dressed.'

'Of course. Would you like me to get you a cup now?'

She said impatiently: 'No. I'll wait till breakfast. The Islands – one of them's Oahu?'

'Yes. Oahu and Hawaii.'

'And we're sailing what – south?'

'South-east by south.'

'And what lies ahead?'

He grinned. 'A lot of ocean.'

'No land?'

'Not for a couple of thousand miles.' She made no response to that, and he went on: 'Plenty of time for everybody to get acquainted.'

He was a type of man that she had encountered before, generally in some similar, subservient capacity. The attitude was obsequious, fawning and at the same time verging on the familiar. Behind the cringing glance lay the knowing look, the mute innuendo. She could well remember the first, a groom, when she was only fifteen: the sordid devotion that lasted the whole of a summer holiday and which drove her to greater and greater cruelty, more and more cutting words and glances, the unpleasant excitement of exercising power over another, older human being. There had been other occasions; she had been forced to realize that she had a great attraction for the type. She was angry with this one, and angry with her own anger. She said sharply:

'Aren't you supposed to be taking tea to the others?'

'It's not quite time yet, miss.'

'I should go and see if you are needed. People were beginning to move about.'

He still lingered. 'Are you sure there's nothing I can do for you?'

'Nothing.'

She turned her back on him, and heard him pad away. She stared out over the sea towards the fading islands. She thought about going to tackle Sweeney in his quarters behind the charthouse, but decided against it. It was better to wait until they were all together, at breakfast. She drew in breath, the clean salt air of the ocean. The rolling of the ship did not trouble her; instead she began to feel ravenously hungry.

Susan Malone was the only member of the party who failed to appear for breakfast, although Toni Marriott looked rather unhappy and confined herself to dry toast and fruit juice ... Sweeney did not arrive until quite late; Lydia had eaten her double egg and bacon and was on her second piece of toast and marmalade when she heard his heavy tread coming down the companionway. He looked at them for a moment before moving to his seat at the head of the table.

'Good morning,' Sweeney said. 'Susan not with us, I see. How is she, Lydia?'

'Sick,' she said. 'Just where the hell do you think you're taking us, Sweeney?'

Sweeney sat down, unfolded his napkin, and spread it across his lap. He said:

'Why, child, is something troubling you?'

'I thought the idea was that we should cruise round the islands here. Now I find we're heading due south. And that there are two thousand miles of empty water ahead of us.'

'That is not strictly accurate,' Sweeney said. 'There are the Line islands, and our course is east of south. But courses can be changed, you know. The idea might be to rest for an hour or two in the great empty embrace of the ocean. We could be anchored off Honolulu again by nightfall.'

Marriott said: 'But shall we be?'

Sweeney shook his head slowly. 'No.'

'In that case, what do you have in mind?'

'Quite simply, a more interesting group of islands. The Marquesas.'

'Two thousand miles away!' Lydia said.

'Slightly more.'

Katey Willeway said: 'What is this all about?' She was frowning, her mouth drawn in a hard line. 'You asked us for a three-week cruise. This is the sort of trip that will take months.' She looked at her husband. 'Won't it?'

Sweeney said: 'I don't think I specified an exact time, did I? I recall speaking of three or four weeks, in a general way.' He surveyed them blandly. 'One thing that concerned me in making up the party was to ensure that no member was likely to be inconvenienced seriously by the loss of a few days.'

Marriott said: 'I don't think that really applies to me, Sweeney. Time is money in my business.'

'Exactly. But some times are more valuable than others, are they not? And there is this project I have been hoping you will be able to help me with. I do think this cruise offers the best prospect for discussing it.'

Marriott stared at him. 'I suppose you couldn't give me a rough idea of what it involves?'

'At the breakfast table? My dear Tony.' Sweeney took his fruit juice and drained it slowly. 'Perhaps it would help if we had plans a little more precisely formulated.'

Lydia said: 'If it isn't going to inconvenience you too much to tell us what we're being let in for.'

Sweeney smiled. 'Not at all. Now. The islands of the Hawaii group are rather dull, I feel. Just another State of the Union, in fact. The Marquesas, on the other hand, have been called the forgotten islands. They are the true South Sea islands, barely touched by civilization. Does Hira Oa mean anything to you?'

There was a silence before Candie said: 'Gauguin.'

'Yes. Paul Gauguin lived there and died there and is buried there. His children and grandchildren live there still. Those are the scenes, the skies and seas, he painted.'

Lydia's annoyance with Sweeney was still extreme, but she was conscious, as she had been on other occasions, of its in-effectiveness against his benevolent indifference. She glanced at the other faces round the table, and saw that most of them were more puzzled than put out. Marriott, perhaps, was an ex-ception, but he was making a gallant effort to contain himself. Willeway lifted his large soft chin, and his eyes blinked.

'It sounds quite a lot of fun, Sweeney. Still, two thousand miles …'

'At the moment,' Sweeney said, 'we have the Trades behind us, blowing from the north-east. We should average a steady twelve knots. About ten degrees north of the Line, a position we should reach in two and a half days, we come to the Doldrums. The stretch is fairly narrow at this time of the year – say two hundred and fifty miles. With the engine we can manage seven knots. A day and a half will find us meeting the south-east Trades, some seven degrees north of the Line. For the remaining distance, just under twelve hundred miles, we will get a little assistance from the wind – perhaps a difference of one knot.

We should make our landfall in another six days. Ten days in all. A week's cruising round the islands and we can be back in Honolulu within five weeks. Or I might decide to go on to Tahiti, and we could fly back from there. That would cut the time considerably.'

'What about the boat?' Marriott asked. 'You've bought it, haven't you?'

'Yes,' Sweeney said. 'One buys, one sells. Honolulu, Tahiti – does it matter?'

'I should think you would be more likely to get something approaching your price in Honolulu.'

Sweeney nodded. 'Yes. It is not very important, though. What is important is how you all feel about this.' He smiled. 'I should hate to think you might regard yourselves as being shanghaied. If there is anyone who would prefer not to come – I am sure the rest of us will not begrudge the few hours that it will take to turn about and put him or them ashore in Honolulu. Your return journey would be arranged, of course, and all necessary hotel expenses.'

Lydia burst out: 'All very well, Sweeney. But why not tell us what was in view at the beginning? Why spring it on us like this?'

'I am careless,' Sweeney said, 'in some ways. I hope you will accept my apologies. May I point out also, for those who decide to stay on the *Diana*, that we are in two-way wireless communication with the outside world. If anyone wishes to tell anxious friends that they are likely to be a week or two longer than they had thought – to cancel the papers or the milk for a few extra days – it can be done very simply.'

Another brief silence followed. Candie said:

'You've never been in these waters before, have you, Sweeney?'

'No.'

'But you feel happy about a voyage of two thousand miles across them?'

'Why, yes,' Sweeney said. 'The first sailors who came into

these seas were happy, too. And they had neither two-way wireless communication, nor the *Admiralty Sailing Instructions for the Pacific*, nor a crew who have spent their lives doing just this, including a Number One boy who has done the trip more times, probably, than you have crossed the Channel. I am entirely happy, Roger. The important question is whether you are.'

The cabin door opened, and Susan Malone came out. She looked pale, but not unattractively so. She was wearing a silk wrap which showed her figure off well. The kind of seeming innocent, Lydia thought, who was never likely to miss a trick. She said, in a low voice:

'I'm sorry to be so late.'

Sweeney said: 'How are you feeling now, Susan? Better, I hope.'

'A little better.' She smiled wryly. 'I can manage some coffee, at any rate.'

Lydia said: 'Sweeney, it appears, is proposing to sail us two thousand miles south to a group of islands he thinks will be more interesting. It will be a long way to go on a diet of coffee.'

'The first few hours at sea always upset me,' Susan said. 'I'm all right after that.' She looked at Sweeney. 'I promise I'm not going to be a nuisance.'

'You would like to come with us, then,' Sweeney said. 'I have explained that we can put back to Honolulu if there is anyone who would prefer not to come.'

'I'd love to come. I take it you will get me back in time to start my new job?'

'The job will be waiting for you.' He turned his attention from her to the others. 'What decision have the rest of you reached? Roger?'

'As long as there's no prospect of having to scrub decks or rig sails.'

'None whatsoever. Joe – Katey?'

Willeway looked up from spreading butter, lavishly and with

care, on a piece of toast. He caught his wife's eye, and shrugged. She said:

'We can send a message back?' Sweeney inclined his head. 'And the rest of you will be going, anyway. I think we'll stay, then.'

Lydia had been watching Tony Marriott: his eyes had not left the curve of Susan's breast, under the wrap, since she came out. When Sweeney spoke his name, interrogatively, he looked at him abstractedly.

'How about you and Toni?' Sweeney asked.

'Why not?' Marriott said. His eye returned to Susan. 'Why not, indeed?' He looked back at Sweeney. 'And we can get down to discussing that big project you have in mind.'

'Of course,' Sweeney said. 'Well, my dear Lydia, that leaves only you. But our little world is one of extreme democracy, setting one voice at equal importance with all the rest. Shall we turn back and take you to Honolulu? You can be at London Airport tomorrow. You only have to say the word.'

Her resentment against him found no purchase. She said sharply: 'Why couldn't we have had all this out before we left Honolulu? Why keep it until this stage?'

'Does it matter? I assumed none of you would object to a slightly more adventurous voyage. As far as the others are concerned, it seems that I was right. If I was wrong in your case, then at least there's no harm done.'

If you were filthy rich, there never was any harm done: whoever failed to fit in with the plans could be packed off, first class, by air, and forgotten. But she was not going to let herself be disposed of in that way.

'I'll stay,' she said. 'I think you've behaved badly about this, though, Sweeney.'

'But you will stay,' he said. 'That is what matters, after all. And I was right in my estimation. We shall not need to put back into Honolulu. Our little company remains together, unforced, uncompelled. We can settle down to enjoy the long lazy days of sun and sea, relaxed and at peace, the world forgetting, by the world forgot. And I almost think I might settle down to enjoy my breakfast now. Are you leaving us, Lydia?'

'I've finished, thank you.' She stood up from her chair. 'I think I'll take another turn on deck.'

'A good idea,' Sweeney said. 'If you see Billy, perhaps you would tell him that I am ready for my bacon and eggs.'

5

L ATE IN THE AFTERNOON there was a school of flying fish, some way off on the port bow, with dolphins in pursuit; and most of the party went forward to watch. Willeway stayed aft. He had learned, to his surprise and delight, that the *Diana*'s food supplies included muffins; and Billy was bringing him some. The notion of tea and muffins in seas which were now technically tropic was one that fascinated him. An awning had been fixed, and from its shade he looked out over the thousands of tiny burnished mirrors which the sea offered up. Not far away, one of the Hawaiians, stripped to red cotton shorts, held the wheel and sang. He had a pleasant tenor voice and strong silky muscles under bronze skin.

Billy, coming along the deck with the tray, paused by the wheel and said something to the man, as a result of which the song ended. Billy put the tray down on the table beside Willeway's deck-chair. He said:

'Here you are, sir. Tea and muffins. Dripping with butter.'

They were: the butter had soaked golden into the honeycombed surface and still unmelted dabs offered their soft creaminess to the eye. Willeway looked at them with pleasure.

'Very nice, Billy. Leave it there.'

'And China tea. That's right, sir, isn't it?'

'Exactly. Why did the boy stop singing?'

'I thought he might be disturbing you, sir.'

'No. I quite liked it.'

'I'll start him off again, in that case.' He called out to the helmsman: 'Go on singing, boy.' His voice had taken on an unpleasant edge. 'Mr Willeway's listening to you.'

The boy did not respond at once; either because the reversal of command had unnerved him or because he was trying to think of a suitable song. Billy walked quickly across the deck to him. He kicked him, sharply and viciously, with one of his white pointed shoes; the kick landed just above the ankle and the boy twisted down, rubbing the spot with his hand.

'Carry on with the singing,' Billy said.

The boy did not look round, but after a moment began to sing – the same song which had been interrupted earlier. Billy came back to the sun-deck.

'Anything else I can get you, sir?' he asked.

'I don't think so,' Willeway said. 'Was that necessary?'

'Kicking him? They don't feel much. And they have to get into the habit of jumping to it when they're told to do something.'

Willeway put one of the muffins into his mouth, and felt the butter run as the crust broke under his teeth.

'Might it not cause trouble?' he asked. 'Kicking a citizen of the United States? They are American citizens now, aren't they?'

Billy looked with contempt at the sweat-sheened back of the helmsman.

'These boys are from the outer islands. They won't give any trouble. Not as long as they're kept in place.'

Willeway finished the muffin and sucked a fleck of butter from one of his fingers.

'I'm not sure that I agree with you, Billy, particularly about something like this. You can't kick a person into song. It needs to be spontaneous.'

'He's singing, sir.'

'Yes,' Willeway said. He reached for another muffin. 'It sounds different, though.'

'I'll see to that, then.'

Billy began to move towards the helmsman again. Willeway said: 'No. Leave him alone. I was wondering – what kind of strawberry jam might you have in that pantry of yours?'

'I'm not sure of the name, sir.'

'Not Cooper's?'

'No. Some American brand.' Willeway shook his head slightly. 'We have a mango preserve I can recommend.'

Willeway thought about this. 'No,' he said. 'I'll continue with what I have.'

'Then you won't be requiring anything else, sir?'

One muffin remained on the plate. To order more, Willeway decided, would be a sign of greediness. A little regretfully, he said:

'No, thank you, Billy.'

He took his time over the final muffin, alternating its richness with the astringent delicacy of sips of China tea. He was pouring himself some more tea when he saw Sweeney approaching. Sweeney took one of the vacant chairs and eased his great bulk into it. Willeway said:

'Have you had tea, Sweeney? Shall I ring for some?'

Sweeney shook his head. 'I don't care for afternoon tea.'

Willeway nodded, and drank his own. He said:

'That steward – he's not a particularly pleasant character, is he?'

'In what way?'

Willeway recounted the incident with the helmsman. Sweeney listened with grave attention. He said:

'No, not particularly pleasant, I would agree.'

'Are you going to do anything about it?'

'In the line of reprimanding him? I think not. It scarcely seems my affair.'

'But you're in charge of the ship, aren't you? I mean, you are responsible for the crew as well.'

'I don't imagine,' Sweeney said, 'that Billy has suddenly taken on brutality because I have taken over the *Diana*. The hands have been with the ship for some time, and so has Billy. No doubt they have grown used to each other.'

'Is that a good reason – for not intervening?'

'I can't think of a better one. My dear Joe, intervention in human affairs is something that always requires a great deal of justification, and generally offers very little. The man who intervenes is himself suspect – rightly so because his motives are invariably mixed – and the chances of working an improvement are not, I would say, much better than even.'

Willeway said: 'But wouldn't you agree that the human race has progressed, and that the progress is a result of intervention? Didn't somebody have to do something about, for instance, slavery?'

'You mistake me,' Sweeney said, 'but it is my own fault for not expressing myself plainly enough. Intervention in small things does no good – interference with little people is a mistake. Intervention on the grand scale is a different matter altogether. The Wilberforces and the Lincolns are great men, self-justifying. To kill for the sake of private honour is absurd, but the slaughter of a tyrant is something that rightly rings through history. To place the spanner that may wreck the mightiest machine is an act that is right, as well as satisfying.'

'But don't you still have to consider values? The machine may be doing good.'

'People may be persuaded that the machine is doing good. In fact, good is only capable of being done on a small scale. Evil is more versatile. You can hate those you have never seen, all the vast multitudes of them, but you can only love those you know – and that with difficulty.'

'Even if one accepts that,' Willeway said, 'in wrecking the machine one may still be injuring people who have done no harm. Don't you have to consider them?'

'No,' Sweeney said. He shook his head slowly. 'Thousands of men died young and in violence because of Lincoln. Many of them had done no harm.'

'I don't see it, Sweeney.' It was pleasant, he thought, to indulge in mild academic argument, shaded from the hot sun, a deck tilting regularly but not excessively beneath one, mind and stomach replete. 'In the end you can never be sure. Lincoln claimed he was doing right. So did Napoleon. So did Stalin and Hitler.'

'I was talking of effectiveness rather than of moral issues. Morality, for all the conditioning to which the human mind has been and is subjected, is always a personal choice in the last analysis.'

'I would put people first,' Willeway said. 'You more or less said that, didn't you? That good can only be done on a small scale. Doesn't stopping Billy kicking the hands qualify in that respect?'

'On a small scale, and by saints. Not by me. What about you, Joe? Does your mentioning the matter to me qualify? Can we consider the incident disposed of now? As far as you are concerned, anyway?'

Willeway thought about this. 'I suppose I'm a weak character,' he said.

'No,' Sweeney said, 'I would not agree with you there.'

They came into the Doldrums that evening. The sails hung slack and lifeless, the air itself had a dead quality, as though the great expanse of sky were boxed and shuttered, the sea flowed past in an oily calm marked only by the white scum of the *Diana*'s wake. It was oppressive below in the saloon, and the Japanese cook fell for the first time below excellence: he served them a Polynesian pork dish which was a little greasy. Willeway was glad to go up on deck again afterwards; Katey, the Marriotts, Candie and Lydia Petrie were playing some kind of poker dice in the saloon.

He made his way to the bow and looked out over the port rail. A half-moon hung a few diameters above the horizon; between it and the *Diana* a broad path was crusted with silver, bright against the dark viscid-seeming waters that otherwise ran away to the draped velvet sky and its guttering stars. He was conscious of the absence of accustomed sounds. The engine throbbed below decks, but he missed the creak and groan of stays, the whine and slap of the sails. Far out the crust of silver was broken by a moving speck; at first dark, then fiercely bright, then dark again. Perhaps a giant ray leaping.

He wondered when he had last seen a path of moonlight on untroubled waters and was surprised, after a moment's reflection, to remember that it had been on his honeymoon. They had gone to Capri, at about this time of year, when only a relatively few tourists lingered on an island tired and empested by the long, hot summer. He tried, half-heartedly, to think himself back into the skin of the young man he had been, but it was difficult and did not really seem worth the effort. He and Katey had reached a balance of mutual tolerance, tinged with affection and boredom on his part, affection and boredom and resentment on hers. Year by year they learned to withdraw from each other a little more, so as to bear each other a little more easily. From time to time they shared the same bed, but that was not particularly important. He had always pitied rather than envied over-sexed men: such a straining and striving for so small a satisfaction. There were less troublesome and more abiding pleasures in life. The children had been another source of irritation between them; now they were both away at school, that was removed for the greater part of the year. All in all, he could say that his life was a peaceful one, and likely to continue to be peaceful.

Someone was walking along the deck on the starboard side; he turned with his back to the rail and looked that way. The engineer, Yasha, came into view beyond the companionway that led down to the crew's quarters. Willeway realized that it was the first time he had seen him on deck: his white face was still whiter in the moonlight. He walked round the bow and came abreast of Willeway. In a low but clear voice, he said:

'Good evening, Mr Willeway.'

Willeway returned the greeting. He said:

'It's stuffy below, isn't it? And I suppose we shall be in these sort of conditions till the day after tomorrow?'

'It might be so,' Yasha said.

It was an oddly phrased reply, Willeway thought: scarcely helpful, and yet not spoken in an unfriendly tone, Nor friendly, either; detached, rather. He said:

'You've done this trip before, I take it?'

The engineer brought out a pipe and tamped tobacco into it before replying. Then he said:

'Yes. Several times.'

'So you know the Marquesas?'

'I worked a copra boat among them for some years.'

'They're pleasant islands?'

'Pleasant enough.'

His answers were stoppers, but Willeway persisted. 'Will we make it in ten days, as Sweeney says?' he asked.

Yasha lit his pipe. 'No. I think not.'

'Why? We've been making good time surely?'

'Good time, but on the wrong course.'

Willeway was startled. 'Are you sure?' The engineer shrugged. 'Have you spoken to Sweeney about it?'

'I think he knows what he is doing.'

'But how can he, if the course is wrong?'

'A few degrees nearer south than we should be. It is not important. We are not short of fuel or food supplies, and it can be corrected later.'

'But why say he knows what he is doing?'

'I was thinking he may have something else in mind. One of the high islands, near the Equator. He may have thought of calling there first.'

'The high islands?'

'That only means they are not low islands – fairly recently volcanic. These are empty waters,' Yasha said. 'Scattered in them, here and there, are islands – small, isolated, hundreds of miles, probably, from the nearest neighbour. Many of them uninhabited, none with a profitable trade. Ships do not call at these islands. There is no reason why they should.'

'In that case, why should Sweeney?'

'Perhaps he is a romantic, your Sweeney.' The smell of his tobacco smoke came to Willeway – rich, heavy stuff which reminded him of childhood, his grandfather. 'He brings a party of guests from England to Honolulu, buys a boat which he could charter, so that he may sail it himself. That is romance, is it not? And takes it two thousand miles to the Marquesas. To sail off course in the hope of finding an uninhabited tropic island – that surely goes with the rest.'

'Yes, I suppose it does.'

'The only thing that does not fit is Sweeney himself.'

'In what way?'

'The romantic gesture is for small men. One feels that he is large – not only in body, you understand. One would not expect him to be romantic. Apocalyptic, possibly.'

'He's a man who has always been able to indulge his whims.'

'Yes. That does not make a romantic, though. If anything, the reverse is true.'

Willeway said: 'How about you? Are you quite happy about a skipper who is sailing off course, in waters he knows nothing of?'

'Happier than I would have been sailing round the Hawaiian islands. These are deep waters. No shoals or reefs. We have a good crew, and the wireless. There is no danger.'

'And also, I would guess, you are something of a fatalist.'

Yasha shrugged. 'Possibly. And Sweeney interests me. He is intelligent and capable. I think he may be purposeful, also.'

'Purposeful?'

'Perhaps not,' Yasha said. 'Or perhaps it will emerge.'

6

O N THE FIFTH NIGHT OUT FROM HONOLULU, the *Diana* was
back in the Trades and it was with the breeze whipping
the sail high above their heads that Tony and Toni made love
on deck. He had pulled her down against the coaming which
supported the skylight – it was a poor concealment, and precarious, but that was characteristic of him – and in the quiet
aftermath she could hear the murmur of voices in the saloon
below, and someone laughing. After a time she eased him from
her, and put herself to rights.

Marriott said lazily: 'You're my girl. Do you know that? The
absolute one and only.'

In a sense it was true. She knew that she still fascinated him
even more than his casual adventures, that she could hold him
sexually against all comers and without effort. She wondered
how much her barrenness might have to do with it; it enabled
him to be entirely spontaneous with her, committed yet un-
committed, the true stamp of the mistress image which capti-
vated him. She did not think she would have held him if there
had been children. He was good with other people's children
but, she thought, too much the child himself to tolerate her in
the role of mother.

Not that he had made any positive attempt to prevent her
having children. In the early days of their marriage he had expressed himself as happy over the prospect of their starting a
family right away, and she herself had looked forward monthly
to pregnancy. His assiduousness, she thought, made it almost
a certainty. Her hopes had faded gradually; it was not until
the third year that she went to a gynaecologist and was told

that, unless she had an operation, pregnancy in her case was extremely unlikely. She had taken her news to Tony, expecting him to be pleased to hear that her sterility could be overcome, and had been puzzled by his reaction: at first that they could not, at the time, afford the operation and then, when she told him that it could be done on the National Health Scheme, an indignant rejection of the idea of his wife being in a public ward, followed by a cooler but even firmer rejection – the operation, he insisted, involved an element of risk and he was not going to allow her to take the risk. He would hear of no objection to this and refused to see the specialist who had recommended the operation to her. Gradually she came to understand that he did not want her to have children, that by doing so she would be reduced from mistress-wife to wife-mother in his eyes.

Although, ever since puberty, she had found it easy to arouse emotions in members of the opposite sex, she was not herself a very emotional person. Having grasped the negation, she accepted it. She would have liked children – she would still like children – but the need was subordinate to her need for Marriott. The notion of children was abstract, unrealized; Marriott was real, the most real thing that had happened to her. She enjoyed the fact that other men still found her attractive, and enjoyed his pleasure in that, but their interest produced no response in her. With Marriott she was fulfilled: there was nothing left over. She did not even mind the attention he gave to other women, and the probability – conviction almost – that he was unfaithful to her. He would not stray far, and he would always come back.

They walked now, hand in hand, along the deck, and he talked to her, relaxed and confident, off-guard as he was only when alone with her. He said:

'I tried to pin him down to something again this evening, but it was no good.'

'Sweeney?'

'Yes.'

'Do you think there might not be a project, really?'

He made a faint clicking noise with his tongue. 'But why invent one? To persuade us to come on his cruise? It seems a bit pointless, doesn't it?'

She said: 'He doesn't seem in any kind of hurry about anything, does he? I mean, having the ship hove-to all afternoon. This fishing thing. Nobody caught anything.'

'There never seemed any prospect of catching anything. It was pretty obvious that Billy thought we were all mad.'

Toni thought about this for a moment. 'Do you think – might Sweeney have gone a bit crazy? Not just this fishing – the whole thing. After all …'

'He looks and talks sane enough. He's always been somewhat on the odd side. But he keeps his feet pretty firmly on the ground. He's a good man to have on your side in a business deal.'

She pressed his hand. 'Anyway, whether he's crazy or not we can still enjoy ourselves. You didn't have anything else important on, did you?'

'Well, nothing that looked very hopeful. But it puts you back; and we're still in the red.'

She laughed. 'No housekeeping this month, though! And no drinks bill.'

'Yes,' Marriott said. 'And I could do with a brandy right now. Let's go below and see what Billy can fix up.'

They had a couple of nightcaps in the saloon with the others, and towards eleven there was a general move to turn in. Marriott settled down for sleep in his bunk, but Toni switched on the light above hers and found herself a book. It was a sentimental novel about an unhappy love affair, and she read it, engrossed but sceptical. She could remember having the same attitude towards fairy stories in her childhood. She reached the end of a chapter, hesitated for a moment, and plunged into the next. It was at that instant that the light went off.

She said: 'Damn!' and Marriott muttered something at her

from across the cabin. 'The light's gone,' she told him. 'I was reading.'

'Generator, probably.' She heard the rustle of bed-clothes as he humped over in his bunk. 'It's a bit late for reading, anyway. I should go to sleep.'

He followed the advice himself; after a few minutes she could hear his breathing, deep and steady. She continued to lie awake. The fact of having started a new chapter unsettled her. Her light was still switched on, and she thought that whatever fault there was in the generator might be mended quickly to let her continue with her book. Eventually she abandoned this hope, but she still did not feel sleepy. She tried to settle down, but found herself becoming more awake instead of less. At last she got up, and felt around until she found her wrap and slippers. Marriott did not wake. Feeling in the locker beside his bunk for a torch did not rouse him either. She clicked it on, opened the door to the saloon and went through it and up on deck.

There was some light there; not much, but enough to make the torch seem pointless – she slipped it into the pocket of her wrap. The moon's light waxed and waned behind a varying cloud cover which hid the stars, except in one sector of the sky. The sea was dark all round the ship. Walking forward, she came to the look-out's post and saw him staring ahead into the gloom, humming a song. She kept her distance from him – she had learned that it was unsafe for her to approach any kind of man under circumstances like these – but watched him. His task suddenly seemed particularly lonely and, in a way, sad. Looking out over these dark vast empty waters for the lights of another ship, for the tremendously improbable. She turned her head and looked up at the *Diana's* foremast where their own lights would be, the red and green low down, the white light up aloft between the jib stays. But the lights were out.

She wondered about drawing the attention of the look-out to this. On the other hand, there could be some reason for it and he might construe any remark she made as an invitation: she had once had a pass made at her at a cricket match for asking which side was batting. But it might not have been noticed, and it might be important. She was debating this with herself when there were footsteps on the deck behind her, and she looked and saw Sweeney.

'Toni,' he said. 'Couldn't you sleep, my dear?'

'I didn't feel tired.' She put a hand on his arm, and pointed up at the mast. 'The lights are out, Sweeney. Ought they to be?'

'Not really, but it scarcely matters. We are a long way from shipping lanes.'

'My bed-light went out, too. I was in the middle of a chapter.'

He chuckled. 'Maddening. That was the generator. I could have got Yasha to see to it, but he had turned in and it didn't seem worth while. If you really want to finish the chapter, I suppose I could rouse him. Otherwise he'll see to it in the morning.'

'No. Of course not, Sweeney. I just came up for a breath of fresh air. I'll sleep all right after that.'

'I'm sure you will.' He put his hand over hers, large, comforting, unlascivious. 'If you are really restless, I can give you a pill from the medicine chest.'

She shook her head. 'I don't like taking pills. I'll sleep well enough.'

'Yes. You have an admirable simplicity, Toni.'

'Is that meant to be a compliment?'

'It is a compliment. You are satisfied with your life, are you not? And few people are.'

'Not satisfied. There are a lot of things I would like.'

'For instance?'

'Oh, terribly expensive clothes. And jewels. Particularly jewels.'

For a moment she was surprised with herself for saying that. It was true, but she could not remember revealing it before. It had been a daydream of her adolescence – the man who would find her and shower her with pearls and gold and rubies – and she had always been ashamed of it. But she felt no shame in talking of it to Sweeney. Nor, even fleetingly, was there the thought that he had the power, if he wished, to turn the dream into reality.

'That is simple, too,' Sweeney said. 'Did you think, when you married Tony, that he would provide you with all those things?'

'No. It never occurred to me.'

Sweeney laughed. 'But he might still do so, might he not?'

She turned to face him directly, looking into the shadowed eyes under the heavy brows.

'Sweeney,' she said, 'you do have something in mind for Tony, don't you?'

'So that he can buy you the clothes and jewels?'

'But there is something?'

'A great opportunity,' Sweeney said, 'lies ahead of him. I can promise that.'

She said: 'We are grateful to you, Sweeney. And for this lovely holiday.'

He shook his large head, smiling. 'Are you more tired now?'

'Yes, I think so. Are you turning in?'

'Not quite yet. There are one or two things I have to see to. I suppose those lights ought to be dealt with.'

They walked together towards the companionway leading down to the saloon. Toni said:

'You take your duties seriously.'

'Conscientiously, I hope, but not seriously. Sleep well, my dear. Tomorrow is a new day.'

She looked at him. 'That's an odd expression.'

'Is it?'

'For you. You don't generally use clichés.'

'Banality, like death, is ineluctable.' He pressed her hand. 'Good night, Toni.'

She made her way below by the light of the torch, and so back to her cabin. Marriott was sleeping; he screwed up his eyes as the torch beam traversed his face, but he did not wake.

Toni climbed back into her bunk, and settled herself. Quite suddenly she was very tired: she decided she would sleep late in the morning and skip breakfast. She drifted into a reverie of riches: a car of her own ... a Lancia, perhaps ... and so fell asleep.

She awoke, to her surprise, in the early light of dawn. A luminous grey filled the cabin. She lay still for a while, coming fully awake, and heard the patter of feet on the deck overhead and, a little later, the cry of a seabird. There was something strange about that. She slipped out of the bunk and looked out of the open scuttle between her bunk and Tony's. The island rose directly before her, a darker grey against the grey of sea and sky. She stared at it for quite a long time, before she bent down and shook her husband by the shoulder.

7

THEY CROWDED ON DECK like children, to look at the island which rose sharply out of the glassy sea. The *Diana* had approached from the north-east, and it was possible to see that the eastern coast had high cliffs, and above the cliffs steeply rising wooded ground that presumably culminated in a mountain peak – presumably, because its top was shrouded in cloud. The whole island seemed to be surrounded by a reef, as much as a mile offshore to the east, but lying closer in to the westward. There were breaks in it here and there; elsewhere the sea broke quietly against this narrow curving rib.

Her sails furled, the *Diana* beat round the north of the island under engine alone. The contours of land changed and clarified. There were two peaks, one much lower than the other and unclouded, and a valley between them; the island fell away, in these two steps, from east to west, and in the distance sloped easily to the sea. There was also a spit of land which jutted out, like a curved arm, from the north coast, the reef curving out to accommodate it. It, too, carried trees, but they were relatively sparse and, even from this distance, identifiable as coconut palms. When Sweeney came up from the charthouse, they put up a barrage of questions.

'Silver Island,' he told them. 'The name is a corruption of the original; it was discovered by a man called da Silva, a Portuguese mariner who was blown off course by a typhoon, and found the island when desperately low in water and provisions. There is, in fact, no other land for over three hundred miles. Up to the last war its ownership was in some doubt; then it became a United States Trust Territory and such, I believe, it remains.'

Katey asked him: 'Is it inhabited?'

'According to the records, no. There was a native population at one time, but they died out in the nineteenth century following an epidemic of measles introduced by a passing trading vessel. Whites have never bothered to colonize it. It is too small – about seven miles by three – and too far from shipping routes to make it a worth-while proposition for copra-growing or anything of that kind.'

Marriott said: 'Can you even get ashore? That reef looks as though it goes all the way round, and I wouldn't care to take a ship through the breaks we've seen so far.'

'I suppose you could anchor out here,' Candie suggested, 'and go ashore in the ship's boat.'

'You would need quite a length of anchor chain,' said Sweeney. 'The sea-bed drops sharply from that reef. We probably have a thousand fathoms underneath us now. But there is an anchorage, according to the *Admiralty Sailing Instructions*. The island is volcanic in origin, as all these high islands are, and those two peaks are what's left of the main crater. But there is a subsidiary sunken crater' – he pointed to the arm of land that curved out - 'of which that is part of the rim. And there is an opening in the reef which can be navigated in good weather, such as we have at present. So I see no reason why we should not go ashore on Silver Island. We might even picnic there. Does that seem to be a good idea?'

Sweeney looked at them benevolently. There was a general murmur of approbation and pleasure. He was enjoying it himself, too, Katey thought bitterly. An absolute in gestures: picnic on a desert island. There were all to clap hands and thank the big man for his munificence.

He seemed to catch her gaze on him, and said to her directly: 'How does it strike you, Katey?'

She put a smile on. 'Exotic. Do we need to take any food, though? Can't we live on coconuts and breadfruit?'

'And yams,' Sweeney said, 'and wild bananas and mangoes.

Not to mention wild pig, which very probably abounds on those hillsides. But the pig would need catching and killing and cleaning and roasting. I think it will be better if Cookie puts up a hamper. And a few bottles of champagne, perhaps. We are none of us likely to have this experience again.'

'Can we all go ashore?' Susan asked.

'I think we all should,' Sweeney said.

Susan smiled, looking suddenly radiant. But her features were undistinguished; all she had was youth. Which was enough, after all. Katey saw Marriott's eye on the girl, frankly surveying the curve of breast under a loose red shirt. She was welcome to him, she thought. The lie consoled her, but not much.

They stayed on deck while the *Diana* rounded the headland; they could see the sheltered semicircle of water, rock-edged as far as the promontory was concerned, but with its shoreward side fringed with broad sands and trees. The reef appeared to stretch on, uninterrupted, to the western point of the island, but as the ship continued westerly a channel opened exposing a way through. The *Diana* edged towards it, her engine cut to its lowest power. There was some thirty-foot clearance on either side and then the jagged teeth of coral. It was certainly a passage that required calm seas.

Katey said: 'What happens if a storm blows up while we're in here?'

'In that case,' Sweeney said, 'we wait, in perfect shelter, until it has blown itself out. But there are no storms forecast. The weather is set fair.'

'Let's stay here anyway,' Candie said. 'That beach looks good enough. And this water!'

Looking over the rail one could see far down; it was possible to imagine what it would be like when the sun was on it. From the shore, Katey thought she could hear bird-song, but it might have been a trick of the breeze which blew offshore, bringing a strange scent of wildness with it. She felt a little spring of happiness inside her, a knot dissolving.

Marriott said: 'I wouldn't mind. You can leave Toni and me behind, Sweeney.'

Toni said simply: 'I would like that.' Katey pictured them, bronzed naked bodies locked together beneath the palm trees, and the elation went, the knot formed itself again and tightened. 'I don't suppose we can, though, can we?'

'You'd miss the telly,' Marriott said, 'after a while.'

The engine stopped, magnifying the silence. Sweeney gave an order, and there was the rattling tattoo of metal against metal as the anchor chain went down. It stopped at last, and the *Diana* swung at ease in the middle of the bay. They were about half a mile from shore.

'I think breakfast should be almost ready,' Sweeney said. 'If anyone is hungry.'

'My God, yes,' Lydia said. 'Ravenously.'

Sweeney nodded. 'I told Billy and the cook that we would want it early. I will join you below a little later.'

There was a good deal of chatter and laughter over breakfast, and childish jokes, particularly from Marriott. Katey saw him lean heavily against Susan, and saw her draw away from him. When Sweeney appeared, the hubbub was intensified as they asked him things – what time the shore party was to leave, what they should take with them, and all sorts of questions about the island. He answered them all with composure and good humour. He looked very pleased with himself, Katey thought, but she thought there was something below the surface of the composure – an excitement of his own, a nervousness even? They were all small boys really, she thought, with a generalized contempt, for all their strength and power and money.

The sun had still not risen when the boat was lowered, but the pearl of sky was brightening. To her surprise she discovered that Sweeney's remark about everyone going ashore was to be taken pretty nearly literally: she had expected Billy to be included for serving the food and drinks, but the Japanese cook was on hand, too, and the engineer, Yasha. She said to Sweeney:

'I thought we were having a picnic meal?'

Sweeney nodded. 'It is all prepared in those baskets behind you.'

'But you're taking the cook?'

'I thought he would like the excursion. And if we do kill one of those pigs, he can barbecue it for us.'

The engineer said: 'I would be quite happy to stay on ship. I have seen islands.'

'Not this one, surely.'

'They are all very much alike.'

'It will do you good,' Sweeney said. 'As it is, you spend too much time cooped up with your engines.'

Yasha shrugged. 'As you wish.'

Sweeney was the last to join the boat. Four of the Hawaiian deck-hands were at the oars, leaving the remaining two on board. They looked over the side, grinning, as the boat pulled away across the water.

Katey heard the bird-song distinctly as they came in to the curving sands; and the cry of some animal. The party had fallen quiet: nearer, there was only the splash of water as the oars dipped and rose again. She could see no sign of life on the beach or among the nearer trees. Apart from the bird-song and the strange cry it might have been a deserted empty world on which they were intruding. They rowed in towards the beach, and she saw that the sands were white and unmarked. Not even a crab moved there. Inside her she felt the lift she had felt before, an exhilaration. The boat's keel grated on sand, and two of the Hawaiians, dropping their oars, leapt into the water and began tugging her further up.

Silence was broken as they scrambled out of the boat, for the most part getting their feet wet. Candie cleared the lapping water with a great leap, only to fall prone on the sand, and they laughed. In antiphony to the laughter, a burst of chattering sound came from a clump of trees not far up from the water's edge, and small grey forms leapt from the perches from which presumably they had been watching, and fled inland.

Billy the steward said unnecessarily: 'Monkeys.' From his pocket he drew what Katey saw to be a small automatic pistol and lifted it, cocking his head behind the butt. 'Little bastards!'

Katey was surprised and annoyed at the expletive: it was as though, here on shore, he was assuming an equality with the guests. She glanced at Sweeney, but he seemed to have paid no attention. Susan said:

'Oh, you mustn't! Why kill them?'

Billy grinned, hefted the pistol, and slipped it back in his pocket.

'Not meant seriously, miss. I'm not the kind of shot that can hit a moving monkey at a hundred yards with a Beretta, anyway. All the same, they're nothing but thieving fleabags. Dirty habits, as well.' He rounded on the Hawaiians, who were standing looking about them. 'Come on! Get that gear out of the boat. And get the boat drawn up. We don't want to have to swim for it.'

Candie looked up in the direction of the trees.

'A gun might come in handy, I suppose, if we're going exploring in there. Have you any rounds for it, Billy?'

'Five in, and two or three clips in my pocket.'

Katey said to Sweeney: '*Are* any of the animals likely to be dangerous?'

'They should not be. If you disturb an old boar, or a sow with young, I suppose there is some risk. But they will prefer to avoid you if they can.'

'Snakes?' Toni asked. 'Are there snakes, Sweeney?'

'I doubt it. Nothing terribly virulent, anyway. And snakes, too, will keep out of your way if you make enough noise crashing through the brush. Shall we investigate the interior, do you think, or shall we make our way along the shore?'

'The shore,' Toni said, 'please. It's nicer, anyway.'

She spoke with the easy assurance of a woman who was used to having her whims as quickly obeyed as others' commands. Katey felt like opposing her, but the prospect of going up among the trees was undeniably less attractive than that of walking along the sands. She was still making up her mind to say something when Billy intervened again.

'Be a lot easier round the coast. There won't be any paths in there, except pig-paths. And they're not easy to follow. Dead simple getting lost, too.'

It was the same tone – breezy, almost verging on the truculent. Katey said sharply:

'We'll ask your advice when we want it, Billy.'

He grinned at her. 'Very well, ma'am.'

Sweeney said: 'I am inclined to think we should go round the coast, at any rate to start with. If we wish to explore inland later, we can do so.'

Candie said: 'We could make up separate parties, I suppose.'

'There would be the risk,' Sweeney pointed out, 'of some getting lost. No, let it be the shore path.'

Marriott said: 'Are we taking the food with us?'

'Pick up those baskets,' Billy said to the Hawaiians. 'Don't stand around gawping.'

'No,' Sweeney said. He made a waving gesture. 'We'll come back here to picnic – it is a pleasant spot. They had better be got up under the cool of the trees, though, before the sun rises.'

'If you leave them here,' Billy said, 'those bloody monkeys will get at them, sure as eggs.'

'True,' Sweeney said, 'but simply overcome. We shall leave you on guard, Billy. Accoutred as you are, you should be able to keep the apes at bay.'

'O.K.,' Billy said. 'I'd as soon loaf as walk.'

The sun was still hidden by the jutting headland as they began their exploration to the west, but it had risen clear of the horizon: the ocean was flecked with gold and the sands ahead of them were sunlit. Katey said with satisfaction:

'I'm glad you put that young man in his place at last. I don't care for his manners at all.'

'He's not a very pleasant person,' Sweeney said, 'is he? But one cannot devote all one's time to chiding insolence and ignorance. There is too much of it for that.'

The Marriotts, Candie and Susan led the way; a few yards separated them from Joe, Lydia, Sweeney and herself. Yasha walked by himself, on the same level, but higher up the beach. The cook and the Hawaiians followed behind, the former silent as he usually was, the rest chattering. They should not have been allowed to come, Katey thought: Sweeney should have left them with Billy. But there was no point in saying anything about it. Sweeney was basically indifferent to people's feelings; it was one of the things that came from being as rich as he was.

A spit of sand, at one point, complemented the headland across the bay. Sweeney pointed out to them that this marked the limits of the sunken crater, and that beyond it the beach changed, with the trees coming down closer to the water's edge and the ground behind them rising more steeply. The trees themselves cut off the view of the summit of this hill, but looking back they could see the dip of the valley that ran across the island, and the cloud that rested on the other peak. Its edges were bright with sunlight, its heart black and massive-seeming.

'It looks very steady,' Marriott said.

Sweeney said: 'It probably is. On some of these islands there are clouds which persist the year through.'

Susan said: 'Oh, look. The sun's rising.'

A spot of flame had sprung up between two leaning palms on the headland; it broadened as they watched and the palms stood black against the gold, which sank from its first fulgent shock, but still could turn the eye away.

'It's caught the *Diana*,' Lydia said. 'Look at the brass dazzling. It's almost as though she's on fire.'

'She's smoking, anyway,' Candie said. 'Did you leave something on the stove, Cookie?'

The Japanese shook his head slowly. Yasha said:

'There is smoke.'

Katey could not see it at first, only the brilliance of sunlight on the brass. Then, as she watched, she saw the thin curl of smoke rising from behind the mainmast.

'What is it?' she said. 'There's nothing wrong, is there?'

Yasha had begun to walk back towards the place where they had left Billy, and the boat. After ten yards or so he stopped and called to the Hawaiians:

'Come on! Get moving.'

They went after him at a trot, and he began running himself. Marriott said:

'Shouldn't we all get back? Do you think it's serious, Sweeney?'

Sweeney made no reply, and no move, but went on staring out at the *Diana*. The smoke thickened and deepened in colour. Candie said:

'My God, that looks like the engine-room, doesn't it? And there's all that diesel-oil underneath it. It is serious. Do you think the two boys on board can handle it?'

Sweeney remained silent, concentrated, and the silence spread to the others. They watched Yasha and the four Hawaiians running along the beach, and heard Yasha calling something out, presumably to Billy. He reached the spot where the boat was, and they saw it being dragged down the beach into the water. Sweeney spoke then. He said:

'They're too late.'

There was a puff of blacker smoke from the deck of the *Diana*. Through it licked tongues of flame, pale where they challenged the sunlight, but menacingly bright against the smoke. A figure leapt from the rail and splashed into the waters of the bay, followed by another. Their heads broke water, swimming for shore.

Flame twined, like a climbing flower, around the mast.

8

IT WAS DIFFICULT TO TAKE IT IN. Marriott said: 'She's a goner,'
but the rest of them stood there, seemingly unable to com-
prehend it. Candie himself felt dazed and yet, in a curious
way, exhilarated. The vast distance of ocean all round them
was unimportant; what counted was the fact that they were
safely on dry ground, at least on firm sand, and on an island
whose richness was attested by the unbroken flow of vegetation
along the hillsides, the palms with their coronet of leaves and
heavy fruit only a few yards away. And fish, no doubt, in the
bay, crustaceans among the rocks. It should not be unpleasant
during the days, weeks even, before help came. The sun, fully
risen above the headland, was getting hot. Candie pulled off
the sweater he had been wearing and tied it round his waist by
the sleeves.

More impatiently, Marriott said: 'There's not a lot of point
in standing here, is there? We'd better get back to the boat and
see if there is anything that can be done.'

Candie looked at him with distaste. He was the sort who
would be full of ideas of what to do, and continually hectoring
others to do them for him. Well, at least, he thought, one could
always get away from him. The island was big enough for that.

Joe Willeway said: 'I hope she's fully insured, Sweeney.'

Sweeney said: 'I believe so.' His voice was indifferent. 'Perhaps we should join the others.'

He began to walk back along the beach, and they followed
him without hesitation. Sweeney says, Candie thought. We
all do as he tells us. The surprising thing is that one does not
resent it, as one would in the case of Marriott. Trust in Sweeney

– Sweeney will bring his flock safely into harbour. Safely, at any rate, to Silver Island. Even the two Hawaiians who had been left on board were swimming strongly and nearing the beach. The others had not bothered to put the boat out. It would have been rather pointless to do that now.

Susan said to Sweeney: 'Do you think there's any chance of the fire …' She hesitated over the absurdity of her question. 'We're stuck here, then?'

'Yes,' Sweeney said. 'We are temporarily marooned.'

'How long – temporarily?'

'It's difficult to say.'

Marriott said: 'But you have been in wireless communication with Honolulu, haven't you? As soon as they realize we're lost, they'll come looking.'

'They will come looking,' Sweeney said, 'but not just yet, and perhaps not here. My last message to them was three days ago. Their information is that we are heading for the Marquesas, or possibly the Tahiti group. I should think a search would be concentrated in those areas.'

Marriott said sharply: 'Why Tahiti? You didn't tell us that.'

'Surely I did. Did I not speak about possibly selling the ship at Tahiti?'

'But after visiting the Marquesas. You told us they were our first place of call.'

'I had this little surprise for you. You might have decided to stay here a few days, and perhaps then it would have been preferable to sail direct to Tahiti.'

'But you didn't tell them in Honolulu – that you might be heading for this island?'

'Because I was far from sure that I could find it: a tiny spot in a very big ocean. It is a long time since I did any navigation. I have kept more of the skill than I thought I might have done.'

'So no one has the faintest idea where we are. It sounds bloody …'

Marriott hesitated. 'Yes?' Sweeney said.

'Unfortunate.'

The word which had almost come out would have been something like irresponsible, Candie thought. But even now the tie of deference held. In the fading hope of that business contract, on the other side of the world? Or simply because Sweeney was Sweeney, and one did not use words like that to him.

Lydia said impatiently: 'Bloody unfortunate is right. But how long are we likely to be stuck here? You must have some idea.'

'I believe the Americans keep their uninhabited islands under survey. Inspections are made, I think, every other year. Of course, one does not know when the last one took place.'

Katey said: 'Are you telling us we might be here for two years? It's impossible!'

'Or two days,' Sweeney said. 'Who knows? And there is also the possibility of a casual visit, such as our own. But unlikely. We are, as I have said, a long way from normal shipping routes.'

Willeway kicked his toes in the sand; the sandals he was wearing were of good leather and made Candie's own look flimsy by comparison. How long would his last, Candie wondered, and what did one do when they had worn out? Get used to going about barefoot? Or kill one of those pigs Sweeney had talked about and make sandals out of the hide? How did one do that – dry the skin in the sun? Wasn't there something about tanning hide with urine? Altogether it would probably be simpler to go barefoot.

Willeway said: 'You're painting the picture as black as possible, aren't you, Sweeney?'

'With as much realism as possible. I think that is essential. It is safer to plan on the worst assumptions than the best. Our first task must be to convince ourselves that we are here, that we have no means of getting away or communicating with the rest of the world, and that we must rely entirely on our own resources.'

He spoke earnestly, with an undertone that might almost,

Candie reflected, be satisfaction. The thought crossed his mind: was it possible that Sweeney had engineered all this? He considered it and dismissed it as absurd. He was probably ruthless enough, but there were snags obvious even to his, Candie's, mind, and Sweeney was not the kind of man to overlook them. For one thing, if the fire had been deliberate, there would almost certainly be evidence on which a marine insurance company would, in due course, refuse payment. And Sweeney was not likely to throw away upwards of fifty thousand pounds, merely to see how a group of his acquaintances behaved when abandoned on a desert island. In addition to which, it might not be for more than a few days – they might always be picked up by a passing ship. And Sweeney was here himself, faced with the same deprivations and hardships as the rest.

Susan said: 'We really are marooned, aren't we? It's difficult to grasp the idea. How many thousand miles from London?'

Her voice had a slight tremor. Sweeney said:

'A long way, I'm afraid. Eight or nine thousand miles.' He put his hand on her shoulder. 'But distances matter less than communications. And a communication can be broken without shipwreck.'

Whatever it signified, it seemed to cheer her. She said, with an attempt at a smile:

'I suppose so. Do you think they will keep that job open for me, Sweeney?'

'Or one as good.'

Marriott said: 'But I don't imagine that business deal you talked of will wait.'

'The same applies,' Sweeney said. 'There will be another.' He looked at the rest. 'And an engagement, very likely, for Roger, and Joe will find his rents and dividends have been accumulating nicely and will go back to architecture refreshed and inventive. I am still being realistic. There is no harm in looking forward to our return once we have accepted the fact that we are here, and our stay here may be prolonged.'

'Something for everybody?' Lydia said. 'What about me?'

'Do I need to encourage you,' Sweeney said, 'with thoughts of London? I think you will be happy here.'

She looked across the bright sea at the burning hulk of the *Diana*.

'Maybe I will.'

Billy, Yasha and the Hawaiians were waiting for them beside the ship's boat. The two men who had swum ashore looked guilty, and looked as though they had already had a cursing out; probably from Billy. Billy said:

'All right. You can tell the skipper now.'

The shorter, stockier of the two began talking. He spoke in a liquid flowing accent that made his words difficult to follow, but Candie got the gist of it. They had seen smoke coming from the engine-room and gone to investigate; but flames were already leaping high and the fumes choked them. There was no hope of doing anything, and then there was an explosion – presumably one of the fuel tanks going up – and they dived overboard to save themselves. He finished, and they both looked at Sweeney. They had transparently guilty looks.

Billy said: 'One little thing they haven't mentioned. They both stink of whisky.'

'I had noticed that,' Sweeney said. He said to the men in a detached but not hostile manner: 'You were drinking. Where did you get hold of the whisky?'

'In the saloon, sir. The bar was open.'

'You mean you broke it open,' Billy said. 'I left it locked.'

'No, sir.' His eyes darted from Sweeney to Billy. 'We found it open. We ...'

Billy swung his arm. The Hawaiian tried to dodge, but the blow caught him on the side of the neck and sent him sprawling across the sand. He shook his head, and looked up.

Billy said: 'Don't you call me a liar. That bar was locked. I saw to it last night.'

There had been a dice game in the saloon the previous night, Candie remembered, and Billy had been drinking with the others. He had not been drunk, but he had not been quite in control, either. There had been a business of his trying to ingratiate himself with Lydia, while she had grown more and more cutting in reply. It could well be that he had omitted to lock the bar up afterwards.

Sweeney said: 'Help him up.' Billy looked back at him for a moment, and then put an arm out and dragged the Hawaiian to his feet. 'There is no point,' Sweeney said, 'in squabbling over details. We can do nothing to alter the facts, nor to change our situation. We can improve it, though. We shall need shelter, essentially for the ladies, and then for the rest of us. The boys ought to be able to build some kind of hut. Yasha, will you see to that? And perhaps you, Billy, will report the state of stores to me.'

'What stores?'

'The emergency supplies carried in the boat.'

He said sullenly: 'I can tell you without looking. Canned meat, biscuits and that concentrated chocolate. Supposed to be a week's supply for ten people.'

'But is it?' Sweeney said. 'Perhaps you would be so good as to itemize them for me. And water, too, I take it?'

'There will be fresh water on the island.'

'I am sure you are right. But we haven't located a spring yet.'

He turned, dismissing him. Yasha said:

'There should be an axe in the boat, too. We shall need that.'

'Yes. What else do we have in the way of tools?'

Yasha produced from his pocket a Swiss Army knife. Candie had seen a similar one: they were equipped with various small tools as well as the normal blades.

'This,' he said. Sweeney nodded. He turned back to Billy who was at the boat examining the lockers. 'Billy!'

Billy looked up. 'Yes?'

'Do you have anything we can use as a tool. A knife?'

'No.' He shook his head slowly, staring at Sweeney. 'Nothing like that.'

Sweeney's gaze held his. 'But you do have a weapon.'

Billy put his hand in his pocket and, after a moment, brought out the gun. It lay flat in his hand. Sunlight kissed the blue metal. It drew their eyes. Billy said:

'The little old equalizer.'

'It may come in useful,' Sweeney said.

'Yes,' Billy said, 'I would say so.'

There was a brief silence, edged, Candie thought, with tension. It ended when Sweeney said:

'All right, Billy. Carry on with the inventory.'

Billy stared down at the gun, hefted it in his hand and slipped it back into his side-pocket. He smiled, his cheeky ingratiating smile, at them all, allowing it to linger on Lydia, and turned back to the boat. Marriott, standing between Sweeney and Candie, said in a low voice:

'Wouldn't it have been better if someone else had taken charge of that?'

Sweeney stood, silently staring for so long that Candie thought he had not heard what Marriott said. But he spoke at last.

'It is not so much that I believe in the sanctity of private property as that I detest its opposite. I think a community must show good cause before it redistributes the goods of its members. The pistol is his.'

'But is it safe to allow him to keep it?' Marriott said. 'There's such a thing as self-protection. Doesn't that override the claims of private property?'

'Only, as I said, where good cause is shown. Personal feelings, my dear Tony, are not enough. Ah, they have found the axe, I see. That should make the building of huts a great deal easier. So the boys have a task, and so have Yasha and Billy. And the cook, I trust, will be starting to plan and construct his field-kitchen. The rest of you, I take it, will want to be useful also?'

There was a general agreement. Candie said:

'We might go and see what there is about in the way of fruit and things.'

Sweeney nodded. 'And fuel. Dead branches, driftwood – anything that will burn. You have watches?'

They all had watches. Of all possible superfluities, Candie thought, these were perhaps the most ridiculous. The sun would tell the time for them, as well as anyone could want. He was beginning to enjoy the prospects before them again: an hour or two strolling along the beach or among the trees, and later …

'We will have an early lunch,' Sweeney said. 'Be back by twelve-thirty.'

And later a rest on the beach – in the shade because the day would be very hot by then – and perhaps a swim. Peace and relaxation.

Susan said: 'We have nothing to carry things in; if we do find fruit and so on.'

'For the present you will have to manage. There should be vines on the island from which we can make containers in due course. That is another thing you can look out for.'

Katey said to Sweeney: 'You aren't coming with us?'

'No,' Sweeney said. 'I shall stay here.'

They debated whether to retrace their original path along the beach or cut inland and, at Marriott's insistence, agreed on the first. Candie felt the same resentment against him, even though he himself preferred the beach as easier, but made no protest. They trailed along with Marriott in the lead, followed by Katey, Toni, Lydia and Willeway. Candie walked with Susan, some way behind. Already it was beginning to be hot.

They passed the spit of sand, where they had been when they saw smoke curling up from the deck of the *Diana*, and Candie paused to look back. The ship was blazing furiously, with flames licking around her almost to the water's edge. After a while, Susan said:

'We'd better catch up, hadn't we?'

He touched her arm. 'No. Wait.'

They stood in silence, looking across the bay. It was about ten minutes later that it happened: they saw the *Diana* suddenly yaw and heel over. Her smoke-wreathed stern swung up against the sky, hung there for a moment, and dipped. The ship slid quietly down into the waters of the bay.

9

B Y THE TIME THEY CONTINUED on their journey, the others were out of sight beyond the curve of the beach. They walked on in silence, for which Susan was grateful. A nice thing about Roger was that he was undemanding company; one felt rested with him and at ease. And she needed that badly. Watching the *Diana* sink had removed the last faint illusion that things would come right: the fire go out, the ship prove, miraculously, sound enough to navigate. Or the radio still workable, to bring a rescue party from Honolulu. There could be no illusion now. Here they were and here, indefinitely, they were likely to stay.

Recognizing this, she faced another fact – about herself. She had not, previously, accepted an end with John. Her anticipations had always lain beyond the three or four weeks of the cruise, beyond the new job that Sweeney had arranged. One part of her mind, and the part that counted, had been quiescent, waiting for the telephone call which would surely come – in a day or a week, in a month perhaps – waiting to refuse the first plea, but not sharply, waiting for the next and the next, and finally for the one to which she would surrender. Waiting, therefore, for the moment of walking into a familiar bar and seeing him, hearing his voice, laughing probably … Waiting for the sweet weakness in her limbs, the subduing of the ache of loss.

Nor was this the whole of the calculation. The new job, the cruise – these had been weapons against his indifference, instruments to bring him to heel. Her acts of independence would make him dependent again; he would think of her, cosseted in luxury and pleasure, and want her back, his fancy teased by the thought of tropic nights on deck, the faces of other men near her own. But she saw, now that the immediate future was so different from her expectation, how absurd, childish, the calculation had been. The end had been there – not in her mind, perhaps, but in his. She ought to be grateful for being deprived of those weeks in London waiting for the telephone to ring. It was better, as Sweeney had hinted, to be here, lost to him physically since she had already lost him in every way that counted.

And yet, against all reason, against all recognition, there was this other desolation, the total frustration of knowing that there was no way in which she could touch him now. She would not – she hoped – have done the stupid things other women had done in the past: written letters to him, telephoned on some flimsy pretext, waited outside his office or in a pub where he might run into her. But the fact of being so irretrievably out of touch, and for so long, perhaps, was agonizing. Two years! Dear God, in two years he might not remember her face.

The beach was narrow here, backed by a shelf where palms jutted out, almost overhanging the water. A nut which had fallen rolled with the lapping waves up against the sand. Candie, reaching out and trying to keep his feet dry, fished for it with his outstretched hand. He managed to get his fingers behind it and tossed it up on to the beach. It lay there, smooth and green and heavy-looking. He said:

'Well, I suppose that's something.'

She smiled at him, dragging her mind back from its preoccupation. 'Are you going to carry it with you?'

'Be a bit silly, wouldn't it? We'll leave it here and pick it up on the way back.'

'Unless one of those monkeys we saw gets to it first.'

He shrugged. 'Nothing to worry over if it does.' He looked up at the crown of feathery leaves moving slightly against the sky. 'Plenty more where that came from.'

'Providing you can climb it. I shouldn't think it was easy.'

Candie shook his head. 'Shake them down.' He looked

about him with some satisfaction. 'I think I'm going to enjoy our stay here. Didn't Sweeney say something about bananas? I could devour a hand or two of those right now.'

Misery flowed back over her as she contemplated his contentment. What difference was there between them? Nothing but a sense of loss. She felt she could not resist the question:

'Roger? Have you ever … ?'

Pride, in the last resort stronger than loneliness, bit the words back for her.

'Ever what?' Candie asked.

'Oh, I don't know.' She stared out to sea. 'Imagined this sort of thing, I suppose.'

He talked, and she listened to him, taking in enough to make the right responses. Distance was covered; time passed. It all helped, probably. But she was glad when they encountered the rest of the party returning. Numbers offered cover, and cover was what she needed most.

Candie said: 'Nothing doing further on?'

'We worked round to the other side of the island,' Marriott said. 'Part of the way round. It all looks pretty much the same. And complaints of hunger were beginning to come in, so we decided to turn back.'

'No banana groves?' Candie asked.

'Not a damn' thing but coconut palms and scrub. And there wasn't. much we could do about the coconuts since the only knife is back with the work party.'

'How about pigs?'

'No. Only monkeys.' He grinned at Lydia. 'Lydia claims one of them was white.'

'For Christ's sake, belt up!' Lydia's anger, it was apparent, had been some time in the kindling. 'Keep your feeble sense of humour to yourself, you feeble little squit.'

Marriott shrugged. 'Only reporting what you said.'

'Shut up,' she said. 'Shut up! I can't stand your voice, among other things.'

Marriott said nothing, but continued to smile. Candie said:

'I don't really fancy eating monkey, whatever the colour. Do you think Sweeney's island paradise might not have the Fortnum touch after all?'

'We haven't seen much of it yet,' Willeway pointed out. Marriott had resumed his walk back in the direction of the boat, and they followed him. 'We didn't try to cut inland.' He drew in a deep breath. 'I'm ravenous. It must be the air. I hope Sweeney isn't going to be too strict about the time for broaching the luncheon basket.'

Susan found herself near Lydia. She said:

'It was a white monkey?'

Lydia looked at her, at first aggressively and then relaxing. 'Yes,' she said. 'It was white.'

'An albino, I suppose.'

'I didn't get close enough,' Lydia said, 'to check if its eyes were pink.' She gestured towards Marriott. 'I can't stand that little tick.'

Susan said: 'I don't care very much for him either.'

'Well, you're his number one target. That's pretty obvious. But if you won't play he'll be quite happy to try Katey or me. Nasty little sod. He'll probably wind up among the monkeys himself. And not fussy about the colour.'

'Some men are a bit unsavoury, aren't they?'

Lydia laughed angrily. 'Some men!'

'Not all.'

Lydia said indifferently: 'I wouldn't know. I haven't met them all.'

When they got back to that part of the beach where they had left the others, they found it deserted. The boat was here, drawn up high above the water-line, but there was no sign of Sweeney and the rest.

Willeway said: 'The basket's missing, too. It was under that tree over there.'

'We'd better call for them,' Marriott said.

He cupped his mouth and hallooed up in the direction of the trees. After a pause there was an answering cry. It sounded like Billy's voice. It was not possible to distinguish what he was saying, and they looked at each other uncertainly. Marriott said at last:

'Well, we could have a shot at finding them.'

They made their way up from the beach, through palms and then the scrub vegetation which they had seen further west. There were other trees beyond which Susan did not recognize; they were slender boled and had long glossy leaves. They were so close together that in places it was difficult to find a way through. Here and there was evidence of the passage of the others – shrubs uprooted, occasionally slashed down. They could hear voices ahead now, and quite suddenly were looking down a slight slope into a clearing. It was about as much in extent as a small field, and crossed by a stream at the far end. It was sprinkled with shrubs and saplings which the Hawaiians were engaged in uprooting and carrying away. Billy and Yasha were supervising them.

Candie said: 'Huts up already? That's been quick work.'

'Don't be a damn' fool,' Marriott said. 'They didn't put those up. They've been there some time. Look at the grass on the roof of that one.'

Marriott was obviously right. The huts were, in any case, too big and too solidly constructed to have been the result of a couple of hours' labour by the Hawaiians. They were on the right-hand side of the clearing; she saw three of them, one rather smaller than the others. They were built up on platforms under-pinned with coral blocks so that they perched above the floor of the clearing. It was necessary, because they stood on ground which sloped quite sharply up to the line of vegetation behind them. It was several moments before Susan saw that there was a fourth hut, quite a little one, separated from the three she had first noticed. It was on the other side of the stream and faced towards them. As she watched, Sweeney came out of the open doorway. He waved, and began to walk towards them.

They met in the centre of the clearing. Sweeney said: 'You are back early. Did something go wrong?'

'Joe's belly started rumbling,' Marriott said. 'We were all rather hoping that lunch could be advanced somewhat.'

'Yes,' Sweeney said. 'I think it might. You are empty-handed, I see. You found nothing edible on your travels?'

'Nothing but coconuts, and it was scarcely worthwhile carrying them back. There are enough of them down on the beach. And we couldn't open any, not having the tools.'

'You chose the wrong direction.' Sweeney pointed across the clearing, at the vegetation which stretched on down the valley. 'We've already located banana and breadfruit, and do you see that tree in the far corner? Does anyone recognize it?'

Susan looked at the tree. It was forty or fifty feet high, with leaves glossy like those of the tree they had passed, but more oval, darker green, and reaching, she judged, as much as a foot in length. And there were dark green fruit, too, she saw.

Toni said, in a puzzled voice: 'Not pears, surely?'

'My God,' Willeway said. 'Avocado!'

'Exactly.'

Marriott laughed. 'All we need is a *sauce vinaigrette* and we can kid ourselves we're in the rural annexe of the Caprice or the Mirabelle.'

'It should not be beyond Cookie's powers,' Sweeney said. 'A little coconut oil ... acetified palm toddy ... *aux crevettes*, very likely, if you prefer it that way.'

Willeway said happily: 'Avocado. A whole tree full.'

'Dozens of trees,' Sweeney said. 'Hundreds probably. You shall gorge yourself on avocado, Joe.'

'And bananas,' Willeway said. 'You said ...'

'A little higher up,' Sweeney said. 'But the boys have brought some bunches down. Cookie has them at the kitchen. You can go and sustain yourself on a few if you wish. We shall be serving lunch shortly.'

The kitchen was a pile of stones, put together with rough symmetry, not far from the stream. Willeway headed in that direction and, after a moment, Candie followed him. Katey called after them:

'Bring some back for us.'

Marriott said: 'These huts, Sweeney.'

'Yes?'

'I thought you said the island was uninhabited – had been since some time in the last century?'

'They haven't been used lately,' Sweeney said. 'The boys have done a certain amount of clearing up, but you will find them still showing signs of nature's encroachment.'

'But not sixty or seventy years. It's ridiculous!'

'Well, the island may very well have had visitors during the recent war, of course. The Japanese never got within reach but the Americans may have used it – as a staging post, perhaps. Or merely garrisoned it against the possibility of the Japs moving in.'

Marriott said doubtfully: 'Could be, I suppose. The war's been over a long time, though. I should have thought they would have been completely overgrown by now.'

Katey said: 'There are three huts. What's happening about that?'

'The ladies are to have the one at the end – it is in the best condition. Joe, Roger and Tony will have the small hut next to it. Billy, Yasha, Cookie and the boys will have to make do with the third hut. This is a temporary arrangement, of course. There is nothing to stop couples, or individuals, building their own huts.'

'What about you?' Katey said.

'I shall use the little hut on the far side of the stream.' He spoke with placid assurance. 'It is only big enough for one person.'

Willeway and Candie came back across the clearing, each carrying a hand of bananas. They offered them round, and Susan broke one off. The skin was of a reddish shade, and the fruit inside was tinged with pink.

Toni said: 'Funny sort of banana. Is that because they're not a cultivated variety?'

Marriott was looking at the one he had taken. 'The only thing is, I would have thought the wild ones would be small. These are quite hefty.'

The individual fruits were, in fact, as long as, if not longer than, the high-grade bananas which one found in shops at home. They were slightly thinner, though. Susan tasted hers and found it had a somewhat odd flavour: tangy, not unpleasant. She took another bite. Willeway said:

'I like this. Could it be a new variety, do you think? Might be worth importing.'

'Not an economic proposition,' Marriott said. 'Though I suppose one could try it out on Fyffes. Flog them a few cuttings for a thousand apiece.'

Sweeney said: 'The best profit of all is the profit from adversity. One final word on domestic arrangements. You will notice that there is a small pool there, where the stream leaves the clearing. We must use that for ablutions and laundry and take our drinking water higher up. Yasha and Billy will get the boys working on more complex sanitary arrangements this afternoon. Meanwhile, the bushes provide shelter if not comfort. We have no soap, I'm afraid, unless any of you came provided? I perceive not. Perhaps we shall be able to do something about this in due course – I remember something about fats and wood-ash.'

Toni said: 'Any ideas about making lipstick?'

'No,' he said gravely. 'I'm afraid, none.'

Just another small shock, Susan thought; a reminder of the sharpness of the break between life as it had been and as it must be now. Thinking of the small crosses in her calendar diary, she realized that there would be another complication in a few days' time. How would one cope with that? Presumably as women had coped in all the centuries before packaging and chemists' shops. She contemplated her clothes: sandals, pants and slacks, bra, blouse and cardigan. Entirely adequate for a day ashore, but desperate with a possible two-year stay in prospect.

Marriott, standing near her, said: 'Some will be luckier than others. You don't need lipstick or cosmetics with a skin like yours.'

She ignored him. Handkerchief: she had forgotten that. And they had all got swimsuits and towels in the canvas bag in the boat. It was amazing how cheering the recollection was. One could do a lot with a large towel.

'Well,' Sweeney said. 'I think we could go and see to our picnic now.'

Marriott walked beside her, his arm brushing against hers, and she moved away towards Candie. He said:

'I think, a short snooze after lunch. Don't you find this air tiring, Sue?'

She smiled. 'A little.'

'It's a good job we've got the boys,' he said. 'That's going to save a lot of sweat.'

'But will they carry on working? How is Sweeney going to be able to pay them?'

'He can pay them when we get back. Chalk it up.'

She said doubtfully: 'They may not be so keen on that.'

'He can pay extra. You know Sweeney. Money's no object.'

'But does money *mean* anything now?'

He looked puzzled, and she did not pursue the point. It was obvious that he regarded the whole affair as an unexpected but welcome extension of a pleasant holiday. It was probably as good a way to view things as any.

A white linen cloth had been spread out on the grass – Susan looked at it with an envious and calculating eye – and food, on paper plates, laid on this. Smoked salmon. Cold chicken, beef and ham. Potato salad with pimento, coleslaw, and the

American-style green salad which the Japanese cook invariably offered. And eight champagne glasses.

Katey said: 'Oughtn't we to save some for later?'

'We'll deal with later when it comes,' Sweeney said. 'I did wonder about the champagne – whether it should not be kept against the day our rescuers arrive. But I like my champagne young.'

He worked his thumbs under the cork of a magnum. With a pop, the cork went up and was lost against the green of tropical vegetation. Expertly, Sweeney took the bottle to one of the glasses, spilling none. He poured the drinks out and at last raised his own glass.

'Let us drink,' he said, 'to our stay on Silver Island. May it serve a noble purpose.'

She had no idea what he was talking about, but, a new wave of misery seizing her in the memory of the last time she had drunk champagne, in Le Bourget at the Lapin Sauté, with earnest French businessmen earnestly eating all round them, she did not care. Her eyes pricked as she drank, and she blinked the tears away.

10

AFTER LUNCH, THE PARTY SPLIT into three groups. Billy and Yasha put the Hawaiians back to work: they were to rig two covers over the stream further down and fix flat stones as foot-rests. After that they were to build an annexe to their own hut for the two whites to sleep in; this was Billy's decision, and Sweeney had not demurred. Of the others, Joe and Katey Willeway, Roger Candie and Toni had decided they would go down to laze on the beach. The remainder – Sweeney, Lydia, Susan and Marriott himself – were to explore inland through the valley. Susan had been doubtful. She had made it plain that she preferred Candie's company to his, but her curiosity was greater than her distaste. He was not at all despondent about Susan. Her reaction was an exaggerated one, and that was the kind, in his experience, which could easily reverse itself. Watching her closely he had observed signs that she was more emotional than she cared to show. And Candie was a nonentity; no woman with any spirit could take him seriously.

Marriott was considerably less pleased that Lydia had chosen to join the explorers. She was the kind of woman, as the incident in the morning had demonstrated, with whom he found it most difficult to deal. A woman who though she despised him, individually, could be brought round, but one whose generalized contempt for the male species gave very little scope. Her anger unnerved him. His comment about her claiming to have seen a white monkey had been innocuous enough, but had provoked a storm. She seemed amiable at the moment, but there was a continual uncertainty as to what might happen next.

The ground rose on a moderate gradient as they made their way inland. This area was thickly wooded, but they found what appeared to be the remains of a path which offered easier going. Marriott wondered about this, as he had wondered about the huts. It was twenty years since the war had ended. Even allowing for a garrison staying on for a year or two afterwards, the vegetation, surely, would have triumphed more completely than this. Not that the point was important: there could well have been an attempt to colonize, which Sweeney did not know of and which had failed. It was obvious, at least, that there was no one here now. Or no one, at any rate, in this part of the island, and since this offered, on Sweeney's declaration, the only possible anchorage, there would hardly be a settlement elsewhere.

Sweeney's knowledgeableness was something one did not contest lightly. He drew their attention to things as they progressed. There was the banana plant, bearing both its clusters of yellowish flowers and the bunches of oddly pink fruit which they had eaten earlier. And a little further on he stopped in front of a tree about the same height as the avocado in the clearing. Its leaves also were glossy, but differently shaped, being entire towards the base, but multiple-lobed towards the apex. The fruit which hung among them was large – a couple of feet or even more in circumference – and greenish-brown in colour.

'Our bread supply,' Sweeney said.

'Is that breadfruit?' Susan asked. 'Do you eat it just as it is?'

'You have to cook it. It isn't a very difficult job, though. You merely have to wrap it in leaves and put it in a hole with hot stones. Or you can cut it in slices and fry it.'

Marriott said: 'You seem to have done your homework on tropic islands, Sweeney.'

'*The Coral Island*,' he said, 'was my first bedside book and is still, I think, my favourite. And the disappointment of picking up *The Gorilla Hunters* and finding them all grown up and dull – with beards, even – soured my youth. It taught me that the good and bright and fresh things must always descend to the monotone and monochrome.'

'Once you've learned the lesson,' Susan said, 'does it stay learnt?'

'Not for most people,' Sweeney said, 'fortunately. That plant over there. Do any of you know it?'

Long slender stems carried lobed leaves and clusters of flowers, green and bell-shaped, which were inconspicuous in themselves, but collectively pretty and showy. No one offered comment, and Sweeney went across, gripped the base of the plant and pulled it. It came up, and he showed them a thick tuberous root, two or three feet in length.

Marriott said: 'Yam. But I'm guessing.'

'Guessing correctly. It is becoming fairly clear that we shall not go short of starches. The protein problem remains. No trace of pig so far. Still, we can make do with fish, and I believe young monkey can be palatable.' He saw Susan wince, and added: 'I'm sure we can rely on Cookie to disguise it for us.'

Lydia said: 'I saw a white monkey this morning, Sweeney.'

'Did you?' He looked at her with interest. 'Where was this?'

'Up in the west of the island.'

Marriott was careful to say nothing. Susan said:

'That sort of thing happens from time to time, doesn't it?'

'Albinism? Yes, indeed. But more commonly in some species than in others. White blackbirds are no particular rarity, as you know. But I haven't heard of a white monkey before. Perhaps we can trap it, and present it to the London Zoo on our return.'

He had left the yam lying to be picked up on their way back. They pushed their way now through a more tangled growth of bushes, among which the path was temporarily lost. The ground continued to rise until they reached a brow. They looked down into the sheltered central valley of the island. On the right the hillside sloped up to the crown, wooded except for outcrops of black rock, of the western hill. The ground rose more steeply on the left, interrupted by shelves and small declivities, until it disappeared into the folds – dazzling white with the sun full on them – of the cloud that rested, eddying and shifting slightly, but not substantially changing, on the summit. Marriott began to find its permanence irritating. Ahead of them, a mile or so away, a shoulder of the eastern hill forced the valley to the left, where presumably it continued on to the other side of the island and the sea.

Lydia said: 'That's a bit funny.'

'What is?' Sweeney asked her.

She pointed. 'They're kind of regular. Like fields, almost.'

Marriott saw what she was referring to. Mostly on the lower part of the eastern slope, but continuing down in places to the valley floor, it was possible to trace a geometry of broken shapes. The edges were blurred, and there were incursions of alien elements, but there was an impression of design, a sense of different crops planted in separate plots.

'Could it be accidental?' Lydia asked. 'I don't see how, do you?'

'The best thing,' Sweeney said, 'will be to go and examine things more closely. Don't you agree? If we bear to the right, we should get to the first patch fairly easily.'

They followed the side of the hill. As they got nearer edges blurred still further, but they were eventually aware of standing among a different kind of bush, planted in what might once have been regular lines. The bushes looked vaguely familiar; Marriott felt he had seen them before somewhere, or pictures of them.

Sweeney said: 'Our fortune remains good. This would have been one of the more unwelcome deprivations.'

'Coffee?' Marriott hazarded.

'Coffee,' Sweeney confirmed.

'The bushes have been properly planted?' Susan suggested. 'A plantation? Does it mean someone has tried to run the island as an economic proposition? And abandoned it?'

Sweeney looked out over the hillside. 'It is quite a small plot,' he said. 'Unless there are other plots in other parts of the island, one could hardly pick enough beans to make any kind of export worth while. A patch as small as this does not make sense.'

Lydia said: 'Not for export. It would make sense for home consumption, though, wouldn't it?'

'Home consumption?'

'Perhaps there has been some kind of colony here; more recently than the wartime occupation, I mean. One of those groups you read about from time to time – you know, founding an ideal community away from civilization.'

Reluctantly, Marriott found himself supporting her.

'It sounds reasonable,' he said. 'It would account for the huts, too, wouldn't it? But what became of the colonists? I suppose they might have found the going too hard, and packed it in.'

'If they did,' Susan said, 'at least one of them would have written a best-selling book about it. I don't remember reading anything about Silver Island.'

'They might have died off,' Lydia said.

Sweeney said: 'There are many possibilities. Tony's is as probable as any. The book may still be in proof, after all.'

Marriott stared ahead. 'These patches are of pretty much the same size. That one down there looks as though it's been some kind of wheat originally. What kind of a colony puts down a coffee patch the same size as the wheat patch?'

'A colony of Viennese intellectuals,' Susan suggested.

'It may not have been a colony, in the sense in which you are envisaging it,' Sweeney said. 'Possibly a United States Government experimental station of some kind.' He spoke blandly, tossing them the hypothesis like an adult throwing an idea to children. 'Testing the possibility of growing various crops in these latitudes and conditions.'

Marriott objected: 'That makes less sense than the other. The conditions are pretty well unique. What kind of a test would that be?'

'I don't know,' Sweeney said. 'Though where things fail to make sense I am always reluctant to rule out governmental agencies. Does any of it matter? Surely we should be grateful for what has been left us, whoever left them. It looks as though we shall have a more varied diet than we could have thought possible.'

They crossed from the coffee patch to the next, which was a tangle of what proved to be some kind of green bean. It was difficult to decide exactly what kind, particularly in view of the fact that the beans they found – and, in fact, the plants – showed a wide range of diversity. Some pods were long and tapering, some almost spherical. Opening one of these, Susan found it to contain something like a kidney bean, but bright blue in colour and packed segmentally, resembling the sections of an orange.

She said doubtfully: 'I suppose we can eat these? I've never seen anything quite like them before.'

'We will try them on Joe,' Sweeney said. 'It may be an idea to make him our official taster.'

There was a patch of what seemed, from isolated plants they found, to have been peas, but this had mostly been taken over by an invading weed, a small plant with little sharp adhesive seeds which scratched their bare ankles. They were also able to identify patches of cotton and cocoa, and came down at last to what Marriott had guessed from a distance to be wheat. It was, in fact, maize, but here again showing a great deal of variety in size, shape and colour. Some of the ears were tiny, others large and well packed.

Marriott said: 'Things certainly seem to run riot on this island.'

Sweeney nodded. Touching one of the stalks, he said: 'We can get rid of the poor plants and sow from the good.'

Lydia said: 'Sow! That's pretty long-term stuff.'

'Yes,' Sweeney agreed. He looked thoughtfully at the maize. 'Unleavened bread, of course, unless we can trap a suitable yeast? That might be possible.'

Proceeding along the valley floor, they found root crops: pota-toes, sugar-beet, turnips. Beyond them there was a patch of what might have been wheat, deteriorated almost out of recognition and rank with weeds. It was here that Lydia, going impatiently ahead of the others, turned her foot on a loose stone. She cried out with pain, and sat down to massage her ankle.

'How bad is it?' Sweeney asked her.

'I think I've sprained it.' She winced as he put his fingers to it. 'You'd better go on. I'll wait here for you.'

Susan said: 'I'll stay, too.'

'There's no need. I'll be all right.'

Sweeney said: 'There is no urgency about exploring the island. I should just like to see what lies past the bend in the valley.' He patted Lydia's shoulder. 'We shan't leave you for more than five or ten minutes. Are you comfortable enough?'

'Yes,' she said. She gritted her teeth. 'Take your time.'

They continued round the shoulder of the western hill and found themselves looking at the sea again. The valley dropped gently in front of them and broadened out. On either side it was heavily wooded, but a stream – a river, almost – falling from a cleft of rock on their left, carried on through reed beds and long grass, studded with small bushes, towards the distant blue.

'Nothing remarkable there,' Sweeney said. 'We can turn back and see to our casualty.'

Lydia, when they returned to her, was staring up at the cloud that covered the mountain-top. Sweeney asked her:

'How does it feel now?'

'Stiff,' she said, 'and painful. That cloud … I thought it lifted a bit. Only for a moment. Not really lifted. Thinned, though.'

They looked up with her. The cloud was white, solid-seeming with the sunlight dazzling from it.

'Well?' Sweeney asked her.

'There seemed to be something bright up there.' Sweeney and Marriott had turned their attention to her, and she added defensively: 'I don't suppose it was anything. A trick of the light.'

'Probably,' Sweeney said. 'Let's see if we can get you on the move again.'

She was able to walk, limping, with Sweeney supporting her. Marriott offered to help her on the other side, but she refused him brusquely. He was relieved about that, particularly since it enabled him to concentrate on Susan. He talked to her and forced her into replies; a little unwilling at the outset, but gradually more graciously. She was interested, he discovered, in classical music, and he knew enough about it to say the right things, feeling his way into her prejudices and likings. A reference to the Wigmore Hall brought an animation into her expression which opened up an entirely new range of possibilities. The beginning of a twitch of scorn when he mentioned Bartok alerted him to the probability that her tastes were not modern. He made the best of the information as he turned it up and was rewarded when he put his hand under her arm to help her through a tight spot, and she did not – as she had done previously – draw away. She released herself later, but gently.

Back at the clearing, Sweeney helped Lydia to the hut which had been allocated to the ladies, and Susan, excusing herself to Marriott, went with them. Marriott stood watching the Hawaiians; they had set up a framework for an annexe to their own hut and were roofing it with palm leaves, laid and plaited over a net of branches. One of them, he saw, had a cut cheek and a swelling eye.

Yasha passed him, and he said:

'That boy. Chippy? What happened to him?'

Yasha followed his glance. 'Billy hit him.'

'Why?'

'He said he found him loafing – smoking a cigarette behind the hut.'

'So he hit him?'

'Yes.'

'How did the rest take it?'

Yasha shrugged. 'They carried on with their work.'

'I see.' He let Yasha go and called Billy over to him. 'Billy. Can you spare a minute?'

Billy gave some instruction to the Hawaiians, and came to where Marriott stood. He was smoking himself, and he did not bother to take the cigarette out of his mouth. He looked at Marriott.

'Yes?'

No 'Sir', Marriott noted. He said:

'Do you think it's a good idea – knocking the boys about?'

'If they ask for it.'

'I should have thought that, the way things are, we need their co-operation. It's hardly the best way of getting it.'

Billy removed the cigarette and looked at it. 'Look,' he said, 'do you want to have the labouring done for you, or would you rather take a hand yourself?'

'That isn't the point.'

'Isn't it? I know these bastards. They're not so bad as long as they're kept at it, with a whip cracked over them from time to time. It's when you start letting up that they get tricky.'

'The situation is different now. We aren't on board ship.'

'Dead right, we aren't. All the more reason for making them realize who's in charge.'

'They're Sweeney's employees, not slaves.'

'Are they? Is that what I am, too? What do I get paid in – coconuts? As you said, Marriott, the situation is different. It's not a question of money any more. I would say that so far you're quite lucky. A nice little labour force, and Yasha and me to keep them on the hop. I wouldn't muck about with that, if I were you.'

Marriott said: 'Sweeney is in charge here. Get that into your head.'

'Did I say he wasn't? I've not heard him complaining.'

'He may do when he finds out what's going on.'

Billy looked at him and grinned. 'Take it easy. You worry too much. Sit in the sun and enjoy life. You've got a nice wife and you don't seem to be doing too badly in other directions. I should leave things alone, if I were you.'

They stared at each other for a moment; then Billy turned on his heel and walked away, shouting to the Hawaiians. Marriott, for his part, went to the hut where Sweeney and Susan had taken Lydia.

11

Marriott burst into the hut while Susan was bandaging Lydia's ankle with one of the napkins from the picnic basket which she had soaked in the stream. She did it deftly, and the cool pressure of the linen relieved much of the pain and discomfort Lydia had been feeling. This did not stop her being annoyed with Marriott, whose presence, irritating enough on the *Diana*, had become less and less tolerable during the day. He railed at Sweeney about Billy – about his behaviour to the Hawaiians and to himself – and she heard him impatiently. Before Sweeney could reply, she said:

'Billy! For God's sake, who's worrying about Billy? He'll do as he's told.'

Ignoring her, Marriott said: 'Something's got to be done about him. It will get more difficult to handle if it's left.'

Sweeney raised his eyebrows. 'Do it, then.'

'It's up to you, Sweeney.'

She disliked both his fussiness and his ineffectualness; in combination they aroused her contempt. The incident that morning, concerning the white monkey, had been typical. He had carried on his silly little campaign of poking fun until she had turned on him, and then he had promptly backed down. She said, not troubling to keep the hostility out of her voice:

'Why bother Sweeney with it?'

Marriott acknowledged her briefly with a glance. He said to Sweeney:

'You're in charge, aren't you? So it is your problem.'

'The *Diana*,' Sweeney said, 'is at the bottom of the bay. I have no authority on this island.'

'Of course you do,' Marriott said. He stared at Sweeney with the beginnings of doubt. 'You mean ... You are going to go on paying the crew, aren't you?'

'Billy put his finger on the weak spot in that one, didn't you tell me? Here on Silver Island the cost of life's necessities and luxuries is labour and resourcefulness; and resourcefulness, of course, includes compelling the labour of others. Whether one does it by trickery, by bribery or by force is not essentially important. I can offer the bribe of money – in another place at some indefinite time. It may not be taken, though.'

'If you are paying,' Marriott said, 'you can lay down conditions. For instance ...'

Sweeney said gently: 'You have not made the adjustment yet, I'm afraid. I suspect that Billy has done.'

Susan said: 'You were telling people what to do this morning. And they were doing it.'

'That's true.'

'Well?'

'They were consenting to my commands, just as the Hawaiians appear to be consenting to Billy's. In neither case are the commands enforceable.'

Susan said: 'But if he's bullying them, surely we should do something about that – stop him?'

Marriott said, with exasperation: 'You must agree that it's only sensible to slap him down now, and hard.'

'I don't know,' Sweeney said.

'But, as you've said, we're going to have to live here, possibly for quite a long time. You've got to get things right at the start. Patterns have to be laid down.'

'They establish themselves,' said Sweeney.

'I don't agree!'

'In the form for which the community happens to be ready. Our little microcosm, perhaps, represents at the moment the late Victorian stage, with some earlier undertones. A ruling class, a working class; and linking them a police force and army to keep the workers from proving too troublesome.'

Susan protested: 'Sweeney! You're talking about human beings.'

'No,' he said, 'about the organization and classification of human beings.'

Marriott said: 'I don't think you really give a damn what happens.'

Sweeney smiled. 'On the contrary, I am extremely interested.'

'Interested !' Marriott said. 'And what happens if Billy goads the boys to such an extent that they turn on him? What happens to your ruling class when the underdogs have destroyed the police and the army?'

'There are several possibilities,' Sweeney said. 'But I do know what has always happened to ruling classes that have alienated their police and army. They have invariably gone down.'

Billy's voice, somewhere outside, shouted something. Susan said:

'We ought to let Billy do as he likes with the Hawaiians, in case he turns nasty on us instead? Is that what you mean?'

Lydia burst out: 'Christ Almighty! Why take him so seriously? Little Billy!'

'Little Billy with a gun,' Sweeney said.

Marriott said: 'I wanted you to take that off him this morning. It would have been easy enough to do it.'

'Leaving on one side the interesting question of establishing the point at which society obtains a right to alienate the possessions of its members, there is another thing to bear in mind. It is Billy's picture of himself that is important. And while Billy-with-a-Gun may have its dangers, Billy-deprived-of-his-Gun could be more dangerous still. A great deal more dangerous.'

Lydia said: 'All this talk about Billy. I've met his kind before.' She put her hand out and Susan helped her to her feet. 'I'll go and have a chat with him.'

She hobbled out of the hut into the bright glare of sunlight. Although she shaded her eyes, the harshness of light and the heat invigorated her; a more humid warmth than she liked, but any kind of heat was preferable to cold. If one had to be marooned, she thought, this was as good a place as any. She stared appreciatively at the muscled figures of the Hawaiians, gleaming golden bronze with sweat. They were working on the annexe to the hut and Billy stood near them, white-shirted in the shade. Lydia called to him, and he looked in her direction.

She began to walk, limping, towards him; in response he came towards her, breaking into a trot. As he approached, he said:

'Have you hurt your leg, miss?'

'Not much. Sprained ankle.'

'Let me help.' He put an arm out for her to lean on. 'We'll get you up into the shade.'

He was as he had been on the *Diana*: the obsequious fawning steward. She thought contemptuously of Marriott's concern. He called, and one of the boys detached himself from the rest.

'Lay out palm leaves for the lady to sit down. Moss underneath.' He said to Lydia in explanation: 'We found some soft moss up in the wood, miss. It will do for bedding.'

'You're doing pretty well, Billy,' she said. 'Getting things organized.'

'Not too bad,' he said brightly. 'It's a matter of digging in.'

There was one slight change; his natural South London whine was much more apparent beneath the veneer of accent. She saw no harm in that, an improvement if anything. The whine was not particularly pleasant, but neither had the fake accent been. And a reversion to Catford – or was it Sydenham? - was hardly the sort of thing that seemed dangerous.

He supervised the Hawaiian as he put down armfuls of yellow-green moss and then strewed palm leaves over the top. When it was ready, he helped Lydia to a seat; the moss was more resilient than she would have thought.

'Comfy, miss?'

'Yes, thank you, Billy.'

'Would you like some fruit juice? We've found some oranges further up. I could have some crushed for you.'

'Not just now. We're not doing too badly, are we? It's a well-stocked island.'

She was, she realized, speaking to him more affably than she had done before. She watched him, ready for any sign of familiarity and prepared to crack the whip again. But there were no indications of that. He said:

'Not at all badly, really, miss. I think we'll be cosy enough once things have got running.'

She nodded in the direction of the Hawaiians.

'You don't think you'll have any trouble with the boys?'

'Don't see why we should.'

'If they're driven too hard?'

'Trust me, miss. I've had these boys to deal with for a long time. If you didn't drive them hard enough – that's when you'd have trouble.'

He spoke with conviction: she saw his point and to a considerable extent agreed with it. Whatever was said about democracy, people were happier in the place they were accustomed to. Which was true, of course, of Billy also. He would be impertinent to Marriott because he would recognize Marriott's own unsureness. There was nothing like that in his manner towards her, nor was there likely to be.

She said indifferently: 'Well, you're responsible for them. You and Yasha. But he doesn't seem to bother very much.'

'Yasha? Spends his time day-dreaming. I'll see to them, all right. You don't have to worry on that score, miss.'

'I'm not worrying,' she said. 'By the way – that gun you have.' He looked at her sideways. 'You've got it on you?'

Billy patted a bulge against his right hip. 'Yes.'

'Don't you think Sweeney ought to look after it?'

There was a pause before he replied. 'Why?'

'It might be safer with him.'

Billy shook his head. 'Don't see that it would.'

She said, a sharper tone in her voice: 'It would be more suitable.'

'He hasn't asked for it.'

'Then you'll hand it over if he does?'

She regretted the words as soon as they were spoken. They implied the possibility of refusal: request where there should have been command. That was Sweeney's fault, damn him. For a moment she sympathized with Marriott's frustration.

Billy said slowly: 'I don't know as I would. I don't see any reason. I bought the gun when I was in Tangier three years ago. I've always wanted to have a gun. And I know how to use it, which is probably more than Sweeney does. I reckon it's best in my hands.'

'Can I see it?'

He took the Beretta from his pocket and handed it to her.

'That's the safety-catch,' he told her. 'Better leave it on. She's got a very sensitive trigger action.'

Lydia looked at the small flat, almost toy-like pistol.

'Do you remember what you paid for it?'

'Not exactly. I bought it in Spanish money. I reckon about ten quid.'

'I'll give you twenty for it.' He shook his head. 'Thirty, then.'

He put his hand out and took the gun from her. He did it firmly and deliberately, though not roughly. He looked at it with sly, rather fatuous affection, and tucked it away in his pocket.

'I've always wanted to have a gun,' he repeated. 'I'm not a bad shot with it, either, though this is short-range stuff, of course. That's what I like – feeling I can look after myself at short range.' He stared at Lydia, his smile ingratiating. 'I can look after you, too, miss, and a lot better than if you were carrying her. You won't have to worry about anything going wrong. I can tell you:

whoever else goes short on this island, you won't have to. And it's not a question of money. Money doesn't come into it.'

She said coldly: 'I'm not worried. I can look after myself perfectly well.'

'You'll be all right,' Billy said. 'Are you sure there's nothing I can get you, miss?'

She turned away from him and looked out across the clearing to the cloud-wreathed summit of the mountain.

'Nothing.'

'Then I'll go and see how these lazy blighters are getting on.'

She reflected, as he left her, that she had both lost and won. She might, with a different approach, have got the gun from him; though she doubted that. It would not be easy to pry it loose from him – still harder for the attempt having been made. On the other hand, did that matter when his servility towards her was even more marked than it had been before? As long as he was left alone to bully his Hawaiians, he would be all right. He might cheek such as Marriott, but he would know where to draw the line. Once a servant, always a servant; only a little Scot with delusions of grandeur would think differently. And Billy was no Crichton. She disliked his wretched Secondary Modern mind and outlook, but there was no denying that, in a situation like the present, his flunkeyism might offer advantages. It would do no harm, she thought with satisfaction, to have Marriott made uneasy.

Thinking of Marriott, she thought again of the monkey. She had been the only one to see it; she had called and the others had looked, but it had been hidden by the brown bodies of the rest as they swung away through the trees. She did not think she could have been mistaken about it, but the recollection now was tantalizingly vague. As vague as that other glimpse, earlier in the afternoon, of the bright something caught for an instant in a crevice of cloud. A gleam – of ice, of polished stone, of metal? Or of nothing, sunlight dazzling from mist? Could they have been illusions – her eyes, perhaps? She had had some trouble with her eyes in her late teens, occasional double vision, and her oculist had suggested spectacles. She had ignored the advice, and the trouble had not persisted. It would be hell to have it recur here, thousands of miles from any kind of help.

She screwed her eyes up, and stared at the cloud. Its outlines continually shifted, but only barely perceptibly as a slow distant boil of white vapour against the blue. There was nothing to be seen there but the drifting curves and streamers of mist. Obviously, nothing could lie behind them; nothing except the scrub and rocky outcrops which crowned the smaller hill. And yet, there had been a flash of something. The summit was not nearly high enough for snow or ice, in these latitudes. A diamond, perhaps. She smiled at herself. A brilliant as big as the Ritz, to go with white monkeys, and odd-shaped beans and maize, and funny coloured bananas.

She was roused from this fantasy by the sound of voices, and the sight of the beach party returning. Katey looked a little glum, but the others appeared to be in high spirits. Willeway was carrying a pair of sizeable lobsters. He waved one of them in her direction.

'We've brought supper!'

'Those two won't go far,' Lydia said, 'with the crowd we have.'

Billy had detached himself from the work party, and came over to look at them. He said:

'They look a couple of nice ones.'

Willesway said: 'I'm not much of an underwater swimmer without proper gear. I saw more, but they were a bit deep for me.' He looked at Billy. 'I wondered if you could get one of the boys on it. They're used to this sort of thing, aren't they?'

His tone was tentative. He was soliciting Billy's help, not instructing him. Billy nodded, and she saw the satisfaction, none the less real for being furtive, in his expression. He said:

'They're busy right now. They've got to get the hut finished before sundown. Yasha and I need to have somewhere to sleep tonight.'

Lydia said sharply: 'You can spare a couple of them.'

Billy looked at her. His grin was part sheepish, part conspiratorial.

'Yes, I can do that, miss. And we want to give Cookie more than a couple to work on, don't we?' He shouted an order, and two of the Hawaiians detached themselves. 'Go and see what you can bring up in the way of shellfish, Jillo!'

The others drifted away in various directions, but Toni stayed with Lydia. This was not unwelcome; she was a pretty little thing, and amiable, her only flaw possibly her tolerance of a husband like Marriott. She looked at Lydia's ankle – apparently she had done some nursing at one time – approved of Susan's bandage and said it would probably be all right in a day or two. She sat down on the couch of leaves beside Lydia, drew up her knees and clasped her hands round them.

'Lucky it was nothing serious,' she said. 'We shall have to be careful of accidents. No medical attention, I mean.'

Lydia said: 'Probably Sweeney knows something about medicine, too. Along with everything else.'

'Yes,' Toni said, 'I suppose so.' She shifted her position slightly. 'What was that?'

'What?'

She heard it as she asked the question, a small rustling sound somewhere behind them. Turning, she saw that Toni was looking back at the line of vegetation which here was about ten yards distant from them. Something moved among the low spiky bushes, something grey-brown in colour, scuttling away into the thicker undergrowth. Toni stared after it, her face puzzled and also – what? Surprised? Disgusted?

Lydia said: 'It was a rat, wasn't it?'

Toni nodded her head slowly. 'Yes.'

Lydia said: 'Hideous brutes, aren't they? But they don't seem as bad in the wilds as they do in cities. They seem different.'

'Different!' Toni gave a small shivering laugh. 'That one certainly did. My God.'

'That one? How?'

'I must have been mistaken,' Toni said. She kept her eyes on the place, where the rat disappeared, in fascination and repulsion. 'It was facing this way when I saw it. Just for a moment. But I thought …'

'What?'

'It looked as though it had two heads.'

12

BY THE END OF A WEEK the basic work of setting up camp was finished. The site had been properly cleared and more permanent cooking and sanitary arrangements were made. Under Billy's supervision, the boys had constructed beds of a kind: rectangular frames were made from fairly straight saplings, laced together with vines, and covered with moss and palm leaves. With the corners supported by large stones they proved comfortable, and were clear of the ground and possible vermin. Vines had been used to make bags for bringing food into camp, too, and, on the initiative of one of the Hawaiians, for catching fish. He cut the vine into short lengths, pounded it and bound it into cylinders which he trailed in the water. These gave off some substance which at once attracted and stupefied the fish: they drifted helplessly close to the surface and the other boys easily speared them with pointed wooden spears, previously hardened in the fire.

Working on the orthodox lines of stranded mariners, Billy had also had a pile of dry wood set up on the headland, ready to be fired if anyone should sight a ship. There was talk about setting a watch there, but Billy would not spare any of his work party, and the others, in the end, could not be bothered. That, Katey thought, was Sweeney's fault. It was up to him to organize this sort of thing. In fact, as the days passed, he withdrew more and more from the others; he remained courteous and friendly, but in a distant way. She found this as irritating as his previous magnificence of gesture had been. He had been responsible for their coming to the island, if not for their being stranded on it, and he had no right to cut himself off from the problems that faced them.

It was true that so far the problems had not been very difficult to overcome. In default of Sweeney's leadership, decisions tended to be taken by Marriott or by Billy. They showed that they did not much like each other, but they did not generally come into conflict. Billy, without prompting, was keeping the Hawaiians at work on the things that needed to be done, while Marriott confined himself to trying to organize the passengers. Katey resented, on her husband's behalf, the assumption that Marriott was the one entitled to do this, but the resentment was one to which she was habituated. She had known, for some years, that Willeway was too soft to take control of a situation, just as Candie was too lazy.

In so far as there was liaison between the working group and the rest, it was Lydia Petrie who provided it. Billy, Katey saw with disgust, appeared to be slavishly devoted to her, offering her small attentions and luxuries, doing what he could to please her and, as often as not, being snubbed in return. Whatever she asked for, Billy strove to provide. Her complaint, early in their second week on the island, of the continual diet of fish, was enough to launch a pig hunt the following day.

Some limited exploration had been done by groups of the passengers, and pigs had been seen in different parts of the island. There appeared to be quite a large herd in the thick brush on the far side of the western hill, and Billy made his plans for hunting over there. The Hawaiians had already equipped themselves with wooden spears, and that evening he got them busy with the vines, weaving nets into which the animals could be driven. When Marriott and Candie expressed an intention of going along he shrugged his shoulders in indifferent acquiescence.

In the event they all went, apart from Sweeney and the cook. They travelled along the beach, rounded the western point, and came to the stretch of bush where the biggest number of pigs had been seen. Marriott said:

'Are you going to hold a line with the boys, and have us beat them into it?'

'If you want to be helpful,' Billy agreed. 'If you just want to watch, you can get over on that hillock and I'll detach a couple of the boys to do the beating.'

'We might as well lend a hand,' Marriott said. 'It will increase the chances.' Their antagonism was subdued, for the moment, in the anticipation of the chase. 'We could ...'

'Carry on along the beach,' Billy said. Marriott seemed inclined to argue for a moment, but said nothing. 'Cut inland from about that point where the rock comes down to the water level.' Billy pointed to the place he meant. 'I should go a couple of hundred yards inland, spread yourselves out and start walking this way. Take it slow and easy. We'll have the nets ready by that time.' He turned to Lydia. 'It would be best if you and the other ladies went up on the hillock, miss. You'll see it all from there.'

Lydia said: 'The others can do as they like. I'm joining the beaters.'

'They may run the wrong way,' Billy said. 'And an old boar or a sow with young can be nasty.'

'I'll take a chance on that,' Lydia said.

She looked flushed and excited, an overgrown tomboy. Katey said:

'I'm going to watch.' She turned to the other women. 'What about you?'

'Watch,' Toni said. 'I can't stand pigs.'

Susan said to Billy: 'Will you have enough beaters? I think I'll stay out of it, too, in that case.'

The hillock was close to the sea and covered with coarse grass and a few bushes. They made themselves comfortable and settled down to wait. Toni exhibited a tear in her frock. 'How did that happen, I wonder? That patch of thorn, I suppose. It's almost indecent.'

'We shall be in rags in a few weeks,' Katey said. 'Then what happens?'

'Nudism, I suppose,' Toni said.

She spoke with a hint of complacency; she had a pretty enough figure, damn her. They would all come out of it better than she would if that happened, Katey realized, even Lydia – scragginess would be less unattractive than fatness. After all, none of them had borne children. She said bitterly:

'Well, those of you who've got the figures for it can let me have any spare cloth there is. That table-cloth, for a start.'

Susan laughed. 'Oh dear! I had *my* eye on that.'

'Steward's 'department,' Toni said. 'It will go to the one who gets round Billy best. Guess who.'

'That whole business is repulsive,' Katey said.

'I don't know,' Toni said. 'Do you think they'll make a match of it?'

'I don't think that's very funny.'

'Well, you know. Propinquity makes strange bed-fellows.' Toni stretched her arms back, a voluptuous movement. 'And tropic islands make you sexy. At least, I find it so.'

Katey thought of saying: so does your husband, from the way he looks at the little Malone girl. She refrained, not to avoid embarrassing Susan but because she doubted if the remark would have any effect. She had the impression that Toni saw as much of her husband's manoeuvres as anyone else.

Toni said to Susan: 'How about you, honey? Haven't you begun to feel like throwing your arms round someone?'

There was a glint in her eye; tolerant and amused. She had certainly kept abreast of Marriott's activities. Susan said:

'Not so far.'

'And Katey?'

'No. I don't think we all have your low boiling-point.'

She spoke emphatically, but it was not entirely true. There had been moments, in the evenings particularly, with the air still warm but softer, light draining swiftly out of the purple sky, the first stars springing overhead, when she had felt her blood stir, pulses leap in a way she had almost forgotten. So far she had repressed these feelings: there had been practically nothing between her and Joe since the birth of their second child. She had not felt the lack and nor, as far as she could tell, had he. She contemplated, for a moment, the possibility of some other man. Marriott, for all his attentions to Susan and presumable capability with Toni, would not need much encouraging. But the thought was no sooner framed than it disgusted her.

Toni said, without resentment: 'I'm not the boiling kind, actually. I just simmer gently.'

Katey said abruptly: 'I'm not fond of this kind of conversation.'

'Aren't you?' Toni asked lazily. 'I am, rather. Have they started the drive? They look as though they're heading this way.'

The heads of the three men and Lydia could be seen in the distance above the brush; they were at intervals of ten or fifteen yards and moving slowly towards the place where Billy and Yasha and the Hawaiians stood. At that spot the brush was a good deal thinner, and one could see that the Hawaiians were holding the vine nets between them, with Yasha flanking them at the top and Billy at the bottom.

'Any sign of pigs?' Susan asked.

'No,' Toni said. 'Yes. There's something moving down there, at any rate.'

Between the two lines of figures, the brush rippled as though caught by a gust of wind. The ripple moved forward, slowly then with increasing speed. It reached the point where the undergrowth became patchy and there were glimpses of white bodies – a dozen or more of them – hurtling through the bushes. The wave sheered up against the Hawaiians with the nets and, with barely a pause, was through and lost in a new ripple of the vegetation behind them.

Toni laughed. 'God! They've gone right through the nets.'

'There's another one.' Susan pointed out.

It was considerably in the wake of the rest and travelling more slowly. The Hawaiians, as it approached, converged on it. A couple of them threw themselves on the pig; there was a scuffle on the ground and, after a moment or two, a cry of triumph.

Toni said: 'Heaven be praised. Pork for supper after all. I think we can go and join the hunters now, don't you?'

They reached the scene of the kill almost simultaneously with the beaters. The pig lay on the ground with blood oozing from wounds in the chest and throat. One of the Hawaiians had blood smeared across his chest. Blood was soaking into the dry soil, where a small column of ants had already found it. In death, Katey thought, the pig looked foreshortened.

Marriott said: 'Well, you got one. What happened to the others?'

'The nets didn't hold,' Billy said. 'We'll need stronger ones next time. And they came at us all together.' He contemplated the dead pig with satisfaction. 'Anyway, we were ready for this chap. He'll do very nicely for a first off.' He prodded the body with his toe. 'Plenty of lard on him.'

'He was a slow starter,' Willeway said.

'Not so much that as a slow traveller,' Billy said. 'And low to the ground. He just didn't have the legs. I reckon he must have been crossed with a dachshund.'

Marriott bent down and fingered one of the legs.

'They are short, aren't they?' he said. 'Deformed, almost. That's odd.'

'Plenty of shoulder, anyway,' Billy said, 'and nice hams. Ham and fresh pineapple. How does that strike you, miss?'

Lydia said: 'I'd rather have something simpler. Ham and eggs. Lay some eggs on, Billy, will you?'

'Might get you some seabirds' eggs, miss.'

'No. Too fishy.'

'Frigate-birds aren't so bad. I think I saw some nests in the cliffs as we came in. I'll get the boys over there to have a look.'

Susan said: 'I'm almost sure I saw a hen yesterday, further along the valley.'

'Not very likely,' Marriott said.

'Why not?' Candie asked. 'All those crops and stuff. Who-ever lived here might have left hens and they've gone wild.'

'They don't have much survival value,' Marriott said. 'They need human beings to look after them. The eggs are so vulnera-ble – large and toothsome. The rats would finish them off; pigs, too.'

'It looked like a hen,' Susan said.

'We'll have a hen hunt, anyway,' Lydia said. 'If there's a chance of ham and eggs I'm not going to miss it. O.K., Billy?'

'Right, miss. Now, you lot – get him strapped on to the pole and we'll haul him back to camp.'

The mood on the return journey was happy, almost hilari-ous, and Katey found herself relaxing with the others. They continued in high spirits, aided by a drink which the cook had prepared by fermenting juice drawn from the young stems of the palms. He had mixed fresh pineapple and other fruits with it: the result was a sweeter drink than Katey usually liked, but a distinctly heady one. They drank this, as afternoon faded into brief evening; Sweeney came and drank with them. Across the clearing, mingling with the by now familiar scents of the island, drifted the smell of roasting pork.

'A great moment,' Sweeney said. 'The hunters home from the hill. Adrenalin pumping through the veins, and the sweet smell of burning flesh in the nostrils.'

Susan laughed. 'I suppose you are going to say no to the burning flesh, Sweeney, having missed out on the adrenalin.'

'My appetite is gross enough to need no quickener. Our mountain looks pretty tonight, don't you think?'

The cloud had caught the sunset light. Its crest was glowing pink, a pink that deepened as they watched into orange and red. Pretty, Katey thought, was not the word she would have used. The colours were exotic, sinister, lifting above the dark sunless slopes where a breeze furrowed the tree tops, below the heavy dark blue sky. She finished her drink, and handed the glass for replenishment to Billy who had, without prompting, resumed his steward's duties for the occasion.

Sweeney said: 'A challenge, surely. Once the belly is satisfied, the spirit cries out. When do you launch your expedition to conquer Mount Proteus?'

'Is that its name?' Susan asked.

Sweeney shrugged. 'There are no names on unpeopled islands. But da Silva called it that. He was an educated man, a classicist, and the cloud impressed him.'

'What does it mean, anyway?' Toni asked.

'Proteus was the one who was always changing shape, wasn't he?' Candie said.

'Yes,' Sweeney said, 'Poseidon's herdsman. The cloud was there in da Silva's time, always changing shape, but always the same. And standing guard over Poseidon's broad acres.'

The top of the cloud was purple now, a shade or two lighter than the sky. Marriott said:

'Is there any point in climbing it? Nothing to see.'

'Lydia thought she saw something the first day.' Sweeney turned to Lydia. 'Is that not so? Something bright?'

'Probably nothing. Still, it would be fun to climb it. I don't see why we shouldn't.'

'Good,' Sweeney said. 'After all, it is there.'

Katey asked: 'Are you leading this expedition, Sweeney?'

He shook his large head, smiling. 'I think not.'

'You don't do very much these days, do you?'

'I am not needed,' Sweeney said. 'All is for the best in the best of all possible islands.' He smiled. 'I have interfered sufficiently in your lives by bringing you here.'

They were called to their supper, the food set out on leaves which were roughly circular, a foot or more across, and glossily smooth. The taste of the pork, roasted over an open fire, was exquisite; with it the cook had served green beans from the patch in the valley and a root which he had told them was *taro*. Its colour when cooked was an unappetizing violet, but with night falling on the clearing this was not much in evidence.

The taste was excellent. They had water and palm wine to accompany the food, and the glow from the fire on which the pig had been cooked to cheer them. The cloud on the mountain was invisible now, except where it blotted out stars. After they had finished eating, some of the Hawaiians began singing, at first softly and then loudly and more rhythmically.

Katey felt the lift in her blood again, moved by the night, the singing, the dimness of faces in the flame-edged dark. She was a little drunk too; pleasantly so. Joe was sitting beside her, humming the tune the boys were singing, and she was suddenly, sharply, aware of him – of his voice, a sudden movement of his leg. She turned to him, touching his arm. She saw him look her way.

'Pretty good,' he said. 'A cigar, now. A cigarette, even.' He sighed. 'Can't have everything, I suppose.'

'I'd like to walk,' Katey said, 'down by the beach.'

'Watch your step,' he said. 'It's dark till the moon gets up.'

'I thought you might like to come with me.'

There was a silence while he worked things out. She let her fingers tighten on his arm. After a moment his other hand came round and closed on hers.

'Slip away?'

'I think so.'

The path between the clearing and the sea was a well-beaten one by now, but it was still possible to stumble in the dark. He steadied her, and she relaxed against him. They kissed there, with the singing still loud and the figures of the others, black against the firelight, visible through the screen of trees.

He said: 'Better move on a bit, old girl.'

They walked down with arms intertwined; it had been like this once, she remembered, after a dance. She had been not much more than sixteen and he, anonymous now but important, frightening, then, had touched her breast through her dress, and put a clumsy timid hand on her knee.

'You don't have any kind of kit, I suppose?'

She laughed. 'Would you expect me to bring any, on a day trip to an island?'

'I suppose not. Does it matter?'

She knew what he meant, but deliberately, wilfully, chose to misunderstand him. This was time out of life, thousands of miles from the world of calculation and coping. The path led downwards, and now they could hear the sea.

'No,' she said. 'It doesn't matter.'

13

BILLY HAD HAD THE BOYS MAKING CRAB and lobster pots out of a springy cane-like plant that had been found not far from the camp, and this morning he had taken them all off to set these in the lagoon. In their absence the project for scaling the mountain was suddenly picked up. Willeway did not at first take it seriously, and certainly had no intention of joining it; it struck him as both uncomfortable and pointless. Marriott, however, had developed enthusiasm for the idea, and the women had decided that it would be fun. He thought for a time that he would have Candie's support in backing out, but Candie's curiosity outweighed his laziness for once. Finding himself isolated, Willeway was surprised to see how much he needed the reassurance of group action. It was a reminder how different this life was from the one they had left behind. Sweeney was not going, but he felt that staying with him would not do much to alleviate the sense of separation. Making the best of things, he packed his plaited-vine haversack with cooked breadfruit spread with avocado, put in some bananas and wild mangoes, and readied himself for the departure.

Marriott chose the ascent route. He had decided that, rather than attempt a direct climb, they should take the easier course of traversing the northern slopes of the mountain in the direction of the cliffs. He had the impression, from what he remembered of the view from the sea during their approach in the *Diana*, that the ground did not rise so steeply there; and it was an additional advantage that they could watch out for nesting places, possibly even bring back eggs if the nests were reasonably accessible. This was the only part of the expedition, in Willeway's view, that made sense.

The going, at the outset, was easy. Occasionally they were forced to detour round impenetrable tangles of undergrowth, but for the most part trees and bushes were widely enough spaced, and the gradient steep without being too laborious. Twice they flushed monkeys who swung away, shrieking, through the branches, and once an old sow, teats pendulous, faced them at bay for a moment or two before lumbering off into a thicket. Despite the evidence of maternity, there was no sign of her young.

They came to an outcrop of sleek black rock which reached up twice or three times a man's height. It stretched further down hill than up, and Marriott elected to cross it from above. They toiled up over the shoulder and Willeway, coming last with Katey, found them grouped together and looking down. As he in turn passed the outcrop, he saw that on the other side the ground fell away in a fault which widened out to form a pocket-size valley having access to the sea.

They were several hundred feet above the valley floor, and their vantage point had a diminishing, prettifying effect; they looked down into a small toylike dell. It was attractive enough in itself, though. Some fifty feet below them the rock face yielded a spring which sprayed a plume of water far out, to fall in a cascade from ledge to ledge and at last to the valley floor. It shimmered with rainbow colours in the sun. In the valley it formed a stream which widened out into a pool, its edge framed with rocks and trees and grass, and then, discharging at the pool's far end, ran brightly over pebbles to the shore.

There were tiny trees, quite widely spaced around the pool and set in what, from above, looked like close cropped lawns. At the sides of the valley the trees were thicker; a smell of oranges came up and Willeway could see yellow fruit among the branches. The mouth of the valley was lightly screened by palms; one could see golden sand through them and the blue of the ocean. Nothing moved except the water and the branches of the trees, fluffed by a light breeze: it was a vest-pocket paradise, untenanted, flawless.

Candie said: 'Let's not climb any mountains. Let's go down there and sit in the sun.'

Toni nodded her head emphatically. 'I'm with you. Look at that pool! The colour of it.'

'You would have a job getting there,' Marriott said. 'And you'd get wet. The only way is down through the waterfall.'

'There must be another way in,' Candie said.

'Along the beach, probably. Which would mean going back the way we've come.' Marriott stared down. 'It looks pleasant enough. We'll try from the beach some time. Meanwhile, we'd better be getting on.'

'We could have a rest here,' Candie said. 'I like the view.'

'The worst possible place,' Marriott said sharply. 'We're in the direct sun.'

No one answered him for the moment, and no one moved. They had found perches on various spurs and ledges of rock and were staring into the valley. Candie said:

> 'And in the afternoon they reached a land,
> In which it seemèd always afternoon.'

Lydia stood up, then, stretching herself.

'It's not afternoon yet, though. We'd better press on, hadn't we?' She treated Marriott to a derisive smile. 'Coming, Herr Bergmeister? We've got to have you to lead the way.'

Marriott did not reply, but looked at her bitterly before moving on up the side of the hill. They had to climb another fifty feet to get above the fault; the ascent was steep, with loose stones rolling underfoot, and Willeway found himself slipping and sweating. He reflected on the antagonism between Marriott and Lydia, and the other less obvious signs of antagonism within the group. Resentment and hostility were such a wasteful process; he could never understand why people bothered to indulge in them. Even the years of living with Katey had failed to make him understand it. It was so much less trouble to take people as they came, accepting disappointments and difficulties without fuss.

They passed through another wooded area, which thinned out as they approached the cliffs. Over the last couple of hundred yards before the cliff face there were a few stunted bushes growing among coarse grass and ribs of basalt. At the edge itself there was only bare rock. The roar of the sea came up from below, mixed with the cries of sea birds. A dozen or so feet below them there was a ledge about six feet wide; beneath the cliff seemed to fall sheer to the sea. To the south the whole face was visible, a fantastic sweep of rock – black and then, near the bottom, dazzling white, a blinding glitter in the sun.

Katey said: 'That white – is the rock different down there? And what kind? Not chalk. It's too brilliant.'

Susan said: 'Salt crystals, I should think. A coating thrown up by the spray. Look, there's a patch in the distance where it's broken away.' She stepped back with a wry face. 'I can't take this, though. I've no head for heights.'

They could see the line of the reef far out, a thin unbroken fringe of white. It did not seem to do much to check the long roll of the ocean which broke against the foot of the cliffs rhythmically, the crash awesome even at this height. Between cliff and reef, perhaps, a quarter of a mile out, there was an island. Like the base of the cliffs, it was white. Pointing, Willeway said:

'Will that be salt, too? It doesn't seem as bright.'

Toni said: 'It's moving. Is it … ?'

'Birds,' Marriott said. 'Covered with them. It's where they nest, probably. Look, there's a batch taken off. Well, we know where to send Billy for eggs now.'

Candie said: 'Would you get a boat to it? I wouldn't fancy being thrown against those rocks.'

'When the sea moderates,' Marriott said. 'That's quite a swell. Been a storm somewhere between here and Panama.'

'No sign of it here,' Toni said.

There was a fine shawl of cirrus over towards the horizon. Apart from that, and the white cloud shrouding the peak behind them, the sky was a clear blue.

'More than four thousand miles,' Marriott said. 'Room for a dozen storms. And nothing in between to stop those combers.'

There was silence for a time. The sense of isolation, Willeway realized, was renewed and made more real by their position here, high above the waves which stretched out to the hazy skyline. One could almost visualize those four thousand miles of emptiness.

Marriott said: 'Time to renew the ascent. Unless anyone wants to rest here?'

There was no answer. Willeway turned away from the brink. The ascent, the clouded mountain itself, looked more attractive after the plunge of cliff and the ocean's barrenness. There was not much talk as they began to climb again.

As noon approached they were within a few hundred feet of the cloud's edge, moving up a fairly easy gradient through scrub. The sun beat down hotly. Willeway tried to mop the sweat from his face with his silk cravat, but without much success. Easing off, he said:

'At least it should be cooler up there.'

'You're losing some of that paunch, Joe,' Candie said. 'I can see it melting off you.'

Marriott, fifteen or twenty yards ahead, called back: 'Come on. Almost made it.'

'And what do we do when we get there?' Candie asked. 'Plant a flag?'

'Bit pointless when it's in cloud all the time,' Toni said. 'We haven't got a flag, anyway.'

'One of you ladies,' Candie suggested, 'might spare something. How about a petticoat?'

'If any of us had one,' Toni said, 'we most decidedly wouldn't give it up. What's the matter with Tony? He seems to have called a halt.'

They saw why as they came up with him. Ahead stretched a thicket of thorny scrub; the bushes were only a couple of feet high, but they were covered with needle-sharp spines and grew like a close-set hedge. The thicket seemed to reach up to the cloud's edge and also stretched as far away as they could see on either side. Willeway put a hand out and felt the sharpness of the thorns. There was no hope of ploughing a way through it without heavy protection for the legs.

Katey said: 'What do we do now?'

'Work our way round, I suppose,' Lydia said. 'It can't go all the way round the peak.'

'There's some of it down in the valley,' Marriott said. 'I think Sweeney called it lantana. There's a hell of a lot of it up here. And thick, too.' He straightened up. 'I don't suppose it matters which way round we try, but right takes us nearer to our home.'

Candie said: 'Then by all means right wheel. I've just about had enough of this particular mountain.'

The thicket offered no break as they skirted it, and as they came to a point where the rest of the island – the valley and the western hill – was visible, it was also possible to see that the lantana hedge continued ahead of them. Something else that was apparent was that the cloud lay lower on this side of the peak; it rolled down to a point below that which they had reached. In about five minutes they found themselves surrounded by the outermost tendrils of mist, which thickened rapidly as they went on. Soon the figures of the others were wraith-like, and lost completely at more than a few yards' distance.

Candie said: 'Is it still thorny up above?'

His voice had a deadened sound. Marriott's, in reply, was similarly drained of tone. 'I think so. Christ, yes!'

Lydia giggled. 'Little Tony seems to have stumbled on something.'

Willeway said: 'This is bloody silly, isn't it? Blundering round in a fog. I don't know about the rest of you, but I'm heading down to a place where I can see what I'm doing.'

Marriott said: 'Your eyes get used to it. I can follow the lantana now without running into it.'

'You follow it,' Lydia said. 'Joe and I are going down. How about the rest of you?'

All except Marriott scrambled down the slope. The deep grey of the mist lightened, turned white, dazzled with emergent sunlight and at last thinned to nothing. They stood blinking their eyes against the sky's brightness. Below them the valley stretched, in various greens, and over to the right it was possible to see the camp – the clearing and the tiny huts. Willeway sat down and most of the party did the same.

'Home, sweet home,' Toni said. 'I'm glad to be out of that cloud, anyway.' She gave a small shiver. 'Not at all pleasant.'

Now that they were in the open again, Willeway was prepared to admit, though only to himself, what his own feeling had been up there: an uneasiness poised on the edge of fear. There was no one thing which accounted for it; probably a combination of factors. Being in mist on a mountainside was unsettling anywhere – he could recall a bad couple of hours in Derbyshire – and very likely made worse by the contrast with the tropic brightness all round. And this ludicrous business of the thorn scrub didn't help at all. At any rate, he was, he reflected, damned glad to be out of it, and quite determined not to go back. If the others wanted to scale Mount Proteus, they would have to do it without his cooperation.

'How long do we wait for Tony?' Katey said.

'No reason why we should,' Lydia said. 'He can find his way back all right.'

Toni said: 'I'm staying.'

Susan and Candie expressed their intentions of staying with her. Lydia said:

'All right. We'll give him a little while.'

They did not have to wait long. A few minutes later they heard the scramble of feet somewhere up behind them, and Marriott emerged from the cloud twenty or thirty yards away. As he came to join them, Lydia said: 'Well, did you plant the flag?'

He shook his head. 'That lantana seems to go on for ever.' He was somewhat out of breath; as though, Willeway thought, he had been hurrying to get back to them. 'I suppose we could get round to the other side again, and see if there's a break in the thorn below the cloud level?'

The suggestion was tentative, the look that accompanied it uncertain. Lydia said briskly:

'You can, if you like. We're making for home.'

For once Marriott did not seem to resent Lydia's usurpation of command. He said:

'Yes, I think we might as well. There didn't look as though there were any breaks in that direction, did there?'

Susan said: 'I don't think I like this mountain.'

Candie laughed. 'That's a fine rational remark from a lady scientist!'

'I don't like it either,' Katey said.

'Well, we've had our shot at it,' Marriott said. 'Whatever Lydia saw up there …'

She broke in sharply: 'Brightness for a moment – that was all. Probably the sun shining off the cloud.'

'Or salt,' Candie said. 'Like the foot of the cliffs. There's a bloody great salt lick up there, and someone's planted thorn round it to keep animals from licking it bare.'

'Let's get down,' Lydia said. 'There'll be time to have a swim. I'm filthy with sweat.'

The way down was easy and they were all light-hearted. They crossed a stream at one point and refreshed feet and faces in the clear cold water. It was a much heavier flow than the stream back at camp, and Marriott suggested it might be the one that gushed eventually into the valley they had seen that morning. He said it might be interesting to follow it and see if it went underground, but got no support for that. They were only about a mile from the camp, though still a thousand feet or more above it.

Despite the concentrated heat of mid-afternoon, they were very cheerful indeed over the last stretch. They broke into the clearing just behind Sweeney's hut, and saw Sweeney sitting in the shade of the avocado tree on a stool he had made himself. He got to his feet as they came up.

'Well,' he said, 'did you make the ascent?'

'Not quite,' Lydia said.

Candie said: 'We decided the last bit was sacred to the gods. Or that particular one, anyway.'

'There's a wide patch of lantana not far below the summit, Sweeney,' Marriott said. 'Just about impassable, I would say.'

'All the way round?' Sweeney asked.

'As far as we could tell. It was difficult to follow it inside the cloud.'

Sweeney did not seem surprised, merely interested. He said: 'So the expedition was a failure.'

'I wouldn't say that. We know more about the island. There's a very pleasant little valley to the east of this. And we've located a possible egg supply – a nesting island.' He looked around. 'Where is Billy? Has he still got the boys out diving?'

'All but one,' Sweeney said.

There was something in his tone which caught their attention.

'All but one?' Marriott echoed. 'Has there been an accident?'

'It depends what you would call an accident,' Sweeney said. He was bland, unperturbed by what he had to say. 'Billy shot him.'

14

T ONI SAID: 'Oh, no! He isn't ... ?'
'Dead?' Sweeney said. 'No. The bullet went through his shoulder. A clean wound and he seems fairly comfortable. He's resting in the hut.'

'Perhaps there's something I can do.'

She started to move off towards the hut, but Sweeney stopped her, a large hand waving in negation.

'Yasha and Cookie are seeing to him. I should leave them to it. Cookie has rigged up some kind of poultice – ancient Oriental healing, I gather – and Yasha has approved it. Yasha, believe it or not, has done a spell as ship's doctor some time in the past. With what medical qualifications, I have no idea.'

Marriott said: 'Was it an accident, Sweeney? Did the gun go off by accident?'

'I wasn't present. It happened at the beach. I gather that when they knocked off for the midday break, the boys got hold of some of Cookie's special palm wine; and that when Billy tried to get them working again they raised objections. According to Billy, this chap went for him with a spear. So he shot him.'

'Was Yasha there?'

'No. He'd taken a couple of the boys up here to get something.'

'What do the boys say?' Candie asked. 'The ones who were there.'

'I saw no point in asking them.'

Marriott said: 'No point! What do you mean, no point?'

'Is there any advantage in doubting Billy's version of events unless one is proposing to do something about it? A trial, perhaps, on a charge of malicious wounding?' He shrugged. 'You can arrange that if you think fit.'

'Something's got to be done,' Marriott said. 'He's goaded them beyond endurance, and when one of them hits back, he damn' near kills him. A bullet that goes through a man's shoulder could easily have gone through his heart. You can't tell me Billy's a good enough shot to discriminate to that extent.'

'Then fix up your court,' Sweeney said. 'You be judge, they'll be jury.'

Lydia said: 'Don't be bloody stupid. Whatever actually happened, the boys would blame Billy. They're bound to. They'll tell any kind of lies.'

'I would expect you to back him up,' Marriott said. He was angry enough at the moment, Toni saw, to stand up to Lydia. 'He looks after you well enough. He can do what he likes to the poor god-forsaken Hawaiians.'

'Well, isn't it true?' Lydia said. 'Haven't you said yourself that they hate his guts? And who's going to control the boys if Billy doesn't? Can you keep them working?'

'Yasha can,' Marriott said. 'Without bullying, and without waving a revolver at them.'

Sweeney said: 'There are one or two other things to consider. In the first place, Lydia is, of course, right in pointing out that the truth of the matter would be difficult to arrive at. One would not expect justice in such a court. But it might seem, of course, that justice was the less important thing – that expediency counted for more and that it was expedient to condemn Billy without having convincing proof of his guilt. That leaves the question of punishment to be decided. You could banish him, perhaps, but I think you might feel uneasy to have him wandering the island under no surveillance. Or you could imprison him. The Hawaiians, doubtless, would be happy enough to build a stockade, but could you trust them on guard duties? And would you care to carry them out yourselves? They would be likely to prove tedious.'

'So you think we ought to do nothing?' Susan asked. 'Even though, as Tony says, someone might have been killed?'

'I think,' Sweeney said gently, 'you will do whatever you think best. My only concern is to draw your attention to some small details that might otherwise have been overlooked in the heat of the moment.'

Nothing, Toni saw, would be done. She was sick of their joint and several ineffectualities. Nor could she understand what Sweeney was up to. If he had wanted to, he could have got everything organized, instead of just pointing out difficulties. At least there was action she could take.

She said: 'Yasha and the cook may have things under control, but I'm going to see how the Hawaiian is, anyway.' She looked at Sweeney, challenging him to stop her a second time; but he merely smiled and nodded. Turning away, she said: 'You can sort things out whichever way you like.'

She could still hear them arguing as she ducked into the cool interior of the hut. Yasha and the cook were there, on either side of the bed on which the wounded man was lying. He was the rather squat, broad-shouldered one; she remembered him as having been less docile than the others, and she could well imagine that, intoxicated, he might have turned on Billy. He was moaning slightly now, while the cook held a cloth pad against his shoulder. There was green leafy stuff under the pad; trickles of sap as well as blood ran down the bronzed skin of his chest.

She asked Yasha: 'How is he?'

His blue eyes surveyed her from the square white face.

'Not too bad. I do not think there will be any permanent injury.'

'Sweeney tells me you have some medical training.'

'Some.' He stared at her, smiling slightly. 'In this case, enough.'

She pointed to the poultice. 'And that stuff?'

'Cookie tells me his grandmother had it from her grandmother. I am inclined to put my faith in traditional herbal

117

remedies, particularly when more modern medicines are not available.'

Toni said: 'It looks unsavoury enough to be healthy. You are sure the bullet isn't still inside?'

'Quite sure. A clean hole through, not touching the bone. He has been lucky.'

She looked up at Yasha. She had not noticed him much before, but he spoke now with an authority that impressed her. She said submissively:

'Can we bandage it? It would make him more comfortable.'

'Later, I think. At present the poultice must be changed quite often.'

'So there's nothing I can do?'

'Not at present.'

The cook had not looked at her during the time she had been in the hut. The Hawaiian was staring at her, but with a withdrawn blank expression, twisting from time to time into a grimace of pain. Toni straightened up.

'I'll be outside if you want me.'

She was thinking, as she went out into the open, about violence. It was not her first encounter with its results. She had nursed at a hospital in Glasgow, and had seen, in Casualty, far worse examples than this. But there violence and the effects of violence had been contained by the apparatus of society; epitomized in the blue-uniformed figure, patiently waiting with his note-book. She felt a new shock of realization that there was nothing like that here. There were only individuals, moving through a complex web of their own demands and the demands of others. Their balance was precarious: the act of violence showed how precarious, and something of the gulf that lay beneath.

An argument was still going on between Tony and Lydia; she went past them to where Sweeney had taken up his seat again in the shade of the avocado. He said:

'Well? Is everything all right?'

'It seems to be.' She looked at him intently. 'Sweeney, you must do something.'

'Do what?'

'Organize things. Keep order. You can if you want to.'

'No.'

'You know you can!'

He shook his head. 'It is too late.'

'It will be, if you don't do something.'

'It is already.'

'You won't, will you?' She stared at him. 'Because you don't want to. But why?'

His eyes had left her, and he was looking past her at a tree on the edge of the clearing. After a pause, he said: 'Do you see that?'

'What?'

'The bird.'

She looked, and said impatiently: 'That? It's a parakeet, isn't it? There are lots of them on the island.'

'An unusual one.'

'The bright red crest, you mean? But they do come in all sorts of colours.'

'Not the crest,' he said. 'It doesn't have the parrot beak. The beak is long and pointed, instead of being broad and hooked.'

'Oh God, does that matter? It's the question of Billy that's important.'

'Is it?' Sweeney closed his eyes. 'Well, he's here now.'

She turned and saw the remaining Hawaiians coming into the clearing from the direction of the beach, with Billy directly behind them. He shouted something to them, and they went towards their hut.

Sweeney said: 'You could go and lend moral support to your husband.'

She looked at him. 'Are you coming, Sweeney?'

'No.' He shifted comfortably on his seat. 'I'm not coming, Toni.'

Billy had a little wary smile on his face when he joined the group. He said jauntily:

'Climb your mountain, then?'

Marriott said, in a tight voice: 'What happened to the boy?'

'The one in there?' Billy jerked a thumb in the direction of the hut. 'Nothing much. He got drunk and tried to stick me with his spear. So I winged him. He'll be back at work in a week.'

Marriott said: 'We think you ought to hand that gun over for someone else to look after, Billy.'

'We?' His eyes shifted round the group. 'Who's we?'

Lydia said: 'Count me out.'

Billy grinned. 'Thanks, miss.'

'The rest of us,' Marriott said.

Billy turned to him, with an expression intended to convey reason and patience.

'Look,' he said. 'Say I'd handed the gun over yesterday. Then today when that bastard came at me he'd have had his spear through my guts. You might not think that would be much loss. But what happens next? He's burned his boats, so he runs amok, and the others with him. You'd have had a nice little reception when you got back from your mountain climbing. They'd have finished off the men, and they'd be getting cracking on the women. Not with spears, though.'

Lydia said: 'I agree with that.'

'I don't,' Marriott said. 'The only danger that exists lies in Billy's treatment of them. If we put a stop to that we remove a risk to ourselves at the same time. It's common sense.'

'And what about the risk to me?' Billy asked. 'Do you think that one that went for me today won't have another go as soon as he's able, if I can't protect myself?'

'You can leave that to us,' Marriott said. 'I'll talk to them about it.'

'Sure,' Billy said with heavy irony, 'you'll talk to them. And they'll promise to be good lads. You can trust them if you like, but don't ask me to.'

'All I'm asking you to do,' Marriott said, 'is hand the gun over. We'll see to the rest.'

'You don't know when you're well off, do you?' Billy stared at him for a moment and then glanced, grinning again, at the others. 'Let's get something straight,' he said. 'I've got a gun. I bought it, and I'm keeping it, and if I have to protect myself with it, I will. Miss Petrie offered me good money for it the day we got here, and I turned it down. You don't hold it against me, do you, miss? So I'm hanging on to it.'

'If it's a question of money,' Marriott said, 'we can pay you very well for the gun. I don't know what Miss Petrie offered, but we'll treble it.'

'Will we?' Billy asked contemptuously. 'You mean, Sweeney will. But Sweeney doesn't give a damn, does he? See him sitting over there. He's quite happy. And so am I as long as no one starts interfering with me. It's if they do that there's likely to be trouble.'

He wasn't going to budge, Toni saw, and Tony had only weakened his position as a result of trying to get the gun off him. Her mind swung back to the thoughts she had had coming out of the hut where the wounded man lay. She had a feeling of helplessness. They were drifting towards an end that was increasingly menacing and all the time less avoidable. She put her hand on her husband's arm, looking for help and offering it at the same time. She felt at the same time a fierce pride in him. He might not be doing it well, but he was trying to do something. He wasn't acquiescing as Willeway and Candie were. He hadn't abdicated like Sweeney.

Marriott said: 'I'm offering you a last chance to be reasonable.'

She tightened her grip on his arm, wincing for him. Billy said:

'Last chance? You want to watch it, Marriott. You really want to watch it.' He slapped his pocket where the small bulge of the Beretta was visible. 'I'm going to see what Cookie's up to. I don't mind him doing a spot of doctoring, but he's not to let it interfere with getting the supper ready.'

There was silence as he went away, and after a moment or two they broke up into smaller groups. Toni kept her hand on her husband's arm, and guided him away from the others. He allowed himself to be taken, not even looking – as he usually did these days – at Susan, who was talking quietly to Candie. He had the drained, beaten look she had seen before; when a business deal had gone the wrong way – the time, over the Smythe thing, when he had thought they were going to prosecute him.

'Come away,' she said. 'Let's get away, honey.'

They went down to the beach, and she turned eastwards. They had walked for five or ten minutes before he asked her where they were going.

'A walk.' They were holding hands now as they walked over the hot sands. 'I thought we might see if we could get into that little valley this way.'

He nodded. 'If you like.'

After half an hour they came to what had previously been the limit of exploration in this direction. A high ridge of rock crossed the sand and jutted well out into the sea. Toni pulled off her frock and sandals, hesitated briefly, and then slipped off her other things. She put them in a hollow of the rock and weighted them with a loose stone. She smiled at Tony.

'Let's see if we can swim round.'

He stripped in turn, and cached his clothes. She waded out and he followed her. The sand shelved steeply and soon they were swimming in the warm, almost waveless water. They swam to the point where the ridge ended, rounded it, and were looking into a cove, its beach lightly fringed with palms, and, unmistakably, the little valley beyond.

Leisurely they swam in to shore, came out on sand which stung their feet with heat as they dried, and walked hand in hand up the beach and through the palms. On the other side there was grass; not the velvet lawn which it had seemed from high up on the mountain, but emerald green, soft and springy to their bare feet. They walked beside the stream to the pool which fed it. Its surface had an exquisite diversity of colour: cobalt at their feet ranging to pastel shades of blue at the far side. Lazily she asked him why.

'Deep here,' he said, 'shallow over there. Can you smell those oranges?'

'Stay here,' she said. 'I'll bring you some.'

The orange trees were further up the valley. The fruit were small, but deep gold, and she picked half a dozen without even having to stand on tiptoe; the auriferous branches hung low to the ground. She walked back, balancing them in her cupped hands against her breasts. Tony was lying by the edge of the pool; she saw his eyes on her, admiring, and smiled with pleasure. When she got to him, she stooped and rolled the oranges at his feet. His eyes had not left her.

'Shall I peel them for you, too?' she asked him.

'Not yet.' He caught her ankle with his hand. 'You refresh me.'

'I'm glad.'

'After the mess I made of things back there.'

'Forget it.' She bent to kiss him. 'There's only us here. A long long way from anywhere.'

They touched each other, and kissed, and made love in the warm grass beside the pool. She surrendered herself to him as she always did easily, without urgency, securing and secure. She was in a pleasant haze of warmth and sensuality when, un-accountably, her mind went back again to the hut, and the wounded man, and all the apprehension of what might happen as a result. The thrill of fear and uncertainty mixed with desire; enhancing, not subduing. A wave of ecstasy such as she had never experienced before caught her, and she cried out as treetops and mountain blurred against a spinning sky.

15

THERE WAS A SUBDUED UNEASY ATMOSPHERE in the camp that evening. The Hawaiians, as usual, had their supper apart from the rest, but there was none of the customary chatter, and no singing afterwards. They stayed together close to their hut, talking in low voices, and the cook, when he had cleared things up, joined them there. Yasha, as he often did, sat apart, watching. Sweeney remained on his own, too, but looking somnolent, meditative perhaps, rather than watchful. Billy talked a lot and laughed a lot while he was seeing to their meal, and afterwards sat near Lydia.

The signs of tension disturbed Candie. He suggested a stroll on the beach to Susan, and she agreed. They took the path from the clearing which had now, by constant use, become a marked and easily negotiable thoroughfare. Matters were helped by the moon, swelling to its third quarter and bright enough to light their way. On the beach the sand was silver, as were the lapping waters of the bay. They turned east, knowing that in the other direction their way would be barred by the ridge of rock that jutted out to sea. They walked side by side, their arms not quite touching. The air was warm; it had the smell of the sea, and the other strong heavy scents of the island.

Candie prided himself on the fact that his approach to sex was as leisurely and relaxed as it was to the other activities that life had to offer. He had never grabbed, even as an adolescent; he had never needed to. When he was fifteen and spending, as usual, his school holiday with Aunt Lilian, he had become aware of the greater interest that was being taken in him by Aunt Lilian's friend and neighbour, Mrs Archer-Strode. There had been looks, small touches, occasional treats – a mounting complicity behind Aunt Lilian's back. He had been surprised at first when he realized the direction in which events were moving – Mrs Archer-Strode was in her early forties, her unpleasantly spotty daughter a year or two older than Candie himself – but neither shocked nor repelled. He had waited, with interest and a growing but not immoderate excitement, for her to bring them to a head, which she had done at last on a hot August afternoon when Aunt Lilian was in Cheltenham shopping and the daughter staying a few days with a friend. She had seen him during the morning in the garden and suggested that, if he wanted to listen to the cricket commentary in the afternoon, he should come round and make use of her radio: Aunt Lilian's set, dating from about the time of Candie's birth, was in a late stage of crackling decrepitude. So he had waited for ten minutes after Aunt Lilian's pre-war Morris groaned round the corner of the road, and strolled across. She had asked him if he felt grown up enough to have a beer, and when he said yes had decided to have one with him, and they had sat for perhaps a quarter of an hour in front of the glossy new radiogram, attending to the inexorable progress of Bradman towards a century. He had been pleasantly tense but unruffled, aware of the nervousness and desire of the mature woman who sat opposite, and ready for the moment when she called his name in a different, deeper voice, and, when he looked up at her, smiling, asked him if he felt like leaving the cricket for a while to let her show him the Japanese carving she had mentioned once before. To his surprise they had gone not to her bedroom but to her husband's study, and to his surprise also there had in fact been a carving. She had taken it from a glass-fronted cabinet and shown it to him. It was in ivory: a house, with small figures visible through the windows. She showed him what the figures were doing, and asked with a small gasping laugh could one imagine the sort of person who would spend months, years, carving *that* sort of thing. And while she talked she had touched him, lightly and then more boldly and finally, in a quick shameless grasp, with an indrawn breath and a chiding 'Naughty boy! Oh, you naughty, naughty boy ...'

There had been one other afternoon during those holidays, and when he went back to school she had pressed a pound on him. He had been amused by this, as also by her saying that she would have loved to write to him at school, but perhaps better not, but she would be thinking of him and he must come and see her the day he got back from school. A more lasting impression had been made by her disquisition on his body while, on their second afternoon, they lay naked on her bed, their feet tangled in the hastily flung back candlewick bedspread. He had the Latin physique, she told him, and the Latin face to go with it. No normal woman could help being excited by him. 'You'd better not play cards,' she had told him, running her white, scarlet-nailed hands over the dark fuzz already growing on his chest. 'Stick to love, Roger. You'll never go wrong if you do.'

He had accepted the tribute and the advice as coming from the knowledge and experience of an older person; not so much complacently as realistically. He had, from that point on, expected woman to make most of the running, and had not often been disappointed. He was not, despite his somewhat satyr-like appearance, particularly highly sexed, and was always prepared to wait. Eventually there would be the moment of ripeness. He could read the signals well by now.

On the cruise, and later on the island, he had been quite happy to wait. Toni was the most attractive of the women, but he was not fool enough to get involved with a married woman when her husband was in such close proximity. The same applied to Katey, who struck him as the most restless and unsatisfied of the four. Lydia was too angular, both in body and personality, to appeal to him. That left Susan, whom he had liked from the outset and with whom he got on easily, without friction. He had watched Marriott's attempts to court her with a slightly contemptuous interest: she was not, he was sure, the kind of girl to respond to that approach or that type of man. In due course the moment would arrive for her to turn to him, with a small gesture, a glance, an intonation of voice that he would recognize. He would be ready when she did.

He reflected, as they walked along the moonlit beach, that the moment had not yet come. She was friendly, talking at ease, but the barrier was still in place. He wondered about that a little. Marriott's efforts, however unwelcome, should have stimulated her; and there was the forcing effect of the island itself. There should have been some sign by now: an intimation if not an invitation.

They walked about a mile along the beach and sat down facing the sea. She was puzzled over Sweeney, and talked about him at some length. Candie, when she forced him to comment, said:

'He's never really given a damn about anything, has he? Not in the time I've known him. He organized the cruise and skippered the boat because he had the whim to do that. Now he's lost interest.'

She shook her head. 'It doesn't make sense.'

'Nothing about Sweeney ever does make sense.'

'He has that look,' she said, 'of – not quite satisfaction. Completion? Something like that.'

Candie said comfortably: 'He's an oddball. There are plenty of them around, but not so many with the money and power Sweeney's had. He knows everyone who counts. He can have anything he wants. So he's bored.'

'No.' She stared out at the different silvers of sea and moon and breaking surf. 'I don't think he's bored.'

Candie looked at her profile; she had the kind of face, pleasant rather than pretty, which grew more attractive as one came to know it. Not very experienced, he would say. Quite possibly not experienced at all. It was unlikely, in the case of a girl in the latter half of her twenties who had been leading a bachelor life in London, but one of the delights of the female sex was its variety and capacity to furnish surprises. Could that be the explanation of the lack of signals? Could it be that she quite genuinely did not know how to give them? Under normal circumstances the thought of such depressing innocence would have been enough to put him off, but these circumstances were not normal. On such a night, in such a place … he felt his own mild blood tingle, and decided that, even without signals, there was a ripeness to the moment. It was a time and place for transformations.

He took her arms and drew her round to kiss him. She did not resist, but did not respond either. She waited till he released her and said, in a quiet voice:

'Thank you, Roger. I do like you.'

It was not only the words that were damning; he had already taken the message of the firm unmoving lips. He said easily:

'I like you, too. Do you want to go back now?'

'I think so.'

She began to talk, as they walked, and he listened to her, attentive but bored. It was a conventional little story. He sometimes felt that he deserved credit for having diverted at least a few girls, for a time, from the married predators who otherwise, almost infallibly, scooped them up. This one was no exception to the generality: he knew her John and could have forecast every turn of plot before she reached it.

As for the girl herself, she was hurt and miserable, lonely and looking for comfort. Not sexual comfort – at least, not yet. What she wanted was Elder Brother, or Understanding Father, a strong male shoulder on which to rest her head. There was, he felt, a very good chance that time and sympathy would divert her attention from the pub in Fetter Lane to a nearer and more available object; in fact it was a virtual certainty. But between now and then there would have to be all this talk, all this dreary concentration on her. It was a daunting prospect, and having managed to avoid getting entangled in feminine emotional problems in England, he did not relish the thought of having to put up with them here.

He listened politely, and said one or two of what might be regarded as the right things afterwards, but he made no effort to show much interest. She seemed to sense this, and the flow of narrative dried up abruptly. They walked the remainder of the way back to the camp in comparative silence, and parted with a brief good night. She would get over it, Candie thought – sooner here, probably, than anywhere – and after that there would be time to take another look at things. There was no hurry, anyway. The prospects seemed to favour an indefinite stay on the island.

He slept well that night and awoke in the morning to something more than the usual confusion of sounds and voices. Normally he drowsed his way through this prelude to the day, not moving from his bed until breakfast was unmistakably imminent, but the voices were louder, and had a disturbing edge which roused him to wakefulness. He opened an eye, and looked about him. The beds of Marriott and Willeway were empty. He was wondering whether it was worth while getting up to investigate, when Willeway came back into the hut.

'Better get up, Rodge,' he said. 'All hands on deck. Trouble down below.'

'Trouble?' He yawned, and rubbed the sleep out of his eyes. 'What trouble's that?'

'The boys.'

'The Hawaiians?' Candie sat up. 'What have they done – cut Billy's throat while he slept?'

'They've cleared off.'

Candie sat up. 'Cleared off? Off the island?'

'Hardly that.' Willeway stared at him. 'Could they, though? We assumed they'd pushed off to another part of the island. My God.'

He went out again, and Candie heard him talking excitedly to Marriott. He decided that the occasion justified getting out of bed, and pulled on his shirt and trousers. His sandals, he noticed, were already showing noticeable signs of wear and tear, and he thought enviously of Willeway's. By the time he got outside, a group of figures were leaving the clearing and heading for the beach – Marriott and Willeway, Billy and Yasha. Candie followed them, breaking into a trot.

They could see at once, as they came through the palms directly above the beach, that the boat was gone. The sand was deeply scored where it had been dragged down to the water level, and there were the prints of feet on either side. Automatically their eyes went out to the bay, and the broad reach of ocean beyond. The early sun dazzled on emptiness.

Willeway said: 'Is that something? Over there.' They peered out in the direction of his pointing arm. 'Perhaps not. The light's bad, isn't it?'

Billy said: 'Wouldn't do much bloody good if we could see them, would it? Unless you're proposing to swim out and haul them back.'

'No,' Marriott said. 'They've gone.' He stared at Billy. 'They've decided they'd rather take a chance on the ocean than put up with you any longer.'

Candie asked: 'The chap who was shot?'

'He's gone, too,' Willeway said. 'At least, there's no sign of him.'

'I suppose they stocked up with food and water,' Billy said. 'That won't do them much good.' He spoke with bitter satisfaction. 'They won't make it.'

Candie said: 'Cookie?'

Marriott nodded. 'Yes, with the others.'

'Christ.'

Willeway said hopefully: 'I suppose they still could have pushed off to another part of the island? The boat would be useful to them, and at the same time make us think they'd gone off into the blue.'

'No,' Billy said. 'They've gone, all right. I know those brown bastards.'

'Do you?' Marriott said. 'It's a pity you didn't handle them better, then. Who's going to cook breakfast, for a start?'

'The women will take over eventually,' Billy said. 'But I reckon Willeway can have a go at it this morning.' He grinned. 'He's fond enough of his food.'

There was a pause, before Marriott said: 'You're forgetting something, aren't you? You're the steward. Food is your department.'

'Get knotted,' Billy said indifferently. He turned to Willeway. 'You'd better go and see if the fire's gone out. I don't suppose that slant-eyed sod bothered to make it up before he cleared off.'

Marriott said: 'You don't give orders around here.'

'Don't I? Somebody's got to. There'll have to be a bit of organization now that the boys have gone. You're not on a luxury cruise any longer.'

The remark, like the instruction to Willeway, was a deliberate notice of intention. Marriott said:

'We'll do the organizing. And we'll tell you what we want you to do as well.'

'Will you?' Billy said. 'Will you, then?'

The two men faced each other. It was a confrontation similar to that of the previous afternoon, but aggravated both by the present situation and by Marriott having already backed down once. Candie wondered whether he ought to weigh in on Marriott's side, but realized that it wouldn't help. It was Marriott's problem. Marriott had provoked the clash and would have to carry it through. It wasn't as though one could have much sympathy with either of them, Candie reflected.

Marriott said, in a cold low voice: 'Are you going to start waving your gun around again? You're not dealing with boys from the islands now.'

'I don't need the gun,' Billy said. 'I can manage well enough without it.'

'You're a liar, aren't you?' Marriott said. He was tensed up,

Candie saw, concentrated to a pitch of provocation and defiance. 'You wouldn't feel safe without it.'

Moving quickly and unexpectedly, Billy hit him. The blow landed on the side of his jaw, but not cleanly enough to do more than rock him. He stepped back and then came in at Billy, punching. The other men moved back to give them room. They fought savagely, their feet slipping and dragging in the sand.

Marriott, Candie saw, had had some experience of boxing: his blows were cleaner and more professional and he knew how to make Billy miss. It was an advantage which compensated, to a considerable extent, for Billy's superior height, reach and weight. Billy was no better than a rough-house fighter. Marriott had probably guessed that and reckoned that if he could damage him a little Billy might very likely crack up. The old business about the bully being a coward.

It looked for a time as though things might be going to work out that way. Marriott dodged the rushes of the other, parrying most of the wild blows, and got in some useful jabs in the process. He drew blood from Billy's nose and, a little later, ducked beneath a savage swing and hooked an equally savage right-hander to the heart. Billy gasped, doubled up for a moment and was hit hard on the jaw before he could recover. He jumped back, looking extremely unhappy, and paused, breathing heavily and painfully, before he came in again. He looked an unhappy spectacle with blood running over his mouth and down his chin. The disconcerting thing from Marriott's point of view, though, was that he showed no sign of being prepared to throw in the towel. In fact, the sly, somewhat shifty expression which his face usually carried had been replaced by vicious determination. Marriott hit him again on the body and he winced, but came on: a flailing arm caught Marriott's neck and almost sent him sprawling. He recovered himself, but clearly he was shaken. There was only one way it could end, Candie saw. Billy was much too strong for him.

It was several minutes before Billy managed to knock Marriott down for the first time. He began to get to his feet and Billy hit him again. He clutched at the taller man, mouth open, eyes pathetically distended. Billy, looking down, chopped at his neck with the edge of his fist. He groaned horribly, letting go of Billy's shirt, and slumped on to the sand, plainly unable to rise. Billy kicked him in the side, but not very hard. Not out of any desire to avoid doing him serious bodily harm, Candie reflected, but to save his toes: he was only wearing canvas shoes.

Billy said: 'All right.' He looked at the others a touch defensively, as though feeling a need to justify himself. 'He asked for it. I don't like people calling me a liar.'

Candie and Willeway stared at the fallen man; he was not unconscious, but moaning slightly. It was Yasha who stooped down and lifted him into a sitting position.

'He'll be all right,' Billy said. 'Take him down to the water's edge and soak him a bit.' He looked at Willeway. 'You can go and see about breakfast. I've got a bit of an appetite this morning.'

16

Susan passed the weeks immediately following the flight of the Hawaiians and the cook in a daze engendered by optimism. She no longer felt marooned, in the absolute sense. The Hawaiians were somewhere out there and, despite Billy's reiterated conviction that they had gone to their deaths, she could not believe that they would not make some kind of contact – with a ship, another island – and from this contact, she was sure, would come their own rescue. She awoke each morning with a consciousness that this might be the day in which smoke would appear on the horizon, a ship swell towards them over the broad sunlit acres of the sea. After that ... Honolulu inside a week ... London another forty-eight hours away. Theirs would, she supposed, be a fairly big news story. If John was not, in fact, waiting for her, she could at least ring him, light-heartedly, and ask him if he would like to buy her a drink in exchange for a full account. At that point she drifted into reveries of the way he would look when they met again, the sound of his voice, the things she could say to make him laugh ... and so, shivering, to the thought of his hands, the remembrance of his body against her own. She shied away then, but returned soon enough.

She was regretful and ashamed of having talked to Candie that night on the beach. It had embarrassed him to no purpose, and the recollection of it embarrassed her. He had done no more than make the nicest, most civilized pass, and she had repaid the compliment by unloading her own dreary worries and unhappiness on him. There was more to it than this. At a deeper level she registered that she had reached out to another human being, and that he had rejected her: excusing him and berating herself did not disguise that. Had things been different, she might have turned to Candie as part of the hope of forgetting John; but she knew she would never do that now. There were moments of irrevocability in all relationships, mature or immature, and that had been one.

None of this mattered during the time of optimism; but the optimism itself broke in the storm that swept in, late one afternoon, from the west. It was heralded by thickly piling cumulonimbus and oppressive sweltering heat. Within an hour the first thick drops of warm rain were starring the packed earth of the clearing, and soon after that the downpour started. The wind rose later. By the time the night fell it was tearing savagely at the trees and the roofs of the huts. The cooking fire had gone out and all they had to eat was breadfruit cooked earlier in the day, spread with avocado. They went to bed early, and lay awake listening to the wind and wondering when the hut was likely to collapse.

At the height of the storm, Susan thought of the small boat and the Hawaiians. It was an irrational point on which to admit defeat – they might already have been picked up or made land – but she knew then that Billy was right. There was no hope of rescue through them. She wept silently for them, and a little for herself. It was no easy thing to learn despair a second time.

Morning saw the sky a bright washed blue, the winds moderating, but the seas beyond the reef still mountainous and the great waves spilling over the reef to crash against the shores of the island. They had gone to the beach immediately on getting up – except for Candie who was still in bed – and stood grouped together staring out at the waters that hemmed them in. It was Katey who drew their attention to something nearer at hand, something that rolled in the ripples of the ebbing tide. She pointed.

'What's that?'

Billy raced down and waded in to get it. He held it up in triumph.

'Bit of luck!'

It was a cylindrical tin, some eighteen inches tall and about a foot across.

'What's in it?' Willeway asked.

'God knows.' Billy held it to his ear and shook it. 'Could be beans or cooking oil. We'll find out soon enough.' He stared out at the bay. 'I suppose the storm has broken her up and set things rolling. We'll have to keep a watch on the beaches. Never know what's going to turn up.' He turned to Susan. 'Another little job for the cook's helper: beachcombing first thing in the morning.'

She nodded. Billy had established a roster of cooking duties for the women, and she was at present on duty as assistant to Toni. Katey was to take her place at the end of another week. Lydia, it was accepted, was exempt from this. The men, apart from Sweeney, worked under Billy's direct instructions. It was a little surprising, now she came to reflect on it, how meekly they had all accepted this state of affairs. It was standard herd animal stuff – the two bulls fight and the winner takes over. Except that the winning bull had not driven his rival away and had not, thank God, showed signs of any urge towards exercising certain other primitive rights. The only woman he appeared to be interested in was Lydia, and as a suppliant rather than a conqueror.

Something else was moving in the pull of the tide further up the beach. She said:

'I'll start right away. Over there. Is it … ?'

'One of the lobster pots,' Billy said. 'That's a clever girl. I'll keep you on the ration strength, after all.'

He threw the tin he had been carrying to Marriott, who caught it awkwardly, and set off after the other object. They had lost all the pots that had been put down because they had been set too deep for any of the present party to recover them. Lydia had had a shot at getting one of them, but had been forced to give up. The recovery of one of the pots was in itself a tri-umph, since it would offer a pattern on which others could be constructed. Billy and Yasha had tried to duplicate the work of the Hawaiians, but without success.

Billy returned, carrying the pot. They could hear a rustling, the clank of shell, and he said:

'We've got something.'

He opened the top of the wicker pot and spilled the contents on the sand. There were two small lobsters and a larger one. It was the larger one which drew their attention.

The colour was wrong for a start; pale blue against the dark blue of the other two. And then there were the claws. One was small and feeble-looking, the other enormously swollen and ending not in one set of pincers but two. The effect was grotesque and unpleasant. It squirmed and hitched itself in the direction of the water; Billy kicked it back with the side of his shoe.

'That's an ugly bugger,' he observed.

Katey cried out: 'Throw it back in the sea! It's hideous. Get rid of it.'

'Plenty of meat on him,' Billy said. 'He'll cook all right.'

'It's this island,' Katey said. 'Everything's wrong. Everything's out of shape. There was that bird yesterday ...'

'That was a man-o'-war,' Billy said. 'They have those little feet and they're stuck if they land in the wrong place. Bloke told me once they have to land on a slope at night and they can only get off with the warm air rising in the morning.'

'God,' Katey said. 'Oh God, God! And that damned cloud sitting over us all the time. Even the storm hasn't blown it away, has it? And all these filthy misshapen creatures ...' She stared at the lobster. There was more than a touch of hysteria in her voice, and Susan felt it communicating, fraying the edges of her own nerves.

'It's a beastly place,' Katey said. 'Beastly, beastly! Why can't we do something – make a raft ... get away somehow?' She turned to Billy, between demand and entreaty. 'There must be some way.'

'There's nothing to get worked up about,' Billy said. 'I've seen funnier shellfish than that before. A crab once with another crab growing out of his back, and that was down at Hastings. I reckon the little claw's just a replacement, anyway. He lost it in a fight and now he's growing another. What do you think, Tony?'

He said: 'That's what it looks like.'

Since the show-down, the two men had got on very well together. Billy treated Marriott as his lieutenant, and if Marriott felt any resentment he kept it well concealed. Billy was given to approaching Marriott for confirmation of his views, and Marriott invariably supported him. It was an improvement, Susan supposed, over the early bickering – things got done, whether well or badly, without argument – but it did not make her like Marriott any the more.

'Well,' Billy said, 'them as don't want it don't need to eat it. And you're not on kitchen duty right now, Katey, so you won't even have to cook it. Anyway, that can wait. We've not had breakfast yet.'

After breakfast Billy announced that there was to be another pig hunt, in which all except Susan were to take part. Toni and Katey were to act as beaters, while Lydia, on her own decision, was joining the men with the nets and spears. Sweeney had opted to join the party also. Susan, Billy said, was to stay behind, look after the camp, and do the necessary cleaning and tidying up. He favoured her with his shifty winking grin.

'Behave yourself while we're gone. No getting up to mischief.'

She watched them go along the path leading to the beach, and then busied herself with various things that needed doing. There were the cries of birds, and the distant shriek of a monkey, but it was the absence of sound of which she was more conscious: the lack of speech and laughter. She had never been alone before on the island. Everything about her was alien. The harsh screech of a parrot emphasized her sense of isolation.

She began singing to herself, and this helped for a time. Later, though, the artificiality of her own voice oppressed her, and she fell silent. The wind had dropped almost to nothing, a gusty breeze which brought damp heat from the surrounding green, steaming now in the fierce sun. She looked up at the white cloud cloaking Mount Proteus, and thought of Katey's outburst earlier. There was nothing sinister in its appearance, but her nerve ends crawled all the same. One must not let it become an obsession, she thought: a cloud and a mountain, nothing more. It was this heat and the loneliness which made things worse. The thing to do was think of something else – get one's mind away from the island, away from everything.

Her thoughts went into the familiar channels, but flatly, without joy or anticipation. She could no longer believe that rescue was at hand and, lacking that illusion, the other make-believe became impossible too. He was, she could have no doubt, busy and happy in his own life – unaware, probably that the *Diana* was not still serenely cruising and, even if aware, no more than regretful, a little concerned, a little guilty. What time of day was it in London now? Early evening. He might be on his way home. She felt a great wave of misery and loneliness. As it swelled round her she heard a sound different from the noises of the tropical forest: someone was coming up the path from the beach.

Her first thought was that it was one of the Hawaiians – that they had, after all, been hiding on another part of the island and were now perhaps returning to make their peace with Billy. Or perhaps, she thought with quick apprehension, they had been watching from some vantage point – had seen the others go off along the beach? They would find her alone here. But the sound was that of the passage of one person, not a party. And at that moment Marriott came through the trees and into the clearing.

She said: 'Tony! It's you.'

He grinned. 'Who did you think it was?'

'I wasn't sure. What have you come back for? Did you forget something?'

'Spear,' he said. 'After spending all that time pointing and hardening it. Careless of me.'

Lacking facilities for shaving, the males of the party were inevitably becoming more hirsute day by day. Marriott, having a beard in the first place, should have shown less change in appearance than the others, but paradoxically showed more. The carefully trimmed and pointed beard was wildly luxuriant by this time – he had very strong and curly hair growth – giving him an unkempt barbarous look. She found him equally unattractive in this new guise.

She turned away from him. 'Yes, I suppose.'

He did not go into the hut where, presumably, the spear was, but stood looking at her. She disregarded his gaze and went on preparing vegetables for the mid-day meal.

He said: 'I thought you might be making a mid-morning cup of coffee for yourself, and that I might be in time for a cup – or a half-shell.'

The coffee beans from further up the valley had proved a moderate success. They had managed to grind them fairly well with the aid of a couple of stones that made up a rough pestle-and-mortar arrangement, but roasting was more difficult. Some beans were burnt and others hardly touched by the heat. But, although odd-tasting and bitter, it was coffee.

Susan said: 'No. I'm not making any.' She looked at him. 'Won't Billy be waiting for you to get back with that spear?'

'Billy won't mind.' She saw that he was smiling. 'Billy and I understand each other.'

She remembered the wink with which Billy had left her, and the admonition. He had probably known then that Marriott would slip back to the camp – very possibly had put the idea up to him. He would be amused by it. At the same time, he was tossing a reward to Marriott for the way he had accepted his leadership.

This realization did not make her apprehensive again: puzzled, rather. Surely Marriott could not think that having the others out of the way would make her any more willing to tolerate his silly innuendoes and advances? She had made it plain from the beginning that he had no interest for her, and in recent days she had felt that the message had been absorbed. The man was not a fool. He might feel more free with Toni absent, but he could not possibly think that that would affect her. She said sharply:

'I suggest you get back, all the same. I have things to do here.'

Marriott was still smiling. 'That's less than kind. I thought you might be glad of a little company. Don't you feel lonely on your own?'

'I don't want your company.'

He stared at her in silence for a moment. 'You're a nasty little bitch. Sex is a funny thing, isn't it? You're not nearly as attractive as Toni, I don't like you, and yet I can hardly wait to get my hands on you.'

'You're going to have to wait. A very long time indeed.'

He shook his head. 'Not very long. In fact, the only reason I'm waiting at all is because there's a certain amount of pleasure in it. The joys of anticipation. An appetizing small *hors d'œuvre*, I'm much fonder of the main course, though.'

She felt a thrill of fear, then; not at the words, but at the flat implacability of tone.

'Don't be silly,' she said. 'You're not a rapist. You're only a squalid little lecher. Run away, and be thankful you've got someone like Toni to put up with you.'

Marriott looked at her thoughtfully. 'If this were London,' he said, '– the cocktail party jungle instead of the tropic one – you'd be quite safe. I might have tried you out, or I might not. You're not the kind of girl I would go for when I had a reasonable choice. I certainly wouldn't have bothered with you for long. But it isn't London, is it? We can't behave in the way that we used to call normal. Billy demonstrated that to me.' Marriott's hand went to his neck, rubbing it gently. 'He hurt me badly. You won't even get hurt if you've got sense enough not to cause trouble.'

She understood something of the effort it had cost him to knuckle down to Billy: his vanity had been hurt a lot more than his body had. She realized for the first time that she really might be physically in danger, that the threats were not empty, but filled with his hatred and frustration. And although Billy had beaten him up, he was a good deal stronger than she was. She looked around for something to defend herself with. There was nothing nearer than the wooden spits over by the field kitchen. And they were twenty yards away or more.

She said: 'And when the others get back?'

'I used to wonder,' Marriott said, 'about men who took women by force. Even when they were drunk they must have had some thought for the consequences. I didn't see that there was anything that could make it worth while. But I was thinking of the ordinary pleasure of sex. Obviously it couldn't be worth while for that. The difference is when it's the forcing itself that counts, when you can use one humiliation to wipe out another.'

He paused, and laughed. 'What happens afterwards has got nothing to do with it, but nothing will happen. They couldn't even take a gun off Billy, so what can they do to me? Billy will be tickled pink by the idea. Sweeney doesn't care about people – as far as he's concerned they can find their own damnations. Roger Candie? Do you think he'll do anything? Joe? I suppose the women won't speak to me for a few days – Katey, anyway.'

'And Toni?'

'I can deal with Toni.'

She wondered at the glibness with which he spoke, and glimpsed a reason. He thought, when it came to the point, that she would accept him or, if not that, accept the fact of having been forced – cause no trouble because in this new primitive world it would do no good to cause trouble. One accepted things here because one had to. There was no law to appeal to. One was on one's own, and under those circumstances submission, for a woman, was the natural thing. The logic of this was more compelling than his outline of the weakness or indifference of the others. She felt it in blood and sinew and deep inside her body. Her ordinary civilized dislike of Marriott – even physical revulsion against him – was a veneer in comparison with the realities of their new life.

But although submission might be part of the logic of their situation, something which in the long run was inevitable, she would not submit. She turned to walk casually in the direction of the kitchen, and the spits. When he called her to stop, she paid no attention. She heard his footsteps running, and began to run herself. He caught her quite easily. His hand gripped her arm, fingers digging in savagely, and she stopped. With head averted, she said:

'You're bruising me.'

The hold tightened, hurting her still more. 'I told you it was up to you whether you got hurt. I don't mind.'

'What do you want me to do?'

'Look at me for a start. I don't like talking to the back of a girl's neck.'

She needed time. She turned her head to look at him. His mouth was open slightly, with teeth clenched. She thought: if he does to my body in hate what has only been done before in love, I shall suffer it, but I will kill him. Sooner or later I will kill him.

He said: 'That's better. Now, a kiss.'

She heard the sound from behind him, and said:

'Someone else is coming.'

He laughed. 'God! That's a childish one to try.'

She looked past him. Raising her voice, she said:

'Yasha. Did you forget something, too?'

Yasha said: 'Yes.' At the sound of his voice, Marriott released his hold on her and turned to look at Yasha, who was standing just inside the clearing. 'I needed to come back,' Yasha said.

He was staring at Marriott. The recognition was unmistakable, and so was the warning. She felt a great pulse of gratitude towards him, the more because of her isolation and helplessness of a moment before. He had watched Marriott, had noticed him slip away from the party, guessed what might happen. She had protection here, and not for this moment only.

Marriott was silent still. Yasha said: 'I think Billy is looking for you.' Marriott did not speak, but he turned away and went to the hut. Yasha said:

'Are you all right?'

She nodded, rubbing her arm. 'Yes. Thank you.'

Marriott came out of the hut, carrying a spear. He said to Yasha:

'Have you got what you came for? Are you coming back now?'

'You go on,' Yasha said. 'I'll catch up.'

Marriott looked from one of them to the other. He was struggling to control his fury; she was afraid he might attack Yasha with the spear, and moved a little closer to him.

'You're a bit hopeful, aren't you?' Marriott said. 'Or have I been missing something?'

'Get going,' Yasha said. He spoke quietly but strongly. 'I have nothing else to say to you.'

With a final look, Marriott went. They saw him cross the clearing, heard him carry on down the path to the beach.

Yasha said: 'You will be all right, won't you? I will keep him in view.'

'Yes,' she said. 'I'll be all right, now.'

17

THERE WAS ANOTHER STORM, about a month after their arrival on the island; it was more violent than the first and lasted all one day, and the night, and the morning of the day after. During this time Katey developed the conviction that when the skies cleared they would clear entirely, that the cloud would be gone from the mountain-top and that with that lifting all sorts of things would be better. It was not until sunset, with the sky deep blue all round and the cloud turning from vermilion to sombre purple, that she dismissed the hope. She tried to be rational about it – it was ridiculous to let herself be upset by a cloud – but in the mood she was in reason did not help. She drank palm wine instead, and later took Joe away from the others and coaxed him to make love to her, and wept in wretchedness under the bright stars. He tried to comfort her, but was bewildered and helpless himself, and in the end she sent him off to the men's hut. She lay for a long time out in the open before she took herself to bed.

The following morning, Sweeney left them. The hut he had been using had been badly damaged in the storm, and Billy had collected a work party to repair it. Sweeney shook his head.

'No, it doesn't matter.'

'With a dirty great hole in the roof?' Billy asked. 'The next rains we get, you'll be swamped.'

Sweeney surveyed them with his mild reflective gaze. 'I am moving away,' he said.

'Why?'

'I feel that I would like to,' Sweeney said.

Lydia asked: 'Where are you going?'

He pointed up the slopes of the western hill. 'There is a pleasant spot I found by chance. It has running water, and a view of the ocean.' He smiled. 'I will be your look-out, and tell you when a ship crosses the horizon.'

The pyre that Billy and the boys had set up in the first few days was still in place on the headland. There had been suggestions from time to time of setting a watch there, but the only one who could have organized it was Billy, and he had not bothered. Looking at Billy now, Katey thought she detected mixed feelings over what Sweeney was saying: some satisfaction, but also an apprehension of loss. She herself said:

'Will you be coming down here for food, Sweeney?'

'I think not.'

'How will you manage on your own?'

He smiled. 'I will manage.'

'What about shelter?' Billy said.

'I will manage that, too.'

They were all bewildered, but there was a reluctance to question Sweeney more closely. They watched him as he went up through the trees. Katey felt herself sharing the feelings she had attributed to Billy. She remembered when she was very little: her father going abroad, the realization that it did not matter now about voices raised in the nursery, but at the same time the sense of emptiness.

Billy said: 'O.K., then. Let's get cracking on fixing this hut.'

Candie objected: 'What's the point? Sweeney won't be using it any more.'

'If Sweeney isn't using it, someone else can.'

There was a pause while they digested this. The hut, by being Sweeney's, had acquired a nebulous but not inconsiderable importance. Did that remark of Billy's, Kate wondered, mean that he felt himself to have taken Sweeney's place? As far as the exercise of authority was concerned, he had done that weeks ago; but there was more to authority than its exercise.

Billy said harshly: 'All right. Let's get cracking.'

The hesitation ended on that. The party, apart from Katey and Toni who were on kitchen duty, got to work on repairing the hut and had it finished in a couple of hours. And apart, of course, from Lydia. She had gone off on her own that morning. She returned about the time the work was completed. Presumably, she had been diving: she carried a vine-pouch with an assortment of crustaceans in it. She threw this to Toni, and went to look at the hut.

'Sweeney's gone,' Billy told her.

'Gone?'

He told her what had happened. She listened, and then said: 'And the hut?'

Billy said: 'Seems a pity not to use it. I thought you might like a place of your own.'

Katey watched her with the others. It made sense: he had not dared to pre-empt it for himself, but he could do so on behalf of Lydia. The question was – would she accept? It was flattering, but it meant accepting it from Billy's hands. If it had been offered to her, Katey thought … her own envy and bitterness shocked her. Lydia was welcome to it. And Lydia, with no shadow of doubt, would take it.

Lydia said: 'Thank you, Billy.' She glanced at the other women with a faint smile. 'Means the rest of you will have more room to move about, doesn't it?'

The effect of Sweeney's departure was something which closed in on them during the day. There was a sense of being abandoned. Sweeney had retreated from them all during the weeks that followed the sinking of the *Diana*, but there had been the awareness of him in the background, the feeling that abdication was temporary and that government might soon - tomorrow, perhaps – be renewed. Going away was an act which closed all avenues. Katey noticed the difference in the behaviour of Billy and Lydia, the one more talkative and aggressive, the other flaunting. They had killed another pig the previous day, a pitiful crippled thing with wizened front legs, which had hopped rather than ran, and that night Billy ordered a roasting. He had palm wine served while the pig was being turned on a spit over the open fire, and drank heavily himself. By the time the meat was ready for eating, he was fairly drunk. He went up to Toni, who was the duty cook, and took the Swiss Army knife from her.

She said: 'I'll bring you yours, Billy. I know the meat you like.'

'No.' He shook his head in a blurred but decisive gesture. 'Ceremony. There's a right way of doing things. Lady of the house pours the tea, and cuts the pig. Lydia!'

She walked leisurely over. She had been drinking along with Billy, but seemed a good deal less affected.

'Yes?'

'Suggest you make the first cut,' Billy said. He stared at her with owlish concentration. 'You first, then the rest of the ladies, then the blokes, and me last.' He widened his gaze to take in the others of the party. 'Got to see the men looked after before the officers dine. Old Army custom.'

Lydia said indifferently: 'Just as you like.'

She cut meat for herself from the carcase while Billy watched, a glass of wine tilting in his hand. He motioned to Susan and Toni, and they followed suit. Then he made the same peremptory gesture to Katey.

'No,' she said. 'I don't want any.'

He looked at her in silence for a moment. At last he said:

'Come here.' She hesitated, and went towards him. 'What do you mean, you don't want any? What's wrong with you? Sick or something?'

'The shape,' she said. 'Those little twisted front legs ...'

He said with exaggerated patience: 'No one's saying you've got to eat the front legs. Take a cut off his arse. Nothing wrong with his hams, is there? Is there?'

She shook her head. 'All the same ...'

'All the same what? Cut yourself a piece. You're keeping everybody waiting.'

'No.' She stepped back. 'It's deformed, beastly. I don't want any. I'll just have breadfruit, and fruit.'

His eyes on Katey, Billy said to Toni: 'Cut some meat off.' She picked up one of the clam shells they now used for plates, and cut a few slices on to it. 'Take it to her.' He leaned forward. 'You're going to eat it, Katey. I'm responsible for you, you know. Got to keep your strength up.'

He was drunk, and she wanted to avoid trouble. She took a small piece of crisped meat and put it in her mouth, hoping by this means to take attention away from herself: she could get rid of the rest later. But in the act of swallowing she remembered what the beast had looked like. In a spasm of nausea she turned her head and was sick.

Billy waited until she had finished retching before he spoke. He said, in a quiet somewhat amused voice:

'That bit went down the wrong way, eh?'

She said faintly: 'I really couldn't manage it.'

'You weren't trying properly. Swallow properly this time.'

'No.' She turned her head away. 'I don't want any.'

The amusement had left his voice. 'You'll do as I say.' He said to Toni: 'Bring that meat over here to me.'

Katey watched as the shell was taken to him. He selected a piece of meat much larger than the one on which she had gagged, and picked it up in his fingers. He waved it in the air. She looked past him at the others, without much hope of deliverance. Joe started to say something, but Billy cut across his words:

'Shut up. There's only one Welfare Officer in this outfit. Come on, Katey. Come on, girl. Are you going to eat it nicely, or am I going to have to stuff it down your gullet?'

She stared at the meat, helplessly and in horror. She knew she could not bring herself to put it in her mouth. She wanted to break and run, but lacked the strength of will. The meat was brought nearer to her, clutched in greasy fingers. It was close to her face when she heard Yasha's voice, and saw him break from the circle of the others and come towards her.

He said: 'I think you are not well, perhaps.' He put an arm round her shoulders and stood beside her, looking at Billy. 'I will take you to the hut, and you can rest.'

There was a moment in which she thought there would be violence, and cowered back. Then Billy laughed.

'All right, Yasha! She's all yours. Take her off and bed her down.' His voice followed them across the clearing. 'Don't be too long about it, Yasha boy, or you'll find the pork eaten when you get back!'

She slept fitfully that night. When she awoke in the morning, the recollection of the scene came back to her so strongly that nausea swept over her again. She managed to get out into the open before actually being sick, but for a long time after she retched, ineffectually on an empty stomach, and at last stood trembling in the rapidly growing dawn light, holding on for support to one of the trees.

She had no breakfast, but ate a little at lunch and more at supper. During the day, Joe and Candie were sent out to gather vegetables from the patches up the valley, and they reported Sweeney's whereabouts on their return. There was a place up on the hillside where an overhang of black rock made a small cave-like recess and a stream ran down by the side of this. That was where he had camped. They had seen him and spoken to him, and said he seemed to be all right.

The following morning, Katey was sick again. She should have been on kitchen duty, but Billy excused her. She stayed in the hut while the others had breakfast and were organized for the day's work. There was no one in the clearing when at last she emerged. She put together a small bundle and set off up the valley. It was hot already and she felt tired; after a time she felt the need to rest and settled herself in the shade of a tree. There was a clump of banana plants a little lower down the slope and while she sat there she saw a troop of monkeys move along the hillside and settle on it. With a little shock she saw that Lydia's white monkey was among them. And its colour was not the only odd thing about it – its arms, she saw, were extraordinarily long, much longer than those of the monkeys on either side of it. But one of those was odd, too – fantastically barrel-chested. There was another in the troop whose face was strangely distorted, and yet another with a flat splayed-out tail. Other small but nightmarish abnormalities became evident as she watched: one animal seemed to have a single eye set centrally above the nose, but she had only glimpsed it as it moved away and could not be sure.

She could not bear to go on looking at them, and rose quickly to her feet. The monkeys, disturbed, fled chattering. Katey stumbled on along the path. She did not look up until she came to the point from which the overhang of rock where Sweeney was said to be would be visible. She stared at it for several moments. There was no sign of life up there; but, having come so far, she would not turn back. She began climbing, wearily, up the side of the hill.

She did not see Sweeney until she had reached the rock. It was hollowed out underneath, forming a cave about four feet high and wide, and perhaps six feet deep. Sweeney sat there, looking out; he had made a rough seat for himself of branches and leaves, with moss underneath. As she approached, he said:

'Hello, Katey.'

She put her bundle down at the mouth of the cave.

'I've brought you a few things,' she said. 'Some fruit, and cooked yams, and a gourd of wine.'

'That's very kind of you. Thank you.'

'Are you all right, Sweeney?'

He nodded. 'Yes.'

'What do you do up here?'

'I forage for food,' he said, 'and cook it.' He pointed to where, on a patch of level ground near the stream, he had arranged stones as a crude fireplace. He smiled. 'Apart from that I sit and watch and wait.'

'What do you watch?'

'The world. Or, at least, the island and the sea.'

Looking across the valley one saw Mount Proteus big against the sky, crowned with its cloud, but on either side of it there was the ocean, blue tipped with silver.

'And wait for what?' she asked.

Sweeney shrugged. 'For whatever is likely to happen. For the ship coming over the rim of the world, to take us back to England.'

She said miserably: 'I've given up hope of that.'

'You must go on hoping.' He spoke as though admonishing a child. 'It is the one thing that matters.'

She felt a comfort in listening to him, however trite and meaningless the words. And an urge to talk herself, to put her wretchedness on show and have it healed.

'The island,' she said, ' … that cloud … I feel I can't bear it. And the animals and plants. They caught a pig two days ago with shrivelled legs. And this morning I saw the monkeys … distorted, horrible.'

'It will all pass,' Sweeney said.

'The cloud doesn't pass! The edges fray and shift, but it doesn't move, does it? It sits there above us, like a …' She hesitated. 'I'm being hysterical, I suppose. It's strange: in the first few days here I felt so much better, but now everything is ugly, and I am, too.'

'One adjusts,' Sweeney said. 'Life adjusts. That is its triumph over the inanimate universe.'

She stared at him. 'Won't you come back?'

'To the camp? No. It would not help.'

She told him the incident concerning the piece of pork, pausing as nausea rose in her again at the thought of it. He listened, looking not at her but the mountain. When she broke off, he said:

'So Yasha came to your rescue.'

She said: 'I'm frightened.'

'Of Billy?'

She thought about it. 'Not of Billy.'

'Of what, then?'

'I don't know. Of everything. Of myself, perhaps. I think I will go mad if I have to stay here long.'

'No.' Sweeney shook his head. 'You are a stable person, Katey.'

She said bitterly: 'I'm the worst kind of neurotic. That was two days ago, and I've been sick at intervals ever since. It's stupid.'

'There might be a reason.'

'I'm not ill.'

'No.'

He was looking at her with comprehending eyes. There was no warmth there nor sympathy, but understanding – an understanding which mirrored and gave back to her the deep inner awareness she had been struggling to keep from the light. She said, in a whisper: 'How am I going to manage?'

'You will be all right,' Sweeney said. He spoke as to a child again, and she listened as a child might, knowing it is being deceived and yet hungry for the false assurance. 'You will be all right.'

He turned his gaze from her again, and looked towards the mountain.

18

MARRIOTT COULD NOT BE SURE whether Susan or Yasha had talked to others about the episode; and the uncertainty of this tormented him. He was aware of capabilities in himself for very different kinds of action, of being poised between forms of behaviour not only antagonistic but mutually exclusive. The humiliations he had had from Billy had shocked him and went on shocking him – under their hammering he was back in prep school, being bullied again by Prettilove minor. He remembered all the details of the tortures and obscenities; and remembered too, the outcome of them. He had become Prettilove's lieutenant, aiding and inventing, with an eye for a rewarding victim. This had gone on until the row over young Dinsdale, and its outcome of Prettilove removed from the school, himself warned and gated for the rest of the term.

The island, like the school, was a world on its own, but at the school there had been, at least, a constant reminder of an outside authority in the gowned figures of the masters, peripheral but real. There was nothing like that here. One was controlled in part by fears and appetites, in part by the conditioning one had had in the world outside, the rules and conventions which made up what one accepted as civilized life. And the latter receded into vagueness and irrelevance as the former sharpened.

Coming back to the camp that morning had been on impulse, but an impulse sparked off by Billy, the ground prepared by what had already passed between Billy and himself. It was Billy who had drawn his attention to the fact that Susan would be alone there; who, before setting out, had said with a wink: 'Better not forget anything, Tony. You'd have to come back for it, wouldn't you?' The implication had triggered excitement in his blood, the kind of excitement that came with the first long look from a new woman, but even more compelling, less resistible. The idea of abandoning restraints was not merely something in which his mind acquiesced, but a triumph in itself.

Yasha's intervention, at a point where force had been threatened but not indulged, had left things unsettled, unresolved. The first impulse had been to pull the tattered cloak of respectability around him: there was a good chance that neither of them would talk about it, Yasha because he communicated so little with the others anyway, Susan for her own reasons. Nothing had happened, and one could forget it; like the Smythe deal. But forgetting it was not easy. Smythe had gone to South America, dodging prosecution but taking the full weight of suspicion with him. Marriott saw Susan and Yasha every day, and Billy, who had drawn his own conclusions, made needling remarks that mocked his ineffectuality.

He also had the impression that Toni was different. At first it only struck him as a remoteness, a withdrawal from all of them, but his feelings changed following an incident in which he made love to her. She did not reject him, but he sensed a reluctance, a withdrawal here, too, where in the past there had always been ease and abandon. That was when he began to think that someone might have talked, after all. Susan, perhaps. He would not have thought of her as the kind who went running to a man's wife, but women were basically incalculable and the situation itself was one in which normal motivations did not apply. By God, he thought, that was true enough. He wanted her, after the first reaction, more than ever, to possess and to humiliate.

Yasha was the stumbling block. Since that morning, he had kept either Marriott or Susan fairly continuously in view. His silent watchfulness was another irritation, and one that rankled. When, over the business of Katey and the roast pork, he defied Billy with the same calm assurance, Marriott was delighted. The following afternoon, as he and Billy made their way through the valley looking for traces of pig runs, Marriott fired the first shots in his campaign to eliminate Yasha.

At first Billy refused to be concerned about what Marriott depicted as the threat to his authority. Yasha was all right, he maintained – not the sort to give trouble. He didn't give enough of a damn about anything to want to run things. When Marriott persisted, Billy gave him a shrewd grin.

'Put a stop to your bit of hanky-panky with little Susan, did he? Is that what's worrying you? I'm not going to beat Yasha up just so as you can get a slice of crumpet you happen to fancy. You can do your own foraging, mate.'

Mate, he thought, wincing inwardly. But he gave no sign and continued with his argument. Billy was unconvinced, but more thoughtful. Marriott returned to the subject the next day, and subsequently. He was patient and assiduous. It was several days later that the opportunity for clinching things came.

Billy had told Marriott to detail a work party to gather wood for the kitchen fire. It would have to be dragged, on a rough sled that had been constructed, a good way along the beach: the driftwood nearer at hand had been consumed already. The job, in fact, could be expected to take up most of the morning. Billy and Lydia, naturally, were excluded from the list, and Susan was on kitchen duty again. Marriott detailed all the rest.

Yasha said: 'Susan?'

'Kitchen duty,' Marriott said shortly.

'And you, yourself?'

'No. I'm staying behind.'

The two men stared at each other. Yasha said:

'I think I will stay behind, too.'

Marriott reported the refusal to Billy. He said:

'Still doesn't trust you, eh?'

'Nor you.'

Billy thought about that. 'Call him over,' he said finally.

When Yasha came, Billy said: 'I want you on collecting wood.' There was a silence, and he added impatiently: 'I'll see nothing goes wrong while you're away.'

Yasha looked at him for a moment before answering. He said: 'I will stay, all the same.'

'Are you refusing to go on work detail?'

'There is plenty of work that needs to be done around the camp. I will be busy enough.'

It was Billy's turn to be silent. He said at last:

'You'll go on wood collecting, as you were told. Susan will go, too. Toni will take her place on kitchen duty. O.K.?'

Yasha nodded. 'All right.'

Marriott's first reaction was of disappointment at the way in which Billy had avoided a direct clash. He began thinking of ways of hammering home to him the fact that, whatever sophistry was put on it, he had actually climbed down to the older man. But his ingenuity proved unnecessary. Watching Yasha go across the clearing to the kitchen, Billy said softly:

'That bastard.' Marriott watched him in silence. 'So he thinks he can tell me what to do, does he?'

'Yes,' Marriott said, 'he does, doesn't he?'

Billy's glance flicked to him; it had something of dependence in it. He said:

'I don't believe in rushing things. Get things organized first, and then – wham. That's my policy. We'll have to do a bit of thinking about Yasha boy. Got any ideas?'

'A few,' Marriott said. 'And I can think of more.'

They talked it out at intervals during the day, and the following morning Marriott detailed another work party, this time on an expedition looking for hens. A solitary fowl had been seen on two different occasions and the party was to search the far side of the island in case there was a colony of them there. Both Susan and Yasha were left out of the party and given work around the camp.

Half an hour later, Susan was sent up the valley to gather beans from the bean patch. Yasha looked up from his work – he was tying saplings together with vines to make a new carrying sled – saw that there was no sign of Marriott following her, and carried on with what he was doing. Billy waited until Susan had plenty of time to get clear, and then called Yasha over. He nodded and came.

Lydia had gone swimming; there were only the three men in the clearing. Billy said genially:

'I've been thinking – I don't reckon it's likely they'll find any hens on that little trip.'

Yasha shrugged. 'Possibly not. Hens are not likely to survive on an island such as this.'

'So if we want eggs, we'll have to look to the sea birds. There's that island off the east coast – Tony and the others saw it the day they had a shot at climbing the mountain. Covered with birds nesting. Must be millions of eggs there.'

'If we could get to it.'

'Right. We've no boat since those stupid bastards of Hawaiians cleared off with it. But the sea has been pretty calm lately. If we had a raft, we could probably paddle it round there, and lay in supplies.'

Yasha nodded. 'It would be possible to build a raft, I think.'

'Right!' Billy said. 'You've got the idea. Now, we want it to be a fairly big raft – carry three or four of us, at least – so we don't have to shift it once it's been built. Also, we want the right kind of tree, and we want them near the water's edge. There are those trees up towards the West Point: they're about the right size and in the right place.'

'Yes,' Yasha said, 'I know the ones you mean.'

'Fair enough,' Billy said. 'Then I'd like you to take the axe along and have a go at cutting a few of them down.'

The two men stared at each other, Yasha's face contracted, puzzled perhaps, Billy with his familiar sly grin. Marriott felt tension rise inside him – the time Prettilove and he had managed to get Bates trapped behind the Fives Court … his bewilderment and Prettilove's knowing smile … He dug fingernails into his hands.

Yasha nodded towards Marriott, and spoke. 'Is he coming with me?'

'No,' Billy said. 'I've got something else for Tony to do.'

The trip to the place Billy had indicated would take an hour at least. Yasha looked at Marriott, and Marriott smiled now. Yasha said:

'I am not going if he is staying here.'

He spoke calmly and with assurance. Marriott wondered if Billy was capable of carrying things through, whether he might not, after all, back down again. But although the smile remained on Billy's face, it was obvious that anger was smouldering beneath it.

He said: 'Who gives the orders round here, Yasha?'

'You can give what orders you like,' Yasha said. 'I am not leaving Marriott alone with Susan.'

'He won't be alone, though,' Billy said. 'I'll be here. Lydia's down on the beach somewhere.'

Yasha shook his head. 'It makes no difference.'

Billy put his hand casually into his pocket and, as casually, brought out the Beretta.

'You're going to do as I say, Yasha,' he said. 'It's the principle of the thing.' His voice had taken on a reasonable tone again. 'Doesn't matter so much with Tony, but the next time you refused to do something I told you, the others might be here as well. We can't have that because it interferes with running things. There can't be more than one boss in a show like this.'

'Put the gun away,' Yasha said. 'It does not frighten me.' He still spoke calmly, but this time the assurance was tinged with contempt. Marriott saw Billy's face whiten, as he realized this.

'Doesn't it?' Billy asked.

There was a sharp cracking explosion as he fired the gun. The two men were facing each other, four or five feet apart. Stunned by the sound, Marriott saw dust plume briefly in front of Yasha's feet. His own excitement curdled into fear. He recoiled instinctively.

Yasha, though, did not move for a moment or two. When he did, it was to step forward, his hand outstretched.

He said: 'You are not safe with that, Billy. I think I should take it off you.'

Billy stared at him as he came forward. His hand lifted, holding the Beretta, and there were two more shots. Marriott was not sure which of them hit Yasha, or whether both did. He was aware only of shock, and the sight of blood spurting from the red line suddenly ripped across Yasha's cheek. This time Yasha fell back, his body jerking as he tried to keep his balance. Already blood masked one side of his face and dropped in gouts on his chest and shoulder. He recovered himself, looked for an instant at Billy and then, as he saw the gun raised again, swiftly turned and ran for the nearest trees.

Marriott, his voice choking, cried: 'Get him, Billy! You'd better get him before ...'

The gun fired twice or three times. Yasha kept on running, and there was no sign of his being hit a second time. He reached the trees and dodged through them. They saw him less clearly behind the screen of branches, and then he was completely lost to view.

'You missed him,' Marriott said.

Birds, silent in the immediate aftermath of the firing, cut loose with cries that had a touch of frenzy. The smell of powder hung in the air, mixed with the familiar scents of the island. But through it Marriott smelled chalk and ink, and heard the far-off monotonous chorus of Form I doing Latin tables. Billy's face was Prettilove's, waiting with him outside the Head's study, knowing, from a glimpse of Dinsdale inside, why they had been summoned. He felt, along with fear, the same savage glee at the other's greater involvement. Prettilove had committed the particular obscenity on Dinsdale that had brought down retribution. Billy had fired the shots.

Billy said: 'Christ! You were a lot of help.'

'What could I do?'

'You could have gone after him.'

'And have you hit me?'

Billy stared at the gun in his hand. 'Better get this reloaded.'

'You don't think he'll come back, do you?'

'I don't know.' He seemed to make an effort to rouse himself. 'Listen. He went for me. You've got that?'

'Like the Hawaiian? It sounds a bit thin.'

'I gave him a job to do, and he wouldn't do it. Said he was fed up taking orders from me, and he was going to get the gun off me. We had a bit of a struggle, and the gun went off. Then he buggered off. You're the witness of what happened. O.K.?'

'I'll back you up,' Marriott said. He grinned. 'That doesn't mean anyone is going to believe you.'

'They'll believe me.'

Marriott shrugged and pointed. 'There's your first chance coming up.'

Susan had burst into the clearing from the opposite side. She came towards them, easing from a run to a walk as she saw the two men standing there talking.

She said: 'What was it? I heard shots.'

'We had a bit of trouble,' Billy said.

'What kind of trouble?'

'Yasha,' Billy said. 'Touch of the sun, I reckon. He came at me, yelling about the gun.'

'You've killed him!' Her look went from Billy to Marriott. 'It was you, wasn't it?'

'No,' Marriott said, 'it wasn't me. And we've not only killed him, we've buried him in the two or three minutes since you heard the shots. You hadn't got far, had you? I thought Billy sent you up to the bean patch.'

'I dug some yams on the way.' She stared at Billy. 'Where is he? Is he badly hurt?'

'He's not hurt, at all. A scratch maybe. And how should I know where he is.' He jerked his head. 'He ran off in that direction.'

'There were several shots.' She stepped back, still looking at Billy. 'I'm going to go and find him.'

'No.' Billy weighed the gun and, with a decisive gesture, slipped it back in his pocket. 'He's all right. You're staying here.'

She shook her head. 'I'm not.' She glanced at Marriott. 'I'm not staying.'

Billy smiled at her. 'You've had a bit of trouble with Tony, haven't you? And you think you might have more with Yasha not here. Don't you worry. I'll see that nothing happens to you.' He nodded at Marriott. 'He'll do as I say.'

'Thank you. I'd rather go, all the same.'

Billy said softly: 'You haven't been listening, Sue. I'm telling you you can't go, and I don't want to have any more trouble. You might say you're only under my protection as long as you obey my orders. As long as you do as you're told, I'll keep Lover Boy on the leash.'

She hesitated. He meant what he said. Marriott knew that and felt the tingle of anticipation. The moment of fear was over, and they were back in their roles again. Things were not happening twenty years ago in Surrey, but now and here.

Susan said: 'All right. I'll go up and get those beans.'

'No,' Billy said. He smiled at her again. 'I think you'd better stay right here.'

19

Lydia noticed that, in the time between her own return to camp and that of the main party, the case against Yasha had been magnified considerably. She had been lazing on the beach when she heard the shots. She made a leisurely way back to find Billy and Marriott garrulous, Susan silent and confused. The others had taken food with them and did not return until the late afternoon. Marriott had a story ready for them – that Yasha had gone berserk, that Billy had had to fire a couple of shots to scare him off, and that he had then fled into the forest.

Their reaction was one of uneasiness. They found the account unconvincing, Lydia guessed, but were reluctant to disbelieve it since that meant giving Billy and Marriott the direct lie. They were here, after all, and Yasha was not. And there was a possibility that the story was true: Yasha had always been withdrawn, uncommunicative, therefore incomprehensible. Going berserk was not something that could definitely be ruled out. The atmosphere in which they now lived was persuasive also. There were signs and wonders, and improbabilities blended with the normal. They had brought back a hen from the expedition, or what passed for one – a bloated brown monstrosity whose body seemed too large for its feet. When they released it from the imprisoning vines it flopped helplessly in the dust, and stared up at them with unwinking beady eyes.

Willeway said: 'If he's really gone crazy, he might come back, mightn't he? At night. D'you think … ?'

'Yes,' Billy said, 'we'll have to mount a guard. Tony, you fix that up. Joe and Roger, and you'd better do a turn yourself. You can make up your kip during the day.'

Candie said: 'Whoever's on guard – ought to have the gun, don't you think?'

Billy gave him a hard look, then smiled. 'Won't be necessary. You only have to give a shout and I'll be on the spot. I'm a light sleeper.'

Katey said: 'Has he really gone?'

She looked dazed and a little sick. There was something wrong with her, anyway, Lydia thought: she was off her food still and seemed to be brooding a lot. Lydia herself said briskly:

'My father used to say that all ship's engineers were cuckoo. I don't think we have to worry about him, though. He'll probably go and find himself a cave somewhere. He'll be better off on his own.' She pointed her foot towards the bird. 'Where did you get that thing from?'

'In that swampy ground near the other coast,' Candie said. 'There were half a dozen of them we flushed. The rest flew off, but this one seems to have hurt its wing. As soon as it took off, it nose-dived.'

'It's as big as a bloody turkey,' Billy said. 'There's a fair chunk of breast there to carve.'

Willeway said, with some deference: 'We thought we might try it for eggs first. Then eat it if it wasn't laying.'

'Yes,' Billy said. 'That might be a better idea, especially if the eggs are on anything like the same scale. You saw others?'

Candie said: 'Four or five at least. I think one was a rooster. They weren't as big as this one, though.'

'I reckon we'll have to have another hunt,' Billy said, 'now we know they're there. Be nice to have a few hens round the camp. We'll all come in on this one.'

He looked at Lydia in inquiry. She nodded.

'Good idea.'

'What do we do with this character meanwhile?' Candie asked. 'She looks helpless, but I don't suppose we can just leave her like that.'

'Make her a little nesting box,' Billy said. 'And Joe can go and find some worms for her.' He stared at the hen in admiration. 'Great big bastard, isn't she?'

They were settling back, Lydia saw, into the customary routine of their life; here again, the fact that Yasha had stood apart from the others helped. She wondered just what had taken place between the three men to cause the shooting, but her interest was no more than academic. Yasha meant nothing to her. And nothing had happened to disturb her confidence in her power over Billy. The more arrogant he became towards the others, the more humble he was to her. As for Marriott – Marriott knew his place.

The guard was duly mounted that night, but there was no sign of Yasha returning. Lydia awoke early in the morning and set off up the valley before any except Candie, who had taken the last sentry duty, was awake. It had become a habit for someone to go up each day and take food from the communal store to Sweeney; he had not asked for it but it was done anyway. Lydia was exempted from tasks imposed on the others, but she included herself in this. She took breadfruit, cold pork, pineapples, bananas and wine with her and made her way along the path. The air was fresh, birds clamorous, the cloud on Mount Proteus lit gold with the bright horizontal strokes of the barely risen sun.

She had thought, starting so early, that she might have found Sweeney still asleep, but in fact he was bathing in the stream beside his cave, stripped to the waist, splashing the cold clear water over his mountainous flesh. Not much like a god, she thought, and wondered why she thought it. He rose from the stream as she approached and rubbed himself with his shirt, which he then tossed into the stream and weighted with a loose rock. He would dry it in the sun later. Laundry was not one of the major problems of life on the island.

'Lydia,' he said, 'how nice to see you.'

She put the food down in the little niche of rock beside the cave where they always put the things they brought him, and he thanked her gravely. There were two flattish-topped rocks just above the stream; he indicated one to her with a gesture that would have done justice to one of the matched and immaculate Heppelwhites in the drawing-room in Bishop's Avenue, and, when she had seated herself, took the other. The valley was in shadow beneath them, but the sun had reached this part of the hillside and was warm on the exposed flesh.

Lydia said: 'We've had a spot of trouble at the camp.'

Sweeney nodded. 'Go on.'

She told him what had happened, and he listened. He attended courteously, but as though to a tale already told. When she had finished, he said:

'Well?'

The interrogation made her suddenly self-conscious. There had been a compulsion, she recognized, in the early rising, the trek to Sweeney, the unburdening. But what compulsion? The incident had touched her least of all, as she had seen it. She was confused now, unsure of herself and a little afraid.

She said awkwardly: 'I'm not sure that Billy and Tony were telling the truth.'

'And does that matter?'

She was silent for a moment. 'Surely,' she began, but broke off. It was because nothing was sure that she had come here. Patterns of behaviour, like the birds and beasts and flowers on the island, were polymorphic. She said with urgency:

'What's happening, Sweeney?'

'Events obey a logic,' he said, 'although perhaps a different logic from the one to which we are accustomed. Is there anything that threatens you, yourself?'

She shook her head. 'Nothing.'

He looked at her. 'Is there anything you want, then?'

'To be rescued, I suppose.'

'Do you?'

She faced it honestly. 'No, not particularly. Is that wrong?'

Sweeney sighed. 'Right and wrong ... In Paradise the words are meaningless; out of Paradise, pointless. Societies faced with problems throw up kings and queens as answers. But there is more than just the offering of a crown: there has to be an acceptance. Thrice did they offer him a kingly crown. After the third rejection they stabbed him to death in the Forum.'

Her brow furrowed. 'I don't see what it has to do with me.'

'Don't you? Do you think Yasha has turned into a raving maniac?'

Again she had the feeling that he knew more about it all than she did. She caught a glimpse of what might be light.

'Has he been here to see you – Yasha?'

'It wouldn't matter if he had. I was asking what you thought.'

She shook her head. 'No, I don't think he has.'

'But will you assert this?'

'No. Why should I assert anything?'

'By reason of the logic I spoke of. All acts are assertions. So are refusals to act.'

'Which is what you've done.'

'Yes,' Sweeney said. 'That is what I've done. I have left you all and come up here. It would not be your solution, would it?'

She said restlessly: 'What ought I to do?'

'There is no ought in logic.'

She stared at him. 'You're not much help, are you?'

Sweeney smiled. 'No, I suppose not. But you will have to make up your own mind about it. You knew that before you came up here.'

'About what?'

'You know that, too. About Billy. About yourself.'

'Then there is an ought. If I have a choice.'

'You asked me,' he reminded her. 'The view out is different from the view in. One of them may be an illusion. Or both of them. Or perhaps neither. I have not helped you, but you may have helped yourself by coming here. Recognition has to come before resolution.'

She left him, and made her way down from the sunlight into the valley's shadow. They had kept breakfast for her. Afterwards, preparations were made for another hunt for wild fowl; the hen that had been caught the previous day, while still apparently incapable of movement, was otherwise healthy. It had not, to Willeway's evident disappointment, so far produced an egg.

It was usual to leave one of the women at least looking after the camp and making food ready for the evening meal, but this time they all went. Lydia wondered whether this showed a lack of confidence in Billy, or whether it was designed to bolster his story about Yasha's insane violence – a single person left behind might be attacked by him. But, if this were so, he did not labour the point by referring to it. He made no reference at all to Yasha, but the looks both he and Marriott directed about them were more searching, Lydia thought, than usual.

She herself spoke about Yasha to Susan, when they were resting at the far end of the valley, looking out across the island's southern shore at waters as bland and empty as the rest. The two of them sat a little apart, eating fruit, and they could talk without being overheard.

Lydia said: 'What really happened yesterday?'

Susan had been very quiet since the incident; so far, on the trip, she had not spoken to anyone. She looked as though she were reluctant to do so now. She said, at last:

'You know as much as I do.'

'You were there before I was.'

'Not long before.' Her head was averted. 'It was all over by the time I got back.'

'What do you think happened?' Susan remained silent. 'You must have some idea.'

'Billy told us, didn't he? And Tony.'

'Do you think they were telling the truth?'

'Why ask me that?' Susan turned towards her now. Her look was steady and mistrustful. 'Surely you know better than I do.'

She hesitated. 'Of course they were telling the truth.'

'Can't we talk about it?' Lydia said.

She tried to speak flatly, but she was aware of a tenseness in her voice and that the tenseness reflected an appeal. She was looking for help, as she had looked for help to Sweeney. She did not know why she needed this girl's confidence but she knew that somehow it was terribly important.

'Can't we talk about it?' she asked again.

'I don't see what good it will do,' Susan said.

She looked at Lydia again, her expression deliberately blank. Then, with a quick decisive gesture she got up and walked over to where Toni Marriott was sitting.

They flushed the hens eventually, but they lumbered into the air and flew on clumsy powerful wings over the scrub and out of sight beyond the curve of the hillside. Billy and Candie threw stones at them, but failed to hit them. They set off back to camp with Billy and Marriott trying to work out some way of trapping the birds. Lydia, initially depressed, found herself becoming noisy, demonstratively cheerful and excited. Willeway slipped and fell in a stream, and she heard her own laughter roaring emptily in her ears.

The mood persisted after they were back in camp. Over supper she made a lot of jokes which she knew at the time were pointless, and drank a good deal of palm wine. At the same time she was aware of a different tension rising inside her. Her hands clenched, unclenched and clenched again. In the end it reached such a pitch that she got up quickly and left the others. She walked back to her hut, a little drunk and detached, conscious of the separateness of her body, and of its restlessness.

Billy, as always, had lit the two night-lights in her hut. They were made after a pattern the Hawaiians had shown them in the early days: there was a plant which, when pressed, gave an inflammable vegetable oil, and another, the thick flax-like fibres of whose leaves could be used as wicks. They burned with a dim oily light, one by her bed, the other near the door.

In the past the light by the door had been her signal for privacy: she put it out before she undressed, and that meant she was not to be disturbed. If it was still burning, Billy would bring her a drink of fruit juice before he turned in himself. He would serve it in as stewardly a fashion as possible, considering his tattered clothing and unshaven face, and sometimes she would have him talk to her for a while before dismissing him. She thought about this for what seemed a long time; the voices of the others came thinly across the clearing, and something, probably a monkey, was howling out in the forest. She picked up the light from beside the bed and took it over to rest beside the other. Then, moving back into the shadows, she stripped the clothes from her body.

She lay on the bed, perfectly still, waiting. She heard Billy's footsteps as he approached, and his voice at the door:

'Ready for your nightcap, miss?'

'Yes,' she said. Her throat was dry. 'I'm ready.'

With surprise, he said: 'Both lights are by the door. Someone's moved one. Shall I bring it over?'

'Not yet. Stay there. Billy?'

'Yes, miss?'

'You were trying to kill Yasha, weren't you?'

'He wanted to take the gun away from me. I had to stop him.'

'By firing the whole magazine at him?'

There was silence. She could see his body against the light but he would not be able to see her, except as the dimmest of shadows. She said:

'You've looked after me very well, Billy. I can rely on you, can't I?'

He said earnestly: 'You can that.'

'The light.'

'You want it by the bed now? I'll ...'

'Put one out first. Bring the other.'

He bent and did as she had told him. Picking up the remaining light he brought it across the hut towards her. She saw his face, the lines of cruel strength and servile weakness, against the flickering light. And saw it change as he beheld her nakedness.

20

THE WITHDRAWAL WHICH MARRIOTT sensed in Toni was not, in the first instance, directed against him. It was a matter, rather, of self-absorption, of ignoring other people because she found a new interest, a fascination, in herself. She could not tell how or why it had come about: a delayed effect, perhaps, of this new kind of life. She spent a lot of time daydreaming, and the dreams were different from those she had indulged in in the past. Then it had been a matter of visualizing material possessions and privileges: the world of riches which she had never had but always felt was her natural habitat. These dreams were less specific and, for the first time, nostalgic. Her thoughts went back past the barrier, and she remembered the house at Chichester, the noisy bustle of the older children, the quietness when they were at school and there was only herself and her mother and Mrs Wainwright who came in to help. They were static, these recollections; scenes and moments which had a timeless quality. And sounds – the clock ticking through hot summer afternoons, the parrot whistling and clucking to herself, the beat of wind and rain against the windows as she looked out. She realized with surprise that she had been a happy child; with surprise because it was something she had never considered before. Life, for her, had always started with the London flat, the dark somewhat frightening man who was Mr Blair, and then Uncle Stephen, and then Daddy. It had been a strange life, full of new things like the Zoo and the park and the never-ending streets, to which neither the words happy nor unhappy could be applied. There was, she felt now, a similar neutrality about all her life since then.

Her body, its rhythms and pulses, fascinated her too. She stared at her hand, the blue network of veins along the wrist, the soft pink of the palm and the brown back, the astonishing effortless flexure of the fingers. She listened to her own breathing, ran her tongue's tip along the miraculous small ramparts of her teeth. Life, her own life in particular, was a wonder of which one could never tire.

It was this which made her turn from Marriott when he made love to her; his body was an alien thing, an invader, a disturber. Self-consciousness here upset her, bringing detachment and with detachment coldness. She knew this, and knew his awareness of it, but could not do anything about it. For Marriott she felt a kind of pity, seeing him as lost, probing and asserting, so feverishly striving when the answer to everything was quietness and contemplation. He left her, she knew, without the satisfaction, the reassurance, she had given him in the past, and she was mildly sorry for him. She thought of calling him back, but found her sympathy did not extend so far. He could go and flirt with Susan. There was a shallowness in the male; he would not be much hurt, or for long.

Although the world of external events had come to mean less to her, she felt some interest in Yasha's disappearance and in Marriott's reaction to it. He showed an elation she recognized – nervous, almost hysterical – but which had never before been apparent except at the crux of some important business deal. The elation was even more marked following the night that Lydia took Billy as her lover: a manic extravert hilarity characterized by pointless schoolboy jokes, made particularly to Billy, and explosive outbursts of laughter. And by attentions to Susan which for the first time were obvious and public.

Her curiosity about Lydia and Billy was of the mildest, which was another sign of the change in her. She was surprised at first that Lydia should seemingly have jeopardized a position of power – like the rest, she had seen Billy's devotion to Lydia as sexual or, rather, springing from sexual frustration – for no good reason that she could see. Not, certainly, through physical desire: a woman like Lydia did not grow to want a man who so plainly and abjectly wanted her. But in this she had underestimated Lydia, and Lydia's self-confidence. She made such a showing of the new relationship – sending Billy sheepishly out of her hut the following morning long after the rest were stirring – as to indicate and underline the fact that she had initiated and he acquiesced. Billy, for his part, not only accepted this but demonstrated that his devotion had been increased, not diminished, by fulfilment. At breakfast he all but carried the food from the clam-shell to her lips, springing to his feet to serve her at the slightest expression of need. He behaved like a honeymoon husband of the most ridiculous kind.

Marriott was Court Jester to the royal pair, a Court Jester with an openly libidinous eye for one of the ladies of the Court. Susan was obviously embarrassed by this, Candie contemptuous, Katey shocked and disgusted. The others seemed indifferent, as Toni herself was. She was aware of the advantage of being left to herself, freed of possible intrusion, and aware, too, that this open sexual aggression represented a change in Marriott as sweeping as that in herself. He had ceased to care whether or not he looked a fool; this new single-mindedness she might have found disturbing if she could have summoned up the interest to be bothered about it.

Two days after he had fled, Willeway, during the midday meal, reported that he had seen Yasha. The remark was picked up by Marriott at once.

'Where was he? What did he look like?'

Willeway pointed up the hillside. 'He was up there. I spotted him as I came down the path. He was too far away to see what he looked like.'

'Did he see you looking at him?'

'I think so. He slipped off through the trees.'

'In which direction?'

'Inland. He would have to, wouldn't he? The scrub's pretty

well impenetrable on the seaward side.'

'If we'd had someone there to cut him off ...' Marriott said.

Billy looked up from his seat beside Lydia's knee.

'What do we want to cut him off for? As long as he doesn't bother us, he can do what he likes.' Lydia put her fingers in his long black hair and tugged playfully. He leaned his head back, grinning at her. 'He can have a bit of a snoop if he fancies it. We've got nothing we want to hide.'

'No,' Marriott said, 'I don't think it's as easy as that.' He spoke in an oddly serious, almost obsessed tone. 'We're going to have to do something about him sooner or later.'

'Forget it,' Billy said, imperially casual. 'We've got something on this afternoon that is important – picking up the lobster pots. And when we've done that I reckon we ought to get cracking on that raft. Lydia still hasn't had her eggs.'

'No,' Lydia said. She nodded at Willeway. 'And that monstrous bloody hen you brought in hasn't laid any yet. I think it will have to go in the pot.'

'We haven't got a pot,' Willeway said. 'I only wish we had. I'm getting tired of baked and singed meat. What I wouldn't give for a casserole. *Poule au Pot.*' He leaned back on his haunches in a reverie of delight. '*Coq au Vin.*'

'Lobster pots first,' Billy said positively. 'Then we work on the raft.'

The whole of the party went down to the bay to retrieve the pots; it was one of the activities which Lydia, who was a good swimmer, enjoyed and took part in. The pots had been down three days and produced a fairly good haul: four reasonable sized lobsters and rather more than twice as many crabs, plus a few squids. Billy selected what they wanted for immediate consumption and put the rest in the store pot, which was secured by a vine rope to one of the projecting rocks on the headland. They went back to camp both tired and refreshed from the swimming.

Katey was on kitchen duty, and Toni was supposed to be her

helper. She went with her to get the fire burning up in the kitchen but was taken by a fit of sneezing and slipped away to the hut for a handkerchief – she was fortunate in having had two with her the day the *Diana* went on fire. As she entered the hut she saw Susan bending down over her bed. She called something to her and Susan straightened up, at the same time turning away. She had something in her hand – a piece of paper?

Toni said: 'I think I'm getting hay fever – it must be the season of something or other. Oh hell, all this and a runny nose.'

'Yes,' Susan said. She sounded flustered but cheerful. 'Never mind. One copes.'

'Yes, I suppose.' She looked at Susan again and shrugged. 'Well, back to work.'

That evening Marriott was still more blatantly attentive to Susan. He began addressing her as Sweet Sue and kept very close, almost but not quite touching her with fondling gestures. She shrank from these, which clearly amused him. Toni wondered if she should not say something, for the girl's sake, but her own detachment and disinterest were such that she was disinclined to intervene at all. He had not, it was true, actually touched her in his antics.

Candie offered mild protest. He said:

'Can't you leave the girl alone? Haven't you the sense to know when you're unwelcome?'

Marriott turned to stare at him. His look was vicious, something Toni had never seen before. Oddly, she was not disturbed by this.

'Shut up,' Marriott said. 'I'll tell you when I want your advice.'

Candie was the bigger and stronger man, but it was Marriott who looked the more menacing. Nevertheless, Candie persisted:

'Susan has a right not to be pestered. She's …'

'Shut up,' Marriott said again. 'Shut up. Shut up!'

His voice had risen almost to a shout. Candie looked at him in silence. There would be a fight, Toni thought: the air was electric with their hostility. But Susan discharged it.

She said: 'It's all right, Roger. Thank you. I'm all right, though.'

Candie looked at her for a moment, shrugged and walked away. Marriott stared at her with lust and affection.

'That's the spirit,' he said. 'You're all right with me, Sweet Sue, aren't you? I'll look after my little honey.'

He made a move towards her which might have become a caress if she had not slipped out of his reach. She smiled warily at him. Marriott shrugged.

'O.K. Give it time. A little time, anyway.'

Toni felt very tired when she retired to bed; her mind rolled on billows of fatigue which time and again plunged her down towards the abyss of oblivion. They never quite released her, though; after each drop there was a swimming up to consciousness. And it was consciousness, in the end, which prevailed. She lay there, quite awake, absorbed and happy in self-contemplation. Moonlight fell through the open door of the hut. She remembered being awake at night in the house at Chichester, sitting at the window watching the silver light on the garden, listening to her sister's deep even breathing from the other side of the room.

A sound, here and now, close at hand, shattered the image. A bed creaked; someone moved cautiously. She watched, and saw Susan pass through the moonlight to the door. She paused for several moments, looking out, and then crossed the threshold and was gone.

The obvious explanation was that she had gone out to meet a physical need; but Toni knew that in this case the obvious was wrong. The furtiveness of movement, the looking out before she left, were proof enough of that. Curiosity roused Toni from the lethargy which had lately become her natural state. Slipping out of bed herself, she, too, went to the door.

The scene outside had the sharpness and at the same time unreality of an over-contrasted television screen. Candie was the first person she saw; he was stretched out between the two huts, lying on his belly, head resting on a small heap of moss. She remembered that he had been given first watch for the night. She wondered at first if he were dead, but realized she could hear his breathing. He was, as might have been expected, asleep.

Looking across the clearing, she saw Susan. She had almost reached the line of trees and seemed to be hesitating, looking for something. Or someone. There was a movement in the shadows, and Yasha stepped out. He put a hand out, and Susan took it. They paused no longer but walked together out of the brightness into the trees.

For some time after they had gone, Toni stayed there, watching the patterns of black and white in the empty clearing. She felt at once excited by what had happened and removed from it. It was a dream event, in a dream world. She looked up and saw faint silver on the cloud which hung, as always, over the top of the mountain. There lies the wizard, she thought, dreaming: when he wakes, all will break up and dissolve – mountain and trees and sand and sea run together, coalesce and fade into wisps and shreds, into nothing. And we, too, she thought happily. We, too.

In the morning, Katey commented on the empty bed.

'Susan up already?'

Toni said vaguely: 'It looks like it.' She got up and stretched herself. 'Shall I lend you a hand with the breakfast?'

'Well, Susan will be doing that.'

Toni nodded. 'Yes. I'd forgotten.'

She went, all the same, to the kitchen, after she had washed. Katey said: 'Any sign of her?' At that moment, Marriott came towards them.

'Sign of who?' he asked.

'Susan,' Katey said. 'She hasn't turned up for duty yet.'

Marriott turned to Toni. 'She's not in the hut?'

'No.'

'When did you last see her?'

He was trying to keep calm, but she saw his hands trembling. He put them behind him, as though aware of this himself. He looked ridiculously Napoleonic, she thought, and felt a brief wave of affection for him. She said:

'Last night. When we went to bed.'

'Not since? She didn't get up during the night?'

He stared angrily at the two women. Toni said: 'No.' Katey said: 'Not as far as I know. I suppose she may have done.'

He stood stock still and silent for a moment, and then yelled: 'Joe! Roger!' His voice cracked with anger. He called their names again, and they came out of their hut. To Willeway, he said: 'I took over from you. Anything happen during your watch?'

'No.' Willeway shook his head. 'What kind of thing?'

Marriott whirled on Candie. 'And during yours?'

'No. What should have happened?'

'One of you was asleep,' Marriott said. He was shouting, and Toni saw Billy emerge from Lydia's hut, Lydia following him. 'You should have been awake. That's what should have happened!'

The ludicrous side of it struck Toni, and she started to laugh. Marriott began shouting at her incoherently; she could not make out what he was saying. Billy cut through it by calling for Marriott. When he had brought him to silence, he said:

'Come over to the hut, Tony. We'd better have a little chat about it.'

His voice was cool and easy. Marriott, after a momentary hesitation, obeyed him. The three of them went into the hut.

Willeway, bewildered, said: 'What's wrong with him? I don't even know what's happened.'

'Just because Susan isn't here,' Katey said. 'She's probably down at the loo, or gone for a swim.'

Candie cupped his hands and called Susan's name out. There was a slight echo here, the tail-end of a more vigorous one further up the valley, and they heard the name come thinly back to them. Otherwise there were only the cries of birds and, very distant, the noise of surf. Candie called again, and Willeway took up the calling after him. Then they were silent, looking at each other, beginning to be aware that this might be something serious.

Billy came out of the hut again, with Marriott at his heels. Lydia followed them in a more leisurely fashion.

Billy said: 'No sign of her, then?'

Candie said: 'No. No sign.'

'Then we shall have to have a hunt,' Billy said. 'As soon as we've had breakfast. For her and Yasha both.'

21

Aᴛᴛᴇʀ ʙʀᴇᴀᴋꜰᴀꜱᴛ, Bɪʟʟʏ had Katey and Toni prepare snack meals to be carried with them; the hunt, it was anticipated, might take up the whole day. Willeway groaned silently at the thought of this, but thought it prudent to say nothing. They would trek through the valley, because Billy thought it reasonable to suppose that the two would be on the other side of the island, having put as much distance as possible between the camp and them. But first, on Lydia's suggestion, they were going up to see Sweeney. She had confided her suspicion to Billy that Sweeney might know more about what had happened to Yasha than he had seen fit to tell her.

They took food up to him – bananas, breadfruit, yams and baked lobster. Sweeney was particularly fond of lobster. He accepted the bundles with equanimity and every indication of pleasure. He was sitting, as usual, on the flat stone beside his cave.

Billy said: 'Sweeney, we're looking for Yasha, and Susan.'

Sweeney raised his eyebrows. 'I was surprised so many of you had come. Did you think you would find them here?'

Marriott broke in restlessly: 'You knew Susan had gone, then? How did you know?'

'I knew Yasha had gone,' Sweeney said. 'Lydia told me that. Perhaps one of you would like to tell me about Susan?'

'She left camp some time during the night,' Billy said. 'We assume she's with Yasha.'

'Have you any idea why she left?'

Billy looked at Marriott. 'No. And it wouldn't matter, anyway. We can't have things breaking up, Sweeney. We've got to stick together.'

'Even if some prefer not to do so?'

'It makes no difference. Yasha's a maniac. We can't have him wandering loose around the island.'

'Is the suggestion that Yasha came into camp, and dragged Susan away by the hair? She would be likely to have made some noise, surely. Enough to waken the rest of you.'

Marriott said angrily: 'That's not the point.'

'Isn't it? Then what is?'

'We thought you might know something,' Billy said. 'That you might have seen something. You sit up here watching all the time.'

'I don't look down into the valley much,' Sweeney said. 'I look out to sea. Or up at the mountain and the sky. I find more of interest there.'

'We're going to bring her back,' Billy said. 'That's certain. And the quicker we do it, the better for all concerned.'

'And Yasha?'

'We'll deal with Yasha at the same time.'

'I see,' Sweeney said.

So did Willeway. He had a moment of absolute fright. He had not given much thought to what was happening up to this point; accepting the initiative of Billy and Marriott was merely a matter of taking the line of least resistance, and he was used to that. But Sweeney, by asking a few obvious questions, opened up fearful possibilities.

Marriott said: 'We have to look after ourselves. And that means eliminating dangerous situations.'

Anger was still predominant in his voice, but there was something else as well – a wheedling tone. Willeway wondered about that. Could it be that which had brought them all to Sweeney? Not the hope that he might have seen Yasha and Susan, but as an act of deference: the bluster of a child, inviting prevention? If Sweeney now were to tell them not to be silly, to go back down to the camp and forget about the fugitives – might they not do it? It would be enough, at any rate, Willeway thought, to justify his own secession. He thought more happily: I will stay here with Sweeney. No one will touch me here.

But Sweeney said: 'You must make your own decisions.' His eyes had gone out again to the mountain. 'You will do what you think you must.'

In despair, Willeway said: 'Sweeney!'

'Yes?'

The others were looking at him – Marriott's eyes beady, watchful. Sweeney's eyes had turned to look at him, too, but blandly, without interest. He shook his head and stared at the ground.

'It doesn't matter.'

Billy said, with relief Willeway thought: 'We'd better get moving. It may not be easy finding them.'

They hunted through the valley in a long line, with Marriott taking the left flank, high up on the slopes of Mount Proteus, and Billy the right. The others were spread at roughly regular intervals between them, Lydia being at the centre. They were easily within call of each other, but not always within sight. Willeway, placed immediately below Marriott, stumbled his way through the brush in increasing discomfort. Apprehension, too. He had all too clear a picture of what might happen if they found Yasha, and also of what would happen when, in due course, they were rescued from the island. He remembered reading somewhere an exposition of the law relating to murder: anyone joining in an act of felony which, whether intentionally or not, results in the death of another person is guilty of murder. Weren't those the grounds on which they had hanged the Bentley boy?

He found an opportunity to communicate his fears to Katey when they stopped for lunch. They had come right through to the far side of the island and had swung right to work their way round what they now called Sweeney's Hill. The two of them sat a little apart from the others, and she listened to him in silence. When he had finished, she said:

'Is what we're doing a felony?'

'Hunting a man down ...'

'A man who's gone mad.'

'Mad? Because Billy and Tony say so? You don't believe their story, do you? You know you don't. They're out to get him.'

She nodded slowly. 'I suppose they are.'

When they were called to move on, Katey said: 'We've had enough of this. We're going back to camp.'

She stood up, and Willeway went to stand beside her. Candie, perhaps, would back out with them, and Toni. It might be easier than he had thought. Billy seemed a bit shaken. It was Lydia who said, in a berating voice:

'You can cut that out! No one is going back until we say so. We're in this together. You're not getting out of it.'

Willeway said placatingly: 'We're tired, Lydia – dead beat. And we've seen no sign of them. We could look for them another day.'

Marriott said: 'I don't give a damn if you are dead beat. You'll drag that fat hulk of yours along until you're told you can stop. That's final.'

Katey said: 'I'm going back.'

She spoke firmly, almost indifferently. Lydia went close and stared down at her.

'You heard what was said. There are no exceptions.'

There was a pause before Katey spoke. She said, in the same cool unconcerned voice:

'I'm pregnant. So I'm going back.'

Willeway stared at his wife in the silence that followed. He remembered the look now: the complacency, the mouth even harder than usual, the defiant posture. Whatever the others might think, he had no doubt of the truth of her statement.

Lydia asked her: 'Are you sure?'

'Quite sure.'

Lydia stared at her. 'All right. Go back if you want to.'

'I'll go with her,' Willeway said.

'No,' Lydia said, 'you'll stay with us.'

He looked to Katey for support, but found none. He said weakly: 'She needs someone to help her.'

'She's as fit as a flea,' Lydia said. 'And it's only an easy walk, anyway. She doesn't have any mountains to climb.'

'She might run into Yasha ...'

Lydia dismissed it with an impatient shrug. 'Don't be silly.' The shrug admitted that Yasha's madness was a fiction, to be used as a justification for the hunt but not for anything else. Marriott, hectoring, said:

'Come on. We've wasted enough time as it is. Let's get you moving.'

He looked back after a time, to see no sign of Katey. Presumably she had already set off on her journey back through the valley. Even though he knew she would not help him – that she had nothing to spare from herself and the child she was carrying – there was a sense of loss at her going. And with the loss, self-pity. He was alone, he saw, and, being alone, there was nothing he could do but go along with Billy and Marriott and Lydia. He could not be expected to do anything else.

They struggled through the afternoon, increasingly hot and tired and frustrated by not seeing any sign of Susan or Yasha. Having combed the slopes of Sweeney's Hill, they crossed the valley and continued the hunt on Mount Proteus. Candie and Toni protested at this, suggesting that things should be called off for the day, but Lydia wouldn't hear of it. She herself seemed less tired than any of the men, and her energy and determination, Willeway thought, cowed them. They certainly cowed him. He floundered unhappily on, for the most part lagging behind the others, spurred on by taunts and threats from Marriott who kept the next station to him. Earlier, he had deliberately not looked for the fugitives, dreading the cry that they had been sighted. He no longer cared now. All he cared about was the tiredness and discomfort of his body, increasing hunger and recurring thirst. When Billy called a halt to rest, he flung himself down in a patch of coarse grass, panting with exhaustion.

They had come up the slopes of the mountain to a point from which they had a view over the cliffs to the eastern waters; it was not very far from the point at which they had rested during the abortive attempt to scale Mount Proteus. A breeze came up from the cliffs, tempering the sun's heat. In any case, it was not quite as oppressive as it had been: the sun was standing fairly low in the western sky.

Candie said, with satisfaction: 'We'll have to pack it in soon, anyway. Can't hope to find them after sunset.'

There was no answer to this: even the fanatical determination which Lydia and Marriott displayed could not contest the logic of the statement. Lydia sat a little apart, looking angry and discontented. Billy chewed on a stem of grass. Marriott, just below him, brooded silently.

Willeway said cautiously: 'We might as well start for camp now, don't you think? It's quite a long way down.'

Toni said: 'I'm dead beat. I could sleep for days.'

'After eating,' Willeway said.

She gave a tired laugh. 'After eating, yes! God, I'm so hungry.'

'I'm more thirsty,' Candie said, 'at this moment. Anyone remember seeing a stream in the last quarter mile?'

'I thought I saw an orange grove,' Willeway offered.

'Did you? Where … ?'

Marriott interrupted, slamming his palms together with a melodramatic slap.

'Orange grove!' he said. 'I'll bet that's it.' He stood up and looked at the others. His face was transformed with excitement. 'Let's go.'

Lydia also rose. 'Go where?'

'The valley,' Marriott said. 'The little valley with the waterfall. We might be able to catch sight of them from above.'

Toni said: 'No, Tony. Not there.'

There was protest, pain even, in her voice. The others paid no attention. Lydia said:

'Do you think they might be there?'

'It's a good chance,' Marriott said. 'It's sheltered, difficult to get at.' He was almost quivering with tension. 'Why not?'

Lydia looked at Billy. He said:

'Why not? It's not far off our route back, anyway.'

It took them about twenty minutes to reach the place from which they could look down into the little valley. Billy and Marriott cautioned the rest against talking above a whisper, or kicking loose stones. They stared down silently together. There was sunlight on the eastern rampart, but the floor of the valley was already in the shadow of sunset. It looked very quiet down there, and very peaceful.

Candie said: 'You're not likely to see anything at this time.' He shifted his position. 'Can't it wait? If they are there, they aren't likely to move out during the night.'

'Quiet,' Marriott said. His voice was eager, imbued with longing. 'Keep still. I think ... There. Yes, there! By the lake. Do you see them?'

Willeway saw something move among the trees by the lakeside. He could not be sure it was a human being, but he realized it was too large to be anything else. Lydia said, with triumph:

'It's them, all right. Can we get down from here?'

Billy said: 'I don't think so. And they would spot us coming. Give them time to get clear. But we've got 'em if we go round by the beach.'

'Good enough,' Lydia said. 'We'll do that. Let's get on with it.'

They had to pass fairly close to the camp, and there Toni left them. She looked at Marriott and told him she was not coming to the little valley with them. He averted his face from her, and said abruptly to Lydia:

'Let her go. There are enough of us.' He whirled on Candie who looked as though he were going to say something. 'You're coming, though. And you, Joe.'

The sun was only a couple of diameters above the horizon on the sea behind them when they reached the rocky headland which barred their way. There was some argument as to whether they should swim round or try sealing it. Billy, and Lydia at first, was for swimming, but Marriott pointed out the near impossibility of Billy keeping the pistol dry if they took that course. So they set out to climb the rocks. It was far from easy, and Willeway slipped and sweated behind the others. But at least the end must be near. He had stopped worrying about what might be going to happen; the proximity of the happening was all that concerned him.

In fact, it was over very quickly. They saw Susan and Yasha from the top of the rocks, and were themselves seen almost at the same time.

Lydia asked: 'Will they try to make a run for it?'

'No,' Marriott said. His voice was raised, almost to a shout. 'There's nowhere they can go, no way out. Come on, Billy!'

He scrambled down the rocks inside the valley; the gradient was much easier on this side. Willeway saw the two figures confer together; then Yasha began to walk towards them. Susan, after a moment's hesitation, followed him. He waved her back, but she came on. He stopped, and called to the invading party.

'Do you want me? I'll come. But let Susan stay here, if she wants to.'

'No,' Lydia said. 'You're both coming.'

Yasha stood there in torn white shirt and frayed duck shorts, white-bearded, shaggy-haired. For the first time in weeks Willeway looked at them all objectively: a collection of ruffians, and he was no exception. How could one expect the standards of civilized life to remain, when the appearances were so conspicuously absent? Lydia stood erect against the skyline: she had discarded her blouse and was dressed in sandals, a skirt ripped down one side, and bra. There was a certain wild magnificence to her stance.

'She will do as I say,' Lydia said. 'So will you, Yasha. Come on, both of you. We've wasted enough time. Shoot them, Billy, if they don't jump to it.'

They obeyed with no further protest, scrambling up over the rocks and down the other side, Billy brandishing the gun in their rear. Both Lydia and Marriott were volubly elated on the way back to camp. Yasha and Susan said nothing, and Candie and Willeway were silent also. As far as Willeway was concerned, all he was thinking of was food and bed.

As they turned inland towards the camp, Marriott pointed to a bird, a small parrot, perched on a branch of a tree. He stooped down, picked up a stone and threw it. It did not hit the bird but went near enough to disturb it; the bird flew off awkwardly and fell in a flutter of wings near Marriott's feet. He grabbed it before it could recover itself.

'Here you are, Lydia,' he said. 'A pet for you.'

'I wonder why it fell,' Billy said.

The parrot bit Marriott. He cursed, and shifted his grip to its neck. Holding it up, he said:

'Its feet. Can't perch properly.'

Willeway looked at the feet. One of them ended in a horny blob, the other had three misshapen toes. They looked hideous, and he wanted to kill the bird, both for its own sake and because of its ugliness. But Lydia said:

'Thank you, Tony. We'll have a cage for him. You'll make a cage, won't you, Billy?'

They came to the camp. Katey was at the kitchen, Toni with her, helping. They looked at the returning party with their captives, but said nothing.

'Food,' Lydia said. 'Good-oh. I want a drink badly, too. Get me some palm wine, Billy.' He hesitated, looking at Yasha. 'Yes,' she said, 'it is a problem. What do you think?'

Marriott said: 'Tie them up. For now, anyway. We can tie them with vines to one of the trees.'

'Yes,' she agreed. 'That should do it. See to it, will you?'

'Right,' Marriott said. 'Go get some vines, Joe. Snap to it.'

Tiredly Willeway did as he was bid.

22

THE STRANGE THING ABOUT THE DAY in the little valley with
Yasha had been the feeling of peace. They had both known
that the probabilities were that the others would come to get
them – they had kept in cover as much as possible and watched
the sea for the sight of someone swimming round the point –
but her fear and anxiety over that were surface things. Deep in
her mind there was a contentment, an ease, such as she could
not recall knowing before. Not with John, certainly. With him,
even in the act of physical possession, there had been the fear
of loss, and even in the best times of companionship a jealous
awareness of the claims of others.

Was it Yasha, she wondered, who produced this? Was it possible that she was falling in love with him? She smiled at the
thought: a White Russian ship's engineer, well into middle age,
who had, in any case, offered her no more than help and protection – which he had offered to Katey, too, she remembered.
More likely it was the release from the company of the others –
from Marriott in particular – which was responsible. And the
valley itself ... the sense of being cut off from the raw polymor-
phous luxuriance of the rest of the island, the quietness. Voices,
one's own as well, seemed to die into the air, and there appeared
to be no monkeys here and none of the more raucous birds. The
sound one noticed most was the sound of water, the splash of
waterfall and stream and the deeper voice of the sea.

But Yasha counted, too. There was no denying that. His presence relaxed and reassured her. It was nothing like the way she
had felt with Candie: she remembered pouring out her troubles
to him, with embarrassment and shame. There was no compul-

sion to talk to Yasha about John, no need to parade a wound. The wound was healing. Here in the little valley, in Yasha's undemanding company, it would heal rapidly. Given time there would be nothing left but the scar, and that no more than a faint pale line which one would look at now and then, amazed to think that it could ever have hurt.

They did talk, but of neutral untroubling things. She told him about her grandfather, who had been a ship's carpenter and had brought her presents back from his voyages – a flaxen-haired doll in peasant dress from Hamburg, castanets and a lacy fan from Lisbon, a model of a liner, in heavy pink and white alabaster, all the way from Calcutta. And Yasha, in turn, talked of his childhood in Hong Kong, and of his long years wandering among the islands. When they were hungry they ate fruit and coconut, and drank water where it splashed over clear polished ledges of rock. If they were left alone, Yasha explained, he could make fire from dry wood and they could probably catch fish, and shellfish under the rocks. But for the moment they must wait and watch. The long day passed too quickly, and the time came when Yasha touched her arm and she looked up the shadowed slope of rock and saw them standing there, silhouetted against the slanting sunlight.

Yasha said quietly: 'Get away, Susan. Run. I will hold them.'

'Run? Run where? There is nowhere to go.'

'Go, anyway. I will talk to them.'

He started to walk towards them and, after a moment, she followed. 'Go back,' he said. 'Please go back.' But she paid no heed.

The journey back to the camp was wretched, made worse by the almost lunatic high spirits of Lydia and Marriott. She was nauseated by the incident of the parrot – the offer and acceptance of that squawking bird with the obscene travesties of feet – and shocked when she realized that she and Yasha were to be tied up. Marriott supervised this; he took over from Candie to make the vines tighter about her wrists. Candie had tried to avoid looking at her as he pulled at them; Marriott grinned in her face and, when she was helpless, squeezed her breasts with his hand. She shrank away from him, but said nothing.

With Yasha she was made to sit by the side of the women's hut, where they could be kept in view. Billy brought out gourds of palm wine and offered them to the rest of the party. They all drank heavily; even Katey and Toni had some while they were preparing supper. Candie and Willeway relaxed from their uncomfortable silence and talked and laughed with the others. But they did not look in her direction.

Billy went to look at the hen, and there was an uproar when he returned. He was carrying an egg. It was larger than an ordinary hen's egg and white, almost unnaturally white. He took it to Lydia.

'How are you going to have it, Lydia?' he asked. 'Fried or baked?'

'Fried,' she said. 'A fried egg!' She stared about her in drunken majesty. 'This is really my day.'

The drinking continued during supper and after. Toni brought some food to Susan and Yasha and Billy allowed them to have their hands released. At the same time he had them brought nearer to the fire; night was falling rapidly and he wanted to have them where he could see them. Later he came to supervise their tying up again. Embarrassed, Susan asked him if she could go down to the lavatory, grateful at least that it was Billy and not Marriott. He thought about this, and agreed. He stood on guard about twenty paces from the privy until she emerged. When they got back, she said:

'Do I have to be tied again?'

'Got to stop you running away,' Billy said.

'There's nowhere to run to. No one.'

He glanced at Yasha. 'Yes. I suppose as long as we keep him safe it doesn't matter much about you.' He thought for a moment. 'You could give us your parole, too.'

She said gratefully: 'I'll do that willingly.'

It was something to be free of the fear of being physically helpless, at the mercy of any mauling Marriott cared to inflict.

Yasha said: 'I suppose I would not be allowed to offer a parole?'

'You're right, cock,' Billy said. 'You've given us enough trouble already.'

'Could the vines be tied a little less tightly?'

He held up his arms and showed red weals on his wrists.

'Shut up,' Billy said. He leaned down and slapped Yasha across the face, with no particular brutality but hard enough to rock his head back. 'Keep the mouth shut if you don't want us to find something to shove in it.'

Lydia and Marriott were clowning about with the parrot, which had been tethered by the leg to a length of vine. Lydia tugged at the end and the bird fell over, squawking and fluttering its wings. She and Marriott roared with laughter. Then, abruptly, she gave the tether to Billy.

'Tie it up for the night somewhere,' she told him. 'I feel like bed.'

She got up and with a deliberate, flaunting gesture unclipped the brassiere and took it off. She stood with shoulders braced back against the firelight; her breasts, although small, were well formed. She looked down at Marriott, smiling.

'You've done pretty well today, Tony,' she said. 'We wouldn't have found them but for you. And I've always wanted a parrot. I'll tell you what – you can come and tuck me in, as a reward.'

There was silence, part shocked, Susan thought, part expectant. Marriott looked at Toni, then at Billy. Billy made a move towards the pair of them, but stopped when Lydia spoke again. She said, in a sharp arrogant voice:

'I hope no one wants to argue about that. I hope everyone realizes that I'm the one who decides on the privileges, and that I can give them as I like and withdraw them as I like. I hope that's quite clear.'

In a low voice, Billy said: 'Lydia …'

'You're tired, Billy,' she said. 'Perhaps you won't be as tired tomorrow. If you're a good boy, I'll be very nice to you to-morrow. But naughty boys don't get any sweets. I think you'd better take a turn on guard duty tonight, anyway.' She giggled. 'Tony's got duties of his own. Come on, Tony. I won't ask you to carry me across the threshold. I won't carry you, either. Wouldn't be proper.'

She was drunk, Susan saw, but it wasn't only the drunkenness that had brought her to this; there was something else, something hideous, working behind it. Fear touched her again; fear for herself but more fear for Yasha.

Marriott looked once more at his wife, and Toni stared back, her face empty of expression. His own face took on an ugly grin.

'Right!' he said. 'Lead the way, your Highness. No delay to the royal summons.'

Billy watched them go to the hut in silence. Then he turned savagely on Candie and Willeway. Candie would take the first watch, he told them, Willeway the middle one and himself the last.

'And stay awake,' he said. He nodded at Candie. 'You, par-ticularly. If anything goes wrong, you're for it.'

Susan retired to bed along with Katey and Toni. No reference was made, either to Lydia and Marriott or herself and Yasha. They said quiet good-nights, and the two other women fell asleep fairly quickly. Susan lay awake, worrying about Yasha. If there was any way in which she could release him ... she would have had no hesitation about breaking the parole she had given Billy. But she could not go and leave him here, at the mercy of Lydia and her men. With a little shock of surprise, she real-ized that she took Lydia's paramountcy for granted. And Lydia, she felt in her heart, had changed more than the others, more even than Marriott. She was stripping convention from her as she had stripped herself of the brassiere in front of the camp fire. And what lay behind convention was ugly and dangerous, possibly insane.

She made one attempt to help Yasha. She went quickly from her bed to the door and looked out. Candie was there, and awake, walking to and fro in the moonlight. She slipped out, calling his name quietly. He heard, and came towards her.

His voice was low, and guarded. 'What is it? What do you want?'

She said: 'Yasha – he's tied so tightly. Can't you ease the vines off a bit?'

'No,' he said, 'I can't. I'm not getting into trouble with Billy over it.'

Yasha, she saw, was awake and watching them, but he said nothing. She took Candie's arm, trying to find some way to reach him.

'Let him loose,' she said. 'Come away with us. You can't go on here, Roger. Terrible things are likely to happen.'

She saw him shake his head in the moonlight. 'I don't fancy being hunted. And they might not keep their tempers as well a second time.'

'Look, there would be three of us! And only three of them that count.'

'Three and a gun.'

'We might persuade Joe to come with us.'

'Joe! Don't be silly.' He shook his arm free. 'You'd better get back to bed before Billy wakes up.'

She said desperately: 'There are only three of them. The rest of us are still sane. We must do something now, before it's too late.'

'I told you to go to bed. I'll have to call Billy if you don't. And that means you'll probably be tied up, too. Go on.'

He meant what he said; and he was right about Willeway. If he himself could not be persuaded to make a stand against Lydia and the others, there was no hope of Willeway doing so. She looked at Yasha, and he looked back at her, smiling. She did her best to return the smile, but her legs were trembling as she went back into the hut.

Lydia, the next morning, repeated with Marriott the gesture she had initiated with Billy, sending him out of her hut late, when the others were at breakfast, and making her own ostentatious entry a quarter of an hour later. Marriott, though, was not shamefaced as Billy had been; he strutted, peacock-like, clapped Billy on the shoulder, whispered something to him and laughed. He met Toni's eye, too, and grinned at her. She returned his look for a moment, and turned away. Her face showed nothing.

The question of what to do with Yasha came up. His hands had been freed to enable him to eat, and Billy, as a concession, allowed him to have his legs free as well. There was small danger of his getting away; when he tried to get up he fell over, and it was some time before his hands had unstiffened enough to let him eat. His wrists were scored raw from the vines. Susan took food to him and helped him with it. She was called back by Marriott.

'Over here, Susan! Can't have you two getting up to mischief. He can manage.'

Billy said: 'Are we going to tie him up again afterwards?'

'We're going to have to make up our minds about Yasha,' Marriott said.

Lydia was feeding fruit to the parrot which was tethered to one of the stakes of the hut. She said:

'You can find him some work to do for a start. He can build a cage for Polly. He's good with his hands.'

'One for himself, too,' Marriott said. 'Why not? We'll put him in a cage.'

'He's safer tied up,' Billy objected.

'We can still tie him up at night,' Marriott said. 'I rather fancy the idea of putting him in a cage. We can get him on cutting saplings down directly after breakfast.'

Lydia said indifferently: 'Just as you like.'

'As for Susan …' Marriott went on. He looked at her with insulting calculation. 'I reckon I might take her up the valley and get her on some digging. We ought to do some planting as well as picking.'

Lydia slapped her hand down on his wrist and gripped it.

'Any planting that needs doing, I'll supervise. And she'll stay here in camp where I can keep my eye on her.'

She favoured him with a steely smile. Marriott laughed: he seemed more flattered than put out.

'Fair enough, Lydia,' he said. 'You're the boss.'

Yasha was put to work as had been agreed. After some further discussion, it was decided that making the bird-cage could be left until he had made the cage for himself: Billy pointed out that he could do jobs like that after he was inside. He worked silently and steadily, cutting and trimming the saplings with the axe. Susan was put on general work around the camp – cleaning up and then preparing food. She found herself doing the kitchen work that normally was divided between two women.

She wondered if a servant class was being created – Katey and Toni had looked somewhat embarrassed but had made no protest about it. There was a disconcerting feeling of permanence about the arrangement. But she had envisaged worse possibilities and felt she ought to be grateful that so far they had been spared these. She made mid-morning coffee for the others and, when they had been served, made as though to take some to Yasha. Billy stopped her.

'He's on hard tack. I don't believe in pampering the working classes. You can have a drop yourself, though, since you've made it.'

She put the coffee down and walked away. Billy called after her:

'Right! You can go on hard tack, too, if that's the way you want it. We don't want any uppishness from you, my girl.'

There was no point in needlessly offending him. She swallowed her dislike and attempted a smile. She said:

'I'm sorry.'

He was partly mollified. 'All right. Don't let it happen again, though. Go on, then – drink it up.'

It almost choked her, but she drank it.

Yasha spent all day making the cage. The saplings were about an inch and a half thick and rather more than six feet long. They had to be stripped of bark and grooved near each end where they were to be tied together. All four sides were tied at the same time, the length spread out across the clearing – three or four inches slack was allowed between the bars. The other men had to help when it came to setting up the cage and squaring it into its proper shape. Longer diagonal poles were laid corner to corner to make the structure stable.

Candie said: 'You don't need a floor to it, really. The ground will do.'

'Too easy for him to lift up and crawl under,' Billy said. 'We'll have a floor all right.'

Watching and listening, Susan felt again the horror of what was happening: the simple, almost schoolboyish interest in the mechanics of so hideous a project. They completed it in a burst of enthusiasm - one whole side made a door which, when closed, could be tied with the vine ropes.

'O.K.,' Billy said. He had completely recovered his spirits. 'We've got your new home ready for you, Yasha. Time to go aboard.'

Yasha went into the cage, and they closed the door behind him. Marriott called to Lydia, who was resting outside her hut:

'Come and look at our new bird!'

23

THERE WERE MOMENTS WHEN LYDIA looked at herself with astonishment and horror, but these were rare, and the insight so unpleasant as to make her look away again at once. She had committed herself to the part she was playing, and took feverish pleasure in it. Her domination over Billy, intensified by taking him as her lover, had been in no way lessened by her taking Marriott as well. It had been increased, in fact. Both men were hers, to do with as she pleased. She had drawn their manliness from them and absorbed it into herself; they would not now challenge her authority. Her savage delight in the act of possession was more emotional than sensual: here and now they abased themselves to her body. The sensation was intoxicating, and addictive.

Marriott was in many ways the more rewarding of the two; he had a fierceness and a frenzy which answered her own. He was still after the Malone girl, and it amused her that she could forbid him this – the prohibition was not jealous but malicious. Probably eventually she would let him have her, she thought, but in a way and at a time of her choosing. She would rule in this, too. And not yet. Certainly not yet.

She started drinking palm wine before sundown, and got through a good deal. She still did not like the taste of it, but the alcohol both soothed her and released her. She flirted with her two men, and amused herself by getting them to satisfy her caprices. She sent Marriott up the valley to get her an orange from a particular tree whose fruit, she said, tasted better than the others; and she made Billy look after the parrot, which he loathed. By the end of the evening she was drunk, and drunkenly took Billy off to her hut. She warned Marriott:

'Behave yourself. No getting up to mischief while I haven't got my eye on you. Katey! You see he doesn't get hold of Susan.'

She had a hang-over the next day and was rough with them all at breakfast. After breakfast she had an idea. Her hut, she decided, was not big enough; she wanted a new one built.

Billy said: 'You can have mine.'

Marriott, following Yasha's flight, had moved in with him.

He went on: 'Tony can move back with the others and I'll take yours over. Dead simple.'

The suggestion that someone else – particularly Billy – should have the privilege of a private hut annoyed her. She said sharply:

'Don't argue with me, Billy. I want a new hut. And I'll decide where the rest of you sleep. On the beach, if I say so. Have you got that?'

Billy said placatingly: 'Just as you like, Lydia. I only thought we ought to get cracking on making that raft we were talking about. To get out to the island for the eggs.'

'It can wait,' she said impatiently. 'The hut comes first. I'll show you where I want it, and how big.'

Billy and Marriott supervised, and the actual work was done by Candie, Willeway and Yasha. There was a distinction drawn here: the former two were given the easier jobs and allowed frequent rests, while Yasha was kept at it and made to do the heavier work. In the afternoon, Candie complained of feeling ill. He said his arms and legs felt heavy and that he was feverish. Billy, at first, accused him of malingering and told him to get on with it, but Toni intervened on his behalf. She said that she had been feeling the same way: they had probably both got a bug of some sort, perhaps a cold coming.

Billy showed himself undecided. Lydia, watching, called Candie over. She put her hand on his forehead; he was hot and clammy; almost certainly running a temperature.

'He can have the day off,' she said authoritatively. 'Go and lie down in the shade, Roger.'

She watched him go, remembering the feel of his skin beneath her fingers. Perhaps later, when he had got over his cold, if it was a cold … There was no point in exposing herself to possible infection. But some other time … as a man there was not much to him, but the lankiness of the lean dark body was attractive. She sauntered across to watch the two men who were still at work. Yasha was cutting trees at the edge of the clearing, and Willeway was hauling them away and stacking them.

Marriott, supervising at that point, said: 'Anything you want, Lydia?'

She felt better, but traces of the headache lingered.

'Yes,' she said. 'You can bring me some wine.'

He raised his eyebrows. 'Just as you like.'

'Yes,' she said. 'Just as I like. Go and get it.'

She studied the two men while he was gone. They were stripped to the waist and sweating from their exertions. Neither, she decided, had much in the way of physique. Willeway was unattractively fat, the stomach above the belt folding into heavy rolls when he bent over. Yasha was in better condition, but a good deal older; his skin showed the slacks and creases of middle-age and there were white hairs on his chest.

Marriott brought wine, and stood beside her chatting while she drank it. She listened to him, half attentively. Her real attention was given to Yasha; there was something about the silence and steadiness with which he worked that attracted her. They were treating him like a serf, but he was refusing to be affected by it. Something in him was untouched, a quiet core of – what? Dignity? She found the notion both pleasing and exasperating. There was a tree a little way off a good deal thicker than the rest. She pointed it out to Marriott.

'Get him on felling that one.'

'There's not much point,' Marriott objected. 'I don't see how we could use it.'

She stared at Marriott. 'I want it down.'

He shrugged. 'Very well.'

Yasha looked briefly from one to the other of them when the order was given him, but said nothing. He went to the tree and began swinging the axe at its base. His strokes were clean and rhythmic; the steel bit into the wood and flung out small white chips. Lydia drank more wine.

'He's strong for his age,' she said thoughtfully.

'Yes,' Marriott said. 'He's taking things better than I would have expected. Scared, probably.'

'I don't think scared.'

'Biding his time, then? That could be dangerous. I'm not sure we oughtn't to do something, well ...'

'What?'

He grinned at her conspiratorially. 'I don't have to dot and cross and underline with you, do I, Lydia? We've got to look out for ourselves. If he's a risk, it might be best to lose him somewhere.'

The implication did not disturb her, but annoyed her a little. She did not need help, from Marriott especially.

She said: 'I can see to Yasha.'

'Can you?'

He was a man, after all. Not young and not handsome, but perhaps with a quality that neither Billy nor Marriott had, a strength inside to match the strength in the arms swinging the axe. The thought grew, and amused her. Where she stood now, nothing was denied her. Incalculability, outrage – they were not merely permissible, but required.

Marriott said: 'Well, we'll talk about it another time. There's no denying that he's useful. As long as we keep our eyes on him.'

What would Marriott do? Try to persuade Billy to make a stand? She smiled inwardly; she only had to say the word and Billy would turn on Marriott eagerly and mercilessly. The alliance between them was of her choosing and she could break it whenever she wished. If she had wanted to, she could have taken the pistol away from Billy; but it was better that he should have it. It made things simpler.

She went on drinking and watching Yasha. The idea, now she had admitted it, engrossed her. She began to be impatient, but found a satisfaction in controlling her impatience. Later. The time would be right then. The very fact that everything was open to her made it important that things should be done in the right way.

By the time they had supper she was pretty intoxicated. Katey had prepared fish as the main course, grilled on wood embers. Lydia ate four of them, savouring the crumbling sweetness of the white flesh beneath the burned, blackened skin. She said to Katey:

'That was very good. Take one to Yasha.'

'He's supposed to be on hard tack,' Billy said.

'Would you like a fish, Yasha?' Lydia asked. He nodded silently. Ignoring Billy's remark, she said again to Katey: 'Take him one.'

She watched while he ate. The sight of him appeasing his hunger excited her. She made Katey take him another fish, and a third. There were no more left. She had pineapple taken to him, and said:

'Wine. Give him some wine.'

Billy said uneasily: 'We don't want to pamper him, Lydia.'

Marriott laughed. 'I don't know.' His little eyes gleamed. 'The condemned man ate a hearty supper.'

She paid no attention to either of them. Yasha was drinking wine from the gourd; she saw the muscles of his throat move as he swallowed. She said:

'Have you had enough, Yasha?'

He put the gourd down. 'Yes. Thank you.'

'In that case,' Billy said, 'it's about time we put him back in his cage, I reckon. Tie him up, Joe.'

'No,' Lydia said. Her own voice sounded far away. 'Come over here, Yasha.'

He came and stood before her. She looked up. 'Kneel down, Yasha.' He remained standing, and shook his head slightly. She said impatiently: 'Well, sit down, then. I want to have a look at you.'

He sat down beside her. Leaning towards him, she put her hand on his face and traced the line of his jaw. The grey-white beard was rough beneath her fingers. Playfully she gave it a little tug.

'An old man,' she said, 'but a strong old man. I don't think you need to go in a nasty uncomfortable cage tonight. I think I can find a better place for you.'

Marriott laughed. She realized he still thought this was a pre-liminary to carrying out his hinted suggestion of the afternoon. That amused her, too. Billy cried:

'No! Lydia, you can't …'

She shook her head. 'That's not a word you use to me. Is it? Is it, Billy?' He dropped his head. 'Well, what's the answer? I'm waiting.'

'No,' he said 'I'm sorry, Lydia.'

The exchange had apparently brought things home to Mar-riott. He said angrily:

'We're not having that, Lydia. We're not going to stand by while …'

'Tony.'

Her voice cut across what he was saying and stopped him. She waited a moment, and said:

'If you're going to be tiresome, I'm going to have to get Billy to deal with you. I wouldn't like to do that, but I will if neces-sary. You do believe that, don't you?'

Marriott's eyes went from her to Billy. The two men stared at each other briefly. Marriott got up and turned away.

He said: 'I'm going down to the beach.'

'Not yet,' Lydia said. He looked at her. 'I'll tell you when you can go.' She turned back to Yasha. 'I feel like going to bed. Are you strong enough to carry me? Well, it doesn't really matter. I can get there without that.'

Yasha said nothing. She stood up and he stood up with her. She put a hand on his arm, her fingers digging at the hardness of muscle.

'Come on,' she told him. 'Don't tell me you're too tired from all that chopping.'

'No.'

'Then let's go.'

'I mean – I am not coming with you.' His eyes were steady. 'You must look elsewhere.'

Her first thought was that the refusal was some kind of joke, obscure because he was, after all, a foreigner. But then she read the meaning of his gaze, the contempt which he hardly troubled to conceal. Fury moved in her, cold bitter fury. If he had waited till they were alone, it would have been bad enough, but here, in front of the others, with Marriott and Billy watching … It was an insult which they would never forgive her for accepting, either. Nothing would be the same again if it were allowed to stand.

She said, in a hard controlled voice: 'All right. Joe, tie him up. If he wants the cage, he can have it.'

Yasha submitted to being bound. The others watched in silence. When it was completed, Lydia said:

'They don't look tight enough to me. Tony, go and tighten them up. We don't want him to get loose during the night.'

'It's a pleasure,' Marriott said.

He drew on the bonds, pulling hard. Yasha winced, but made no outcry. When he had finished, Lydia said:

'Put him in his cage now.'

Marriott led Yasha to the door of the cage and pushed him in the back. He fell forwards, sprawling to his knees, putting his bound hands out in front to protect himself. Marriott pulled the door to and began roping it into position.

'Are you comfy?' Lydia asked Yasha. He stared up at her without replying. 'I wouldn't like to think everything wasn't just as you wanted it.' She drank more wine. 'That will do, Tony. You don't have to spend all night tying the door. I thought we might have some fun, a little after-supper entertainment.'

She went to the cage and stood with her back to it, looking across the clearing. To Willeway, she said: 'Go and get some stones, Joe. There are plenty of loose stones up behind the hut.' She began to walk away from the cage with measured stride. She was counting as she went. ' … twenty-three, twenty-four, twenty-five. I think that's about right. Don't want to make it too easy.'

Except for Susan who had not been drinking, they were all pretty drunk by now. The only one who grasped the purport was Marriott. He guffawed, and said:

'Win a prize with every ball! How do we score points, Lydia?'

Willeway had filled a bag with stones and brought them to where she now stood. She picked one out and weighed it in her hand; it was roughly spherical and about three inches across.

'One point for every hit,' she said. 'Ten for drawing blood. I'll decide what the prize is later.'

Katey burst out: 'I don't think that's a very good joke.'

'Don't you?' Lydia said. 'Come here, Katey.' Katey hesitated and came towards her. Lydia held out the stone. 'You can have first bash.' The silence was heavy, knife-edged. 'Or would you like to watch it from inside instead of outside? We can arrange that.'

Katey looked from Lydia to Billy and Marriott. Billy's face was unconcerned, Marriott's showed something like anticipation. She turned from them to Willeway, and he looked back, lost and frightened.

'Make up your mind,' Lydia said.

Without answering, Katey took the stone. She hesitated, and threw it. It went roughly in the direction of the cage but missed by several feet.

Lydia looked at her for a moment, and decided to accept the gesture. It amounted, after all, to submission. She laughed.

'Not very good, but it'll do for a start. My turn now.'

She picked a stone out of the heap and threw it at the cage. It hit one of the bars and ricocheted off. At once she picked up another and threw again. This time the stone went through. It hit Yasha on the shoulder and he drew himself away. Lydia said:

'One to me. Billy, Tony, your turn.'

They came to her with no hesitation. Susan ran towards her, too, her face frightened and incredulous.

'You can't!' she cried. 'I won't let you.' She scattered the stones with her feet. 'You're all insane.' Lydia stooped down for one of the stones, and Susan seized her arm, trying to hold her. 'I won't let you!'

'You look after her, Tony,' Lydia said. She shook herself free as Marriott grabbed the girl. 'O.K., Billy, we'll make this a twosome. Best of five, for a start.'

They pelted Yasha with the stones. The bars stopped some, and others he managed to dodge, but several landed on him. Susan struggled helplessly with Marriott, crying for help to the others. Toni was not there, having slipped away earlier. Katey and Willeway and Candie heard her but made no move to do anything. They were frightened, Lydia thought exultantly: fear ruled the island and she ruled fear. One of her stones caught Yasha on the side of the face, and in the rapidly growing darkness she saw the spurt of blood. She cried:

'Ten! And three makes thirteen. You're dropping behind, Billy.'

Billy threw quickly, a stone that caught Yasha on the chest and made him stagger.

'There's a ten,' he said.

'One.'

'It's drawn blood.'

'I can't see any.'

She walked towards the cage to see better and Billy followed her. There was a weal on Yasha's skin from which a few drops of blood oozed. Her own cut on his face was a much deeper one. She looked back. Marriott was not simply holding the girl now but making a frank sexual attack on her. The sight annoyed her: it was for her to choose when he raped her. Coming after the Yasha incident, this was too much.

'Let her go, Tony,' she said. He did not respond right away, and she said more sharply: 'I mean that! Let her go.'

Marriott got up from her reluctantly. 'She'll only go for you again,' he said.

'The light's too bad,' Lydia said. 'We can't see when we're hitting him. We'll leave it over till the morning. Billy, you look after him tonight.'

She beckoned Marriott and he came; without enthusiasm but he came. The thought of the mastery she would enjoy again tingled in her limbs.

'My little Tony.' She put her arm across his shoulders and flattened her breasts against his back. 'My fierce little Tony. Now let's see how well you struggle.'

24

CANDIE HAD BEEN TOO PREOCCUPIED with his own aches and pains to care much about what was happening to Yasha: the heaviness in his limbs had become a dull leaden weight which made any kind of movement a sweating agony. Allied to this was the fever which subtly changed the contours of the world about him. Space was unreal – his body was at once immense, swollen with fatigue and a speck in a fantastic overgrown universe. Sounds too. Voices rose and fell in an enormous distorting echo-chamber, inextricably mixed with the background cacophony of island life. Somewhere a bird was sending what was almost Morse code, approximations of dots and dashes from a gruff and lunatic transmitter. He became obsessed with the feeling that there really was a meaning to be obtained from this. He could pick out individual letters, now and then a short word. Again and again the relapse into nonsense infuriated him.

That night he slept fitfully: brief sleeping nightmares were interspersed with more restless waking ones. He was awake when Willeway came in to tell him it was his turn on guard duty, and he lumbered to his feet and out into the clearing with a feeling, although he was desperately tired, of relief. He sat with his back against the side of the hut, dozing and dreaming and aching. There was enough light to see the cage and the figure inside it. Yasha did not seem to be moving. Asleep, despite his bonds; or perhaps dead. He could not feel concerned to the point of checking. A wave of shivering came over him, rattling his teeth. He wanted to relieve himself, but the effort of getting up made him prefer the discomfort. And the relief of one discomfort hardly seemed worth while when every cell in his body groaned silently in protest against moving.

The moon's light faded into the first light of dawn, still not bright enough to tinge with any colour the dark cloud on Proteus. It was not long after this that Candie heard a sound from up the valley; a marauding pig or monkey he thought at first, and then, more clearly, the noise of someone approaching along the path. He looked up, but still did not get up. A figure emerged, at the point where path and clearing met. It was Sweeney.

Sweeney paused for a few moments, as though getting his bearings, and then walked in Candie's direction. In front of him, he said:

'You look a little seedy, Roger.'

Candie nodded listlessly. 'I feel rotten.'

'A touch of fever. You will feel better shortly, I should think.'

'God, I hope so.' The improbability of Sweeney's presence here suddenly impressed him. 'What have you come down for, Sweeney?'

'I believe we must expect a break in the weather.'

'Do you? What makes you think that?'

'The atmosphere. A jangling at the nerve ends. The birds have felt it, too.'

The birds, Candie realized, had fallen quiet. And although the fever continued to distort his perceptions, there was a difference in atmosphere, a deadness in the air. Usually there was some slight breeze, but now the air was deeply, unnaturally still. Far away a monkey shrieked, rawly tearing a hole through the silence. But the silence closed over it again, as solid as before.

He said muzzily: 'Yes, I suppose you would be a bit exposed up above if another storm came.'

Sweeney looked at him. 'Are you all right there, Roger?'

'I'd like to go and have a pee. If I could get up.'

Sweeney put his large hands down and Candie took them. He was brought easily and gently to his feet.

He said: 'Thank you, Sweeney,' and staggered off across the clearing.

He stayed for some time, his forehead resting against the branch of a tree. The bark was cool, smooth, refreshing to his skin. When he turned round, it was to find two people where he had left one. Sweeney had presumably released Yasha from the cage and from his bonds. He was kneeling down, rubbing Yasha's ankles, and Yasha was leaning on him.

It did not occur to Candie to raise an alarm. He walked back and said in something like a normal voice:

'There'll be trouble about that, Sweeney. Trouble with Lydia, certainly.'

'I relieved you,' Sweeney said. 'I took over your watch. Nothing to worry about, Roger.'

He shook his head. 'I'm not worrying.'

That was strange, but it was true. He watched tranquilly as Sweeney chafed Yasha's wrists and ankles back to life. And as Sweeney went to the door of the women's hut and called, in a low voice, to Susan. She came out a moment or two later. None of the others seemed to have wakened. He had the impression that he ought to have been surprised by that, but was not.

'Off you go,' Sweeney said. 'Find yourself shelter, if you can. I think the weather is going to be rough.'

Susan took Yasha's hand, and they went together across the clearing and through the trees in the direction of the beach. Looking after them, Candie said:

'What good does it do? They'll only hunt them down again.'

'Perhaps. But not immediately, I fancy. How are you feeling now, Roger?'

'A bit better.' The aches, although present, were less severe, and his head felt clearer. 'Yes, better.'

They chatted until it was time to wake Katey for the kitchen work. Susan, of course, should have been helping her. Katey asked about that, and the empty bed, but did not seem much concerned by the answers she got. Was there a strangeness in all of them, Candie wondered – a sense of waiting for something? Or was this merely a reflection of his own queer state of mind?

When Billy came out he looked first at Sweeney and then at the empty cage. He did not show much surprise, and went to Lydia's hut to call her. Marriott came out first, buttoning up his trousers. Lydia followed him. She had discarded the last remnants of clothing and stood before the men, arrogantly nude. She looked ugly and splendid and terrible – a virago, Candie thought hazily.

A puff of wind caught at him from behind, pressing him forward. Immediately afterwards the air was still again, but looking up the slopes of Proteus he could watch its progress: trees and bushes heeled over as it passed. There was a quick squawking clatter of birds, but they soon fell silent. He watched as Lydia walked over to the empty cage.

'Who let him loose?' she asked. 'It was your watch, Roger.'

Sweeney said softly: 'I did, Lydia.'

Her gaze went to Katey at the kitchen. 'And Susan?'

'I sent her with him.'

'Why?'

'Because it seemed sensible.'

There was a pause before she spoke again. They were staring at each other, Lydia with deep concentration that did not display any particular emotion, Sweeney with an apparently benevolent interest. Was the waiting for this, Candie wondered? A clash that would solve, and resolve, everything? A wave of giddiness held him briefly.

Lydia said: 'You realize what it means, Sweeney, don't you?' She spoke in a reasonable voice, almost propitiating. His aunt had spoken like that, Candie remembered, when laying guilt on other shoulders, the Young, or the Government, or even God. 'You understand what will happen now?'

'Tell me,' Sweeney said.

'We'll find them again,' Lydia said. 'There's no difficulty about that. It's a small island. It may take us a day or two, but we'll run them down. But we can't take chances any more. They've got away twice already, and that can't be allowed to happen again. It won't be a question of keeping them prisoner next time. We have to think of our safety, Sweeney.'

He did not reply. She said: 'You do understand, don't you?'

Sweeney's gaze left her; he looked up into the deep blue sky, cloudless apart from the familiar shape cloaking the summit of the mountain. Its northern flanks were bright gold from the sun, contrasting with the still unlit slopes beneath.

'I think there is a storm coming,' Sweeney said. 'A severe one, possibly.'

Lydia said impatiently: 'That's not important.'

'It might be useful to make things secure.' As he spoke, another, even stronger gust blew over the clearing and up the side of Mount Proteus. 'It will be worse than we have had before, I fancy.'

Billy said: 'I reckon he's right about that, Lydia. It smells dirty. Typhoon, maybe.'

Lydia said: 'They can't have gone far. We might get to them before the weather breaks.'

Billy shook his head. 'Too risky.' He spoke with more assurance than he had for some time past. 'You don't want to get caught in the wrong place.'

Marriott said: 'Have you been in a typhoon, Billy?'

'On the edge of one. That was enough.'

'Will the huts take it?'

'Not if it really hits us.'

Lydia asked: 'What is the best thing to do?'

Billy shrugged. 'Depends. A kanaka once told me his tribe used to strap themselves to coconut palms when a really big one blew up. That had its risky side, though.'

'In what way?'

'Well, coconuts torn loose from other trees travel in a straight line like cannon balls. They can kill you if they hit you. And some trees get torn loose. Even a big tree may have rotten roots.'

'No one's tying me to a tree,' Lydia said. She laughed. 'Pity Susan isn't here. Tony could have tied her to one, couldn't you, Tony?'

During the breakfast, which Sweeney had with them, the gusts of wind began to come more frequently; and the day darkened as cloud boiled across the sky from the west. It raced over them, at first gleaming white and then, as the sun's rays were cut off, suddenly livid. It seethed like a huge inverted cauldron, but the tension held and the deluge, seemingly imminent, did not come. After breakfast, they did what they could to secure the things that mattered by covering them with palm leaves and piling large stones over the leaves. Then, on Billy's suggestion, they trooped down to the beach.

The sky was bruised purple out to the western horizon, the sea beneath it a fantastic cross-hatching of black and white. Its noise was a roar that had a whine behind it, a dynamo spinning at tremendous speed. The breakers had spilled across the reef and flung themselves in savage crescendos against the beach. The wind was now almost continuous and very strong. The spray in it stung the exposed flesh.

Candie said: 'If we went to the western point ... the wind's steady from that quarter. I mean, one couldn't be hit by anything loose.'

'I wouldn't chance it,' Billy said. 'You get tidal waves with them sometimes. Best to keep off very low lying ground.'

He felt reasonably clear-headed but very weak still. He staggered against the force of the wind. He said to Billy:

'What ought we to do then?'

'We're all right for the present. She's only beginning to blow so far. And the centre may miss us. If it gets really bad, I should think the clearing is as good a place as any.'

Toni said: 'Look.'

Something bobbed on the crest of one of the incoming waves and sank out of sight into the trough. It looked like metal, and cylindrical.

Billy said: 'Something from the old *Diana*, I reckon. I'll bet even down where she is she's getting a shaking.' He laughed. 'Who's volunteering to dive after it? How about you, Joe?'

Willeway smiled feebly. 'I don't think so.'

The spectacle of the sea, fascinating at first, became boring. The wind dropped, almost to nothing and then, five or ten minutes later, suddenly hammered them with even greater violence. By common consent they moved back up the path. Trees all round them were bent over and the wind howled in their branches. As they were crossing the clearing, Candie felt himself pelted by large confetti, flimsy but stinging by reason of the force behind it. It was some moments before he realized that the confetti consisted of small leaves. Then a palm leaf slapped him in the neck, wrapping round him. It must have been carried a hundred yards at least: there were no palms nearer.

There was another lull shortly afterwards, and with it the rain came. It started with a few heavy drops starring the earth of the clearing but within seconds turned into a deluge. Automatically, Candie headed towards the hut, but Billy stopped him.

'Shouldn't if I were you. We're really getting into it now. The next blow may be the kind that rips huts down. You're going to have to settle for getting wet.'

Almost at once, it seemed, he was not merely wet but drenched. The rain, hitting him with the force of a fire hose, soaked through his clothes as though they were rice paper and sluiced his body. It was disconcerting, making him gasp for breath, but it was not entirely unpleasant. Some of the others appeared to have the same feeling. Lydia, in her nakedness, capered about, lifting her arms in some lunatic gesture towards the sky. After some minutes' onslaught, it eased off. It was torrential still by English standards, but nothing more than a refreshing shower compared with what had gone before.

Candie saw the next gust of wind arrive. He was looking across the clearing towards the trees and saw their tops bend right over as an invisible hand pressed them down. A cloud rose from them – birds, he thought at first. But they were leaves. The top of one tree, a little higher than the rest, was stripped bare, as he watched, in one clean swoop. Then the wind reached him. He staggered, almost fell, and leaned against it to keep his footing.

During the morning, wind and rain alternated periods of calm with periods of increasing fury. Candie found himself huddling with the others behind the huts where an outcrop of rock gave some slight protection. In the early part he kept thinking that the worst must be almost over, that each slackening of wind or rain presaged the end. But as time went on, he began to feel that it would never stop, that the storm would go on forever or, at least, until the waters rose and flooded the island. Or the rain washed them all down into the sea – as it was, it had leached the open ground before them, gouging out large channels down which rivers roared, and carrying away whole sections of rock and earth.

It was eleven o'clock, by his watch, when the hut immediately in front of him was torn away, to tumble crazily through the air and smash into the trees further up. A second hut went shortly afterwards, and in the next gust the women's hut disintegrated into fragments which were scattered like matchwood. He was too numbed by now to find this remarkable. All his mind could take in was the thought of relief – from the battering wind and rain, from the cold which made him shiver, from the neverending noise.

The eye of the typhoon reached them two hours later. Abruptly the gale fell to nothing and the rain dropped to a thin drizzle. They were wary at first, expecting a sudden resumption, but as the minutes passed they realized that this cessation was different from those that had gone before. Billy explained it to them. There would be an interval of peace – it was impossible to say how long – before the other side of the typhoon caught them.

Tired, dazed and hungry they hunted for food. Everything that had been in store had been ruined by the storm, mashed and mixed with mud. The avocado at the edge of the clearing was bare, of fruit as well as leaves. Willeway ventured up the valley to the banana plant and brought back the same story. They found a few coconuts, but there was nothing to split them with: the axe had gone, along with everything else. In the end Billy managed to strip off their husks with the knife he had taken from Yasha, and cracked the inner shells by hurling them against rock. There was something to eat for all, but not much.

Candie was hunting for other nuts among the tangle of broken and uprooted trees and torn and littered vegetation when the wind caught him again. He was taken by surprise, particularly since he had failed to grasp that the new wind would be of opposite direction to the earlier ones. Now it came down the valley between Proteus and Sweeney's Hill, bending trees back where previously it had bent them forward. And it was strong, stupendously strong. On his feet he could not move against it. He dropped, in the end, to his knees and crawled forward. His progress was slow and painful; it was like crawling into butter. From time to time the wind lifted him and thumped him down, breathlessly and painfully, against the sodden ground.

Eventually he got back to the comparative shelter of the rock and huddled down with the others. All afternoon the battering went on, as slow and relentless as before, changed only in that the wind came from the opposite quarter. There was no sunset that evening: the dark of storm merged into the dark of night and, some time after that, the rain stopped and the wind fell to light gusts. Candie was aware that some of the others were moving about, foraging for food probably, but he did not move himself. The fever came back and plagued him through another endless night of misery and discomfort.

He drifted off to sleep at last. When he woke, the sky was pearling, stars quietly fading in a cloudless sky. He looked up, wondering if this, too, was part of the fever, a dream, an hallucination. Cloudless. The summit of Proteus stood bare against the first flush of dawn.

25

THE AFTERMATH OF THE TYPHOON found Marriott with a feeling of weakness and helplessness much greater than following his fight with Billy. The battering the elements had given him had been less violent but, going on so long, had dazed him and sapped his strength more. He was also very hungry. He hunted around for food, but there was nothing. In the darkness he stumbled over things: the ground's familiar contours had been changed by the scouring rains, and he fell across a tree which the wind had uprooted and tossed, caber-fashion, into the clearing. Eventually he abandoned the search as hopeless. There was nothing for it but to wait till morning.

Tired and hungry, he looked for other comfort. He came across Lydia, asleep in the ruins of one of the huts. He lay down, and snuggled his body against her. Half-waking, she put her arms out and drew him to her. The warmth of her body soothed and eased him. He felt a wave of gratitude which was almost homage. Hazily he wondered where Toni was, but did not care. Here was his peace, and he surrendered to it.

In the early hours she awoke and provoked him to desire. Past her shoulder he could see the torn and jagged outlines of the shattered trees against the first grey light. Most of the others appeared to be huddled together higher up the slope. Asleep, probably, but it did not matter whether they were or not. We couple like animals, he thought; or like gods.

'We'll get them,' she said. Her voice was a whisper, not for concealment but in delight. 'That's the first thing.'

'Get them?'

'There'll be less cover now that the storm has torn the top off the island. They won't be able to hide as easily.'

'We'll have to get the camp cleared up first. And find food.'

'The camp can wait. And we'll find food on the way.'

She was not to be crossed. In any case, she was the renewal of his strength.

He said: 'All right. If you like.'

'You can have her first. You'll like that, won't you?'

'First?'

'You won't want her more than once. After that she's just a nuisance. It wouldn't be safe to let her go after that – and after we've dealt with Yasha.'

'What do you plan doing with him?'

'I have some ideas.' Her nails dug into his back, and he winced. 'And I'll probably think of others.' There was a pause before she said, in a reasonable voice: 'It has to be a demonstration, you see.'

From the huddled group, a figure detached itself, rose, and walked unsteadily across the clearing. It was Candie. He stopped and stared up at the sky. Marriott followed his gaze and saw that, for the first time, Mount Proteus was bare of cloud. He freed himself, to look more closely, and Lydia said: 'What is it?'

'There's no cloud on the mountain.'

She said indifferently: 'I suppose the typhoon blew it away. Does it matter?'

'There's something up there. A shape ... I can't quite see what.'

They both stood up. Lydia said:

'The first day – I thought I saw something. It gleamed, and then the cloud hid it.'

The outline of the mountain could be seen against the sky, but no details. They strained their eyes, trying to see. Part of a rectangle? Lydia said:

'Could there be a hut up there?'

Another figure advanced towards them across the clearing: Sweeney. Marriott said to him:

'The cloud's gone.'

He nodded. 'So I noticed.'

'Do you see anything strange about the mountain top?'

'I am not sure.' In this half light he looked bigger than ever, and hunched, bear-like. 'We shall see more easily when it's brighter. It can wait, whatever it is.' He had a brooding look, that was half a smile. 'There is no hurry.'

Foraging among the debris of mashed-up trees and bushes, they found some coconuts – nothing much but sufficient to appease the extremes of hunger. Food was going to be a problem to them in future, Marriott saw. There would be fish, of course, and presumably the pigs and monkeys had, for the most part anyway, survived the typhoon, but the fruit must have been stripped from the trees and the vegetable patches up the valley flattened. It might be months before things returned to normal.

He looked, as he had done from time to time, at the mountain top. The sky was perceptibly lightening, and details were beginning to stand out. There was a hut there, or something man-made, at any rate. But who could possibly have built up there, and for what reason? It made no sense at all.

They saw more of it as the sun rose: light gleamed from glass and metal. It was not a hut – at least not like any kind of hut Marriott had seen before. A rectangular shape appeared to be bedded into the side of the mountain, immediately below the summit, and to carry above it what looked like a glass cupola. The design, it was obvious, was sophisticated, entirely at variance with the island's primitive wilderness. That was all that could be seen, though. There was nothing which provided a hint as to its purpose.

They were all curious now, Lydia in particular. The hunt for Yasha and Susan could wait, she said; their immediate objective must be to climb the mountain, to get a closer look at whatever it was that crowned it. Billy made some suggestion about clearing things up around the camp first, but she brushed that aside.

'We'll need something better than coconuts when we get back if we're going to go up the mountain,' Billy said.

'All right,' she said impatiently. 'You stay here and organize things. Tony and I will go and find out what it is.'

Billy looked as though he might query this for a moment, but in the end he nodded.

'Go ahead. I'll get them on tidying up.'

Lydia turned to Sweeney. 'Are you coming up with us?' she asked.

'No.' He shook his head. 'I will stay here until you return.' The two of them set out along the valley path; though path hardly described it – torn-up trees and bushes blocked it in places and they had to climb over or go round them. Lydia was very cheerful. She said:

'We can keep our eyes open for those two on the way – we'll have a better chance of seeing them from higher up.'

But the first recognition was of neither Yasha nor Susan, but Lydia's parrot. They found it dangling from a jutting branch by its string: the end of the string had caught on the splintered wood. It was dead, and had lost a lot of its feathers, presumably from being thrown against other trees. Its ugly twisted feet drooped beneath it.

Lydia studied it. 'Poor Poll.' She laughed. 'Well, there's supper for us, if nothing better turns up!'

Her callousness shocked and fascinated him; and gave him a sense of pride in having been chosen to replace Billy as her lieutenant. They would rule the island together. Or, rather, she would rule and he, serving her, rule the others. He mentioned to her the problem of future food supplies, which had occurred to him earlier.

'We'll be all right,' she said with confidence. 'There's plenty of vigour in this island. Things will grow again very quickly.'

'I suppose you're right.' Her ebullience sustained him. 'Yes, we'll manage.'

There was destruction everywhere and, occasionally, death. Two monkeys, clinging together, in a tangle of broken branches, a large and a small one. Mother and child, presumably. At first Marriott thought that some quirk of the wind had stripped off the mother's fur, but looking more closely he saw that this was not the case: she was practically hairless by nature. The baby seemed to be normal, asleep in its mother's arms, but its head lolled lifelessly to one side.

They toiled on up the slopes. The sea came in sight below them. They could tell it was angry still, but from this height the white caps were no more than a lacy decoration under the smooth blue sky. They stopped and looked down.

Lydia said: 'It's peaceful up here.' Her own voice was calm, without the feverishness that had characterized it lately. 'And fresh.'

The air was fresh. And cool, and sappy. There was the tang of vegetation, broken but not yet rotting, and the lingering smell of rain. Far below they could see the camp, and a small figure moving across the clearing.

'I've always liked mountains,' she said. 'I remember, when I was eight or nine, my father took me to Snowdonia. We stayed at a hotel near Llanberis.' Her voice was dry and even. 'There had been a lot of trouble at home – between him and my mother – and I thought this was a special treat, he was taking me away, perhaps, and we'd live together by ourselves. Then this woman came to the hotel. They met – by accident apparently. But her name was Nancy, and she had red hair, and I'd overheard one of the scenes at home, heard my mother shout at him about his red-headed Nancy. So I knew that taking me there had only been a way of meeting her.'

Marriott, listening to her, looked out over the sea. Those endless empty waters – at the beginning he had watched them impatiently for the sight of a ship that might offer rescue. The thought had faded now, and he was not sure he wanted to revive it.

Lydia said: 'I left the hotel when I realized that. It was about ten in the morning – they'd pretended to introduce themselves over breakfast – with that thick mountain mist everywhere. I walked to the place where the railway started, and began climbing up beside the line. The little trains passed me from time to time, and I hid in the mist so no one would see me. I went on and on – I was cold and miserable and I began to get hungry. And then quite suddenly, from one second to the next almost, I was in clear sunshine and the top of the mountain was right in front of me, only a few hundred feet away. It was wonderful, one of the most wonderful things that ever happened to me.'

'But you had to come down again.'

'Yes,' she said, 'I had to come down. Some people who had gone up by train and who were staying at the hotel recognized me. They gave me chocolate, and took me down by train, and handed me over to my father. He wasn't angry. I'd just been adventurous, he thought, and he liked me to show spirit.'

He said, after a moment: 'I suppose we'd better be getting on.'

'Yes.' She roused herself, shivering. 'I feel clammy suddenly. I'm probably getting that bug Roger's got.'

'Do you want to go down?'

'No.' She shook her head. 'I'm all right.'

In a declivity, a little further on, they found an orange tree. Its fruit had been stripped from it and thrown against a mossy bank: a few of them remained stuck in the thick moss as though growing there. Others were scattered in the tangle of leaves and broken branches. They picked some up, and ate them. They were bruised, split open in many cases, but they were refreshing. Marriott put more in his pockets, and Lydia inside her blouse – she had dressed before starting the climb.

The last part of the ascent was through undergrowth which, even though mostly stripped of leaves and broken down, was thick enough to obscure their view of the summit. They came out of this abruptly, to find themselves on a slope of rock only a hundred feet or so below the lantana scrub which had barred the way on the previous ascent. The typhoon had had no effect on this; the band of thorns stretched unbroken as far as the eye could see in either direction. Directly ahead the lantana ran up almost to the foot of the building.

It nestled into a slight concavity just below the crest. The lower part was of metal – aluminium, Marriott thought – with metal struts bracing it and steps leading to a closed door. There were no windows in that part. The cupola rose above it, a hemisphere of thick glass or transparent plastic. The base would be about fifteen feet across, ten feet high; it was difficult to tell how deep, but a dozen feet at least judging by the cupola, whose base measured about that much. These were approximate estimates. They were still walking towards it, but the lantana would keep them from getting within a hundred feet of it. To one side of the cupola various radio antennae rose up.

The instruments he could see behind the glass baffled him. Casting back to the Physics Lab at school did not help; there was nothing which resembled anything he had known then. And the sun dazzled on the protecting glass and on the glass and metal inside; it was not easy to look at.

Lydia said: 'A door. There can't be anybody there now, can there?'

'No signs. But who built it, anyway? And for what purpose?'

'Something to do with astronomy,' she hazarded. 'What do they call them? An observatory? They do build them on mountains, don't they? And they have domes.'

'With a cloud covering it more or less permanently? It doesn't seem very likely.'

'I suppose not. Those thorns – do you think they grew round it naturally, or were they planted?'

Marriott said slowly: 'If it were being left with no one in charge ... I suppose thorn would be a way of keeping animals out. Monkeys can do a lot of damage, for instance. They wouldn't take long to rip down those aerials.'

'So there is no one there, you think? They built it and left it. Why?'

'I wish I knew. I wish I could recognize just one of those laboratory instruments behind that glass.'

'Laboratory? Is it a laboratory, then? But why would anyone build a laboratory up here, and then leave it?'

He was not sure which came first, the image or the realization. But in his mind's eye he saw the dead parrot hanging by its string, with its pitiful distorted feet, and at that moment knew the answer. It was monstrous, but it was the only thing that fitted. He said, trying to keep his voice from choking:

'No, that's not the laboratory. This is the laboratory. All this.' He gestured. 'The island itself.'

'The island? What do you mean?'

'All these misshapen birds and animals, the odd plants – those patches planted out down in the valley.' She was still bewildered. 'An experiment in the effects of radiation. Gamma rays, I suppose. The sort of thing you get from nuclear tests, atom bomb explosions.'

He saw understanding dawning on her. He said bitterly:

'I suppose this was someone's brain-wave. Tests in laboratories are artificial by their nature. What you want is a field test, going on over a period of years, with the test animals living normal wild lives, mutations in competition with non-mutations and with each other. I suppose the monkeys were brought in as being closest to the human. We ought to have known you don't get them on these islands.'

'Do you mean it's still going on – the experiment?'

'Why not? They put the lantana round it to protect it. It's going on, all right.'

'The dachshund pig …' she said. 'The white monkey!'

'And the hen. The overgrown hen that couldn't fly. We ought to have guessed something like this. There were enough clues.'

There was a pause. Marriott was aware of a faint distant humming noise. Cicadas? Or generators up there behind the gleaming metal? Nuclear-powered, perhaps, to solve refuelling problems. He made a grimace. Convenient, and appropriate.

'Radiation,' Lydia said. 'Isn't there something else I read? Can't you get ill from it?'

He nodded. 'Radiation sickness.'

'Roger,' she said, 'and Toni. Me now. Could it be that?' She considered. 'I suppose it could be.' She shook her head. 'I feel dizzy. Let's get away from here. I don't like looking at it.'

'I don't, either.'

'What are you doing?'

Marriott scrabbled in the dirt, found a stone and threw it.

It bounced harmlessly, with a faint clang, off the metal below the cupola. He picked up another and then, with a helpless gesture, let it drop. They turned and began to walk back the way they had come.

26

IT WAS HUNGER that dominated Willeway after the storm; the few coconuts that they found near the camp served only to put an edge to his appetite. He suggested that he should go out foraging for more, but Billy vetoed that. He needed Willeway and Candie to help clear up the camp and put up at least a temporary hut on the ruins of the old ones. Toni and Katey were to carry out the search for food. Sweeney had wandered off somewhere in the direction of the beach.

Billy kept them at it, despite Candie's claim to be sick. Gradually some order emerged, and they found enough serviceable in the way of poles and struts to be able to start on the erection of a hut. There was a break for a snack when the women returned. Coconut again; Willeway chewed miserably at his portion. The break was a short one before Billy got them back on the job. He told Willeway to sort out good-sized and intact palm leaves from a pile of leaves and branches that the wind had piled up against the hillside beyond the ruins of the kitchen.

Willeway performed his task without much enthusiasm, his mind running on the delights of food. Obsessed with the idea, he almost failed to recognize the reality when it was in front of him. Embedded in the leaves, stridently violet against the green, was a cooked taro root from the kitchen store. He pulled it free carefully, expecting to find it mashed up; but it was whole and undamaged. The leaves had cushioned and protected it.

He looked at it thoughtfully. Under ordinary circumstances he was very fond of taro, but now the thought of eating it was tantalizing and exquisite. It was about eight inches long, three inches across. Divided up there would be enough for a small portion each, tiny if some were kept for Lydia and Marriott, as it certainly would be. Studying it, he felt the saliva flow in his mouth. He would not have minded sharing it with Katey – there was enough for that – but she was in Toni's company, and, in any case, bringing others in increased the chance of Billy discovering it. There was only one sensible thing to do.

A quick look round showed Billy and Candie busy with the poles for the new hut. He was not wearing a shirt so he could not slip it inside. He broke the root in half and pushed a half into each of the pockets of his slacks. Then, as unobtrusively as possible, he began walking down the path beside the stream. He had almost crossed the clearing when Billy yelled at him.

'Where the hell do you think you're going?'

'Only down to the heads.'

'Well, don't take all day over it. We've got plenty to do before nightfall.'

Willeway walked on, quickening his step. As he reached the edge of the trees – the shattered hulks that passed for trees – Billy called him again.

'Fatty! Come up here a minute.'

He called back: 'It's a bit urgent, Billy. I really won't be long, though.'

'You slack bastard, come here when I tell you.'

He went awkwardly, letting his hands fall loosely against his thighs to cover the bulges in his pockets. But it was no good. Billy waited until he was in front of him and roughly knocked his arm away. The end of the half of taro was protruding from the pocket. Billy pulled it out.

'And the rest in the other pocket, I suppose. Hand it over.'

When he had done so, Billy swung his free arm in a sudden blow that caught Willeway on the side of the neck and sent him sprawling against the side of the hut they were erecting. Before he could recover, Billy had grabbed a length of cane and was lashing into him with it. He cowered away, and the blows landed on his back and upper arms. They were painful and he found himself yelling for mercy.

'I ought to cut you to ribbons,' Billy said, 'you fat-gutted twister. Stealing rations at a time like this – and with all the fat you've got on your carcase.'

Katey and Toni had been attracted by the disturbance and came over to see what was happening. Billy told them. Willeway saw their faces, Toni's blank, his wife's contemptuous.

He said: 'I was hungry …'

'And do you think we weren't?' Billy said.

He raised the cane, threateningly. Willeway flinched from it, and at that Billy started hitting him again. The blows rained so savagely and thickly on him that he had the illusion that the others had joined in, that they were all beating him and would go on doing so until they had ripped his flesh to shreds. He bawled helplessly and abjectly for relief. When it came, it was unexpected. He heard, above his own yells, Katey's voice. She was not pleading for him, though. She said:

'Lydia and Tony – they're back.'

The beating ceased. He lowered his arm cautiously and looked up. Lydia and Marriott were coming across the clearing from the valley path. Billy held up half of the taro root in triumph.

'Fatty found this,' he said. 'He was sliding off on his own to stuff his gut with it. I've been touching him up a bit.'

Marriott said: 'Yes. So I see.'

His voice was flat, empty-sounding. Despite his concern for himself and the pain of the beating, Willeway was able to notice that they both seemed strange – vacant-looking, as though shocked. Billy said curiously:

'What is it? Something wrong?' Marriott did not answer right away. 'Did you find what it was up there?'

Marriott said: 'We found what it was.'

'Well?'

'This is an experimental island,' Marriott said. 'That thing up there is for producing hard radiation, to cause mutations in animals, birds, plants. It's a long-term experiment. God knows how long. I suppose it might be geared to run for twenty years or more.'

Billy said: 'You're not saying it might be twenty years before someone comes to take us off? That's not what you're telling us, is it?'

Candie, in a whisper, said: 'All these monstrosities ...' He turned to Toni. 'The two-headed rat you thought you saw that day – it adds up, doesn't it?'

Billy said stubbornly: 'Even if it were meant to go on for twenty years, they might come back from time to time to have a look at things. No reason why they shouldn't.'

'We're not talking about being rescued,' Marriott said. 'That's not important now.'

'It is to me!'

In a terrible voice, Katey said: 'You mean, radiation that deforms things in the womb?'

'Not just in the womb,' Candie said. 'In the seed, too.'

Katey stared at them. 'What am I carrying? A monster? It's not true, is it? Some kind of a joke?'

Toni sighed, and crumpled. Candie got down and raised her head. 'She's fainted,' he said. 'Get some water.'

Billy went for it, docilely, as though the new turn in events had shaken him back into his old role of steward. Marriott, looking at her, said:

'I don't see why it should hit her like that. She's not pregnant.'

Katey said heavily: 'She is. We both are.'

'She can't be! She was told she couldn't have children without an operation.'

'Perhaps the radiation has done something about that, too. She's pregnant, all right.' Her eyes were full of misery and hatred. 'She'll have hers at the same time as I have mine, or soon after. What will they look like? What will they be?'

Lydia spoke for the first time since their return.

'If we live that long.' She looked at Candie. 'That sickness you and Toni had. I've got it now. That's from the radiation, too, isn't it? How long does it take to kill you? Does anyone know?'

'I suppose it could be radiation sickness,' Candie said. 'Except ...' He looked a little more cheerful. 'It hasn't killed the animals off, has it?'

Marriott said: 'Perhaps it kills some, and others survive it.' He shook his head. 'We don't know much about it, do we?'

Billy brought the water back in a half-shell. He knelt and splashed it deliberately on Toni's face. She stirred and opened her eyes, and Candie eased her into a sitting position.

Marriott said to her: 'Is it true?'

She looked up at him, but her face was a mask.

'Yes, it's true.'

'I didn't know ...'

She cut him off. 'It doesn't matter.'

'Nothing matters,' Katey said. 'Nothing. We may die, or we may live long enough to give birth to monsters.'

'I don't understand it,' Candie said. 'It must be a government thing, mustn't it? Surely they couldn't set up a place like this without warning people?'

Marriott said: 'They couldn't publish it. Apart from the question of military secrecy, there would be all the cranks and abolitionists to consider. They would be heading here in rowing boats.'

'Accidents like ours, though,' Candie said. 'Surely they would have to take precautions against that kind of thing.'

'Perhaps they do,' Marriott said. 'A naval patrol round the island. The *Diana* might just have slipped through the cordon by chance.'

'We haven't seen any ships.'

'They would keep their distance – below the horizon, probably. To make quite sure the radiation didn't affect them.'

Toni said: 'That last night on the *Diana* ...'

'What about it?' Marriott asked her.

'She had no lights. Do you remember the lights went out in the cabin?'

He nodded. 'The generator failed.'

'I went up on deck,' Toni said. 'I couldn't sleep. The navigation lights were out, too.'

Marriott stared at her. 'Are you sure?'

'Yes. I saw Sweeney. I asked him about them. He said it didn't matter because we were so far from normal shipping lanes.'

There was silence while the implications went home. Even dazed as he was, Willeway got the point. But he could not believe it. He said:

'Sweeney wouldn't …'

His voice trailed off. Candie said:

'The party at his house – the night he asked us on the cruise – I was talking to a woman – wife of some junior minister – and she was saying how Sweeney knew all sorts of top secret stuff. He'd surprised her husband by knowing about some hush-hush project in his own department. He could have known about this.'

'So he bought the *Diana*,' Marriott said, 'brought us all here – and scuttled her? Could he have done that?'

'Nothing in it,' Billy said. 'A heap of oily waste in the engine room, and a fuse laid.' He jerked his head up, remembering. 'That boy said the bar was open. I knew I'd locked up; but Sweeney could have opened it again. If they were down there, getting drunk, they wouldn't notice the fire until it was too late to do anything about it – or see how it had started.'

'Scuttle a ship that cost him maybe a hundred thousand?' Candie asked.

'What's a hundred thousand to Sweeney?' Marriott said. 'He's paid that much for a painting before now.'

'But why?' Katey said. '*Why?*'

'Why not? A little experiment of his own. Perhaps he thought the one the government were running didn't go far enough. Or perhaps just curiosity – an urge to meddle.'

Lydia said harshly: 'He picked us carefully for it, didn't he? I wondered at the beginning what we had in common. The answer is that as far as he is concerned, we're none of us any loss to society. Sweeney's victims for the sacrifice.'

Toni said: 'He's sacrificed himself, too.'

'I think he's always been willing to do that,' Candie said. 'But only if he could find a big enough funeral pyre.'

It was true, Willeway thought miserably, that the idea was consistent with what one knew of Sweeney. It had a weird and horrible magnificence that was typical of him. Clutching shreds of hope, he said:

'But even so – it might be a practical joke of some kind?'

'With those freak birds and animals?' Marriott said contemptuously. 'And that installation up on the mountain would strain even Sweeney's financial resources. I don't feel like laughing.'

Lydia's eyes darted about, as though suddenly conscious of an absence. 'Where is he?' she asked.

Billy said: 'He went down towards the beach. He didn't say where he was going.'

'We could go after him,' Lydia said slowly, 'or we could wait here until he comes back. I think we'll wait. It's better to let him come back.'

'And then?' Willeway asked.

Lydia turned her eyes on him, but did not answer. Her eyes had a strange light, a terrible intensity. They frightened him, but behind the fear he felt a growing tingling excitement.

27

ONCE SHE HAD GOT OVER the first shock of finding herself pregnant, Katey had found herself taking the idea placidly. She was aware of the difficulties that might lie ahead, but unconcerned by them. She had a supreme confidence that all would be well, whatever happened. Armoured in this assurance, she had watched the antics of the others - Billy, Lydia, Marriott, even Willeway – with a tolerant and indifferent contempt. The only thing that counted was the child in her womb.

The shock of Marriott's revelation about the island was altogether deeper and more shattering, one whose effect grew stronger instead of weaker as the significance bedded itself more firmly in her mind. Anger turned to despair, and despair turned back to anger – more savage, much less rational – and bitter hatred. She wanted them to go and look for Sweeney right away rather than wait for his return, and urged this on the others. She clashed with Lydia over it.

'There's no sense in hunting him,' Lydia said. 'He'll come back.'

'He may not.'

'He will. Sweeney will.'

'I want to find him now!'

As she said that she was conscious that behind the despair and anger there was still a flicker of hope. Sweeney would have an explanation. It was all some kind of joke – monstrous, but a joke still. The truth could not possibly be what it seemed. They must find Sweeney, and he would make things right.

Lydia said: 'Don't be a damn' fool. There's no point at all in going after him. He's got to come back.' She smiled, her thin face terrible with it. 'And we're in no hurry.'

'I don't want to wait.'

'Go, then,' Lydia said indifferently. She turned away. 'The rest of us are staying here.'

But she could not go on her own: she needed the comfort and safety of the group. Half-heartedly Billy got them back on the job of clearing things up and she went through the motions of work, dazed and wretched but glad of some kind of activity. They found food among the debris – cooked bread-fruit and the remains of a smoked ham – and she ate with the same dulled automatism. Then Willeway, on Billy's instruction, cleared the entrance to the hollow in the rock where they had kept the gourds of wine. The gourds were still there, undamaged. One was passed round, and she drank heavily from it.

The drinking, once started, went on steadily. Toni refused altogether, and Candie after the first drink, but the others showed no restraint. Katey herself felt the flush of intoxication fold protectingly round her. Late in the afternoon pretence of work was abandoned. The sun had dropped behind the shoulder of Sweeney's Hill, but it was very hot. They lay on a carpet of tattered palm leaves, and drank the wine, and looked up, from time to time, at Mount Proteus. The summit was still bare, though light tendrils of mist had begun to form, streaming away to the north, and the sun still shone on it, dazzling from glass and metal, confirming that this was reality and no dream. And yet she would not accept the reality. Sweeney would change it. Sweeney would make a sign, and the cloud would cover the mountain again, and that would be all there was: cloud and a mountain. She tipped the gourd to her lips and spilled wine down her neck as she drank.

Without even a tremor of disgust she watched Lydia take first Billy and then Marriott down the slope to the dubious shelter of the shattered trees. She did not look after them, but knew they had not gone far: Lydia's cries, more of triumph than abandon, came plainly enough through the air stripped of birdsong. What had happened to the birds, she wondered? Flung out, those that were not crushed, over the barren emptiness of the ocean, toys of the storm and dropped casually as toys are. A confetti of feathered bodies scattered on the water. How clever of God, she thought drunkenly, to mark each tiny fall.

Lydia had come back with Marriott and was lying between him and Billy, staring up at the mountain. She had stripped herself of clothes again, and the nakedness of her body was wild, rapacious, unslacked. Looking around her suddenly, she said:

'Where's Roger?'

There was no reply, and she repeated the question peremptorily. Marriott started to laugh, but a look from Lydia reduced him to silence.

Katey said: 'They went off somewhere.'

'They? When?'

'Five minutes or so ago,' Billy said. He grinned hazily. 'I thought he wanted to show her something.'

Marriott began to get to his feet. 'He can't …'

Lydia pulled him down. 'Never mind.'

'My wife!'

'What are you worrying about?' She patted him in a proprietary fashion. 'They'll be back. You can beat her. Maybe we'll all beat her. Make a new law; sex confined to the ruling classes. Go and get some more to drink, Tony – this one's empty.'

Katey said: 'Why hasn't Sweeney come back yet? Do you think he's coming back?'

'No hurry.' Lydia waved her arm lazily. 'He'll be back. Amuse ourselves for the time being. Joe!'

Her husband, Katey thought, was even drunker than the rest. He looked at Lydia blankly, but with a touch of apprehension. Did he think, Katey wondered, that he too was being summoned to Lydia's arms? She had an insane urge to laugh at the thought.

'Do something to amuse us,' Lydia commanded. 'Give us a song, Joe.' She giggled. 'Sing us the song you sang at your mother's wedding!'

He said feebly: 'I can't sing, Lydia.'

'Come on.'

'I can't …'

'Sing,' she said implacably. 'We can make you if we have to.'

He hesitated and absurdly started singing *There is a happy land*. Lydia stared and then began laughing. Her laughter, peal on sharp peal, swamped the cracked and faltering voice. It was infectious, a communicating wave, and Marriott and Billy and then Katey herself joined in. She laughed until her body began to ache with it. Willeway looked at them inanely, half scared, half smiling.

The laughter subsided, and Lydia said:

'That was good. That was bloody good. No, we don't want you to sing again, Joe. You can do a dance for us now. Get up and show us a few steps.'

He essayed a laugh of his own, a weak effort which rapidly died away.

'I can't dance, Lydia,' he said. 'Anyway, I'm too drunk to dance.' He shook his head. 'Too drunk.'

'Get up,' she said. 'Get him up, Billy.'

Billy got up himself and, going behind Willeway, jerked him savagely to his feet. His hand, which had gripped the waistband of Willeway's trousers, released that hold to pluck at the roll of fat just above it. He said disgustedly:

'Enough lard to do fish and chips for the whole of London. You need some exercise, all right.' He tightened his grip and Willeway groaned. 'Come on, let's have you.'

'I can't unless you let go …'

'You're not trying.'

'Let him go, Billy,' Lydia said.

Billy released him, pushing him at the same time. He stumbled and almost fell. Katey thought how ridiculous he looked standing there, plump face sweating through the straggly beard. He said:

'I don't know how to …'

He cringed as Billy slapped him hard under the ribs. Lydia said:

'He wants something to dance to. That's what it is, Joe, isn't it?' He nodded quickly. 'We'll all sing, and Joey boy will dance for us. What shall we sing? Something lively. We want something that will really get him going. Something with a beat.'

She launched into *Swanee* and, after a moment, Marriott and Billy took it up. Lydia was beating time with her right hand as she sang. Breaking off, she shouted:

'O.K., Joe, start dancing! Or do you want Billy to beat time on that blubber?'

Willeway began to dance. He shuffled ridiculously from one foot to another, sweating and wobbling. Leading the others, Lydia quickened the tempo and shouted at him: 'Speed it up! You can do better than that. Get a stick and smarten him up, Billy.'

Billy went to do as he was told and Willeway, anticipating more punishment, jigged faster. His mouth was open and he was gasping. Katey felt the urge to laugh again. The impulse rose in her and she was on the point of giving way to it when she noticed something else: Lydia had abruptly stopped singing and was staring past her, past the cavorting figure of Willeway, towards the beach path. Katey turned her head to follow the glance. Sweeney was standing on the edge of the clearing, watching them.

They all fell quiet. Willeway was the last to realize what had happened. He turned to Sweeney and said with relief:

'You've come back.'

Sweeney said: 'Don't let me interfere with your amusements.'

Lydia and Marriott got to their feet and Katey, after a moment, followed suit. Sweeney came towards them across the clearing. The swift tropic twilight was beginning to fall and he seemed to bulk larger than ever against the shadowy trees.

In a controlled voice, Lydia said: 'We've been waiting for you, Sweeney.'

'Have you?' He smiled. 'Not too impatiently, I hope.'

Lydia jerked her arm up towards Mount Proteus. There was no sun on it now but the outline of the mountain was still sharp against the deep blue sky; one could see the thin veil of mist trailing from it and the jutting projection of the building just below the summit.

'We know what it is up there,' she said.

He looked at her. 'Do you?'

'We've been putting some things together. Why did you bring us here?'

'Is that a real question, or rhetorical?'

She said slowly, her speech slurred by drink: 'You tricked us, Sweeney. No lights in the night – Toni told us about that. And the ship set on fire. That was no accident. You knew all about it before you brought us, didn't you? And when we were marooned here – you knew what it was in the cloud.'

He stared at her impassively, making no reply.

'I'm sick,' she said 'Sick! Temperature – the shivers ... Roger had it first, now I've got it. Radiation sickness, isn't that right? We'll all get it. We're all going to rot away and die.'

Her voice was harsh, stark with a despair that may have been alcoholic but here, in the dusk, surrounded by the shattered pillars of the trees, was convincing.

Sweeney said quietly: 'I am here with you.'

'That's right.' Her face twisted into bewilderment. 'Why? Are you mad, Sweeney? Is that it?'

'Define true madness,' Sweeney said. 'Then, perhaps, one might answer that question.' He pointed up at the crest of the mountain. 'Those who put that up there: mad or sane?'

Marriott said: 'But there was some point to that – some purpose.'

'Purpose divides us from the beasts,' Sweeney said. 'But does it set us above or below them? Perhaps we should be happier if we rejoined the universal pageant. Perhaps we will.'

'Is that why you brought us here?' Marriott asked. 'To be the same as the beasts?'

'You must be mad,' Lydia said.

'Maybe not,' Billy said. 'Maybe he's got something that keeps him from getting sick like the rest of us. Some kind of pills.'

Sweeney made no reply to this. It was Marriott who, after a pause, said:

'No. That's not possible.' He had drunk as much as the others but his speech was less slurred, almost normal. 'But why? Why? A sacrifice? For what? Because you thought they didn't go far enough? Or to show them up?' His voice had a pleading note. 'Tell us why.'

They were grouped round him, Lydia, Marriott, Willeway and Katey herself in front, Billy to his right, a little above and behind him. The anger which had begun to rise again in Katey when she saw him standing, motionless, on the other side of the clearing, had become clamant, and Marriott's seeming deference whittled it to an edge. They stood there, waiting, as though for a revelation. Sweeney would say something, anything – it made no difference what – and they would accept it. Because they wanted to accept it. Because Sweeney said it. They would be reconciled to sickness, death even, because Sweeney told them to be, because he was with them. But nothing would reconcile her – nothing. She leaned towards him, and said:

'Sweeney.'

He turned his gaze to her. 'Yes.'

'Up there on the hill – when I went to you … you remember.'

'I remember.'

'You told me to go on hoping. You told me I would be all right.'

'Yes.'

'You didn't tell me I had a monster in my belly, did you? You didn't tell me that.' Her voice rose as she spoke. She was spitting at him, but he did not draw back. 'You knew I was pregnant, and you said I would be all right. You brought me here to conceive a monster.'

He stared at her without speaking. 'A monster!' she screamed. 'A monster, Sweeney!'

He still said nothing. Her hatred spiralled up against him and became fury, blind, senseless, unappeasable by any retribution but that of pain, physical vengeance for the physical outrage which had been done to her. She threw herself forward at him, hands clawing for the broad impassive face that looked down at her. He moved back slightly and her hands caught at his neck. She was aware that Lydia had flung herself at him, too, followed a moment later by Marriott. The three of them hung on him, pulling him down. She heard her voice shrieking, and the voices of the others. His shoulders bowed under their weight: soon he must topple and fall.

But he did not. He braced himself, shook himself as a mastiff might against terriers, pressed his arms forward and scattered them. Katey was pushed, staggering, away, and saw that he had shaken free of Lydia and Marriott as well. Her shrieks turned to sobs of rage and frustration.

'Listen,' Sweeney began. 'Listen ...'

She had seen Billy moving behind him, but until its blade gleamed in a swift arc through the air had not realized he had the axe. Its edge caught Sweeney below the right ear with a dull spongey sound. Blood jetted, and he sank forward, knees buckling and then the great body dropping, a dead weight, to the ground. He lay on his face. His head was half severed from the trunk, and the blood still fountained up from the hideous wound.

They stared at the body in silence for a while. The savage joy Katey felt was mixed with awe. It was incredible that he should be dead – Sweeney reduced to the anonymity of a corpse. When

Lydia flung herself down, she thought this was some revulsion of feeling, that she was weeping – for what they had done.

But it was not that. Lydia pressed herself to the body, scrabbled at the wound itself, daubed herself with blood.

'He's dead,' she crooned. 'Sweeney's dead ...' She looked up, naked and bloody, at the others. 'Drink!' she cried. 'Eat!'

The mist came down, dark and red; and there was no way back.

28

From the moment that Marriott and Lydia came down from the mountain, Toni wanted to get away. She would have slipped off earlier but for her concern for Candie: he had another shivering fit, and he looked ill. She felt helpless in that there was nothing practical she could do for him, but she stayed by him and talked to him, and he seemed glad of that. Their isolation became more marked as the others began drinking heavily; they talked in low voices but no one was paying any attention to them anyway and they were unlikely to be overheard among the raised voices and increasingly drunken laughter around them.

Candie asked: 'What do you think will happen – when Sweeney comes back?'

She shook her head. 'I don't know.'

'Do you think he did – bring us here deliberately?'

'It looks like it, doesn't it? I suppose so.'

'Do you hate him?'

She said slowly: 'No. But it's different for me.'

'But you are …?'

'Yes. I'm pretty sure of that. And it was something I thought could never happen. I'm glad.'

'Even if …'

She smiled. 'Birth is a good thing. Any kind of birth.'

And that was true. Whatever it was that was growing within her, she loved it, and would go on loving it. She had fainted with the shock of the news but, recovering consciousness, it was a wave of love for the unborn child that moved her. She had meant it when she told Marriott that it did not matter. What mattered was that the child lived, that her body nourished it, that, in the end, it would be born, to be cared for, protected – loved, above all.

Candie said wryly: 'And death? Is that a good thing?'

'The animals don't seem to have died,' she pointed out. 'Not even the crippled ones.'

'No.' He paused. 'I don't hate him, either.' He glanced at Lydia, who was preparing to strip her blouse off. 'There are some others I'm beginning to dislike.'

'How do you feel now?'

'A bit better. Fever quietening down again, I think.'

'Well enough to walk?'

'I think so. Where?'

'Away from here.'

'Will they try to stop us?'

'Not if we choose the right moment.'

The moment was not long delayed. Lydia took Marriott off and Billy was lying on his back, staring up at the sky. He might even have been asleep. She touched Candie's arm.

'Now.'

Billy was not asleep. She saw him turn his head to look at them as they walked across the clearing, but he did not say anything. They walked among the stripped boles of the trees. It was very quiet, still and hot: with the leaves gone there was no protection from the sun.

Because Lydia and Marriott had gone the other way, she had taken the inland path, but once the clearing was lost to view behind them she began bearing to the left. Candie made no comment, and asked no further questions about where they were heading; he had some difficulty in walking and stumbled from time to time. She put an arm out to steady him, and for a moment he leaned against her, as though taking strength from the touch of her body.

In a tired, heavy voice, he said: 'You're a good girl, Toni.'

'Can you go on now?'

He nodded. 'Yes.'

They came down to the beach only a couple of hundred yards from the rocky escarpment that barred the way to the little valley, and at this point Candie seemed suddenly to become aware of his surroundings, of the direction they were taking.

He said: 'They'll find us there.'

'They will find us anywhere. But at least we've got away for the moment.'

'That's true.'

They reached the ridge, and she said:

'Climbing or swimming – which can you manage best?'

'Swimming.' He brushed his forehead with his hand. 'It will be cooler, too.'

'You go first. I'll follow.'

She waded out after him, glad of the water's freshness. The sea still showed evidence of the storm, even here inside the reef: long waves rolled in to break in a grumble of surf against the sands. They plunged forward and began swimming. They were clothed – Candie in shirt and trousers, herself in slacks and shirt. Their clothes would dry on them quickly enough, but she worried a little about Candie, unwell as he was. It was a good thing that she felt well now, since he might need looking after. She smiled to herself at the thought. Whatever happened one went on making plans for the future.

Rounding the point, Candie felt weak. She saw him falter, swam abreast of him, and got him to hang on to her shoulders. It was not too difficult; the breakers carried them both in towards shore. She had to help him out of the water, too, and when she had done so he collapsed on the warm sand, only a few feet from the hissing foam of the tide. He began apologizing, but she cut him short.

'Never mind. We've made it, anyway. Rest and get your strength back.'

While he rested, Toni looked about her. There was storm damage here, but not so extensive as in the other part of the island; trees were less shattered and not all had been stripped of their leaves. Presumably the valley's confining walls had provided some shelter. The wall ahead of them, the eastern wall, in particular, was precipitous, almost an overhang. She looked at it more closely. At its foot a rampart had been constructed of loose rocks, a barricade three or four feet high. She saw something move there, and then the figures stood up and were plainly visible. They were Susan and Yasha. They came from behind the wall, and walked towards them.

Yasha asked: 'Is he all right?'

'Roger? Yes. A bit exhausted.'

Yasha made an explanatory gesture towards the barricade.

'We thought the others might be with you.'

Toni shook her head. 'We left them at the camp. They were drinking.'

'And Sweeney?'

'He went off this morning. He hasn't come back.'

Susan said dolefully: 'We thought he might do something.'

'I don't know.' Toni looked up; she realized that here, in this valley, one could not see the summit of Proteus – it was hidden by the mountain slopes. These two knew nothing of what the lifting of the cloud had revealed. She did not particularly want to tell them, but they would have to know sooner or later. She told them, as briefly as possible, and they listened without interrupting. When she had finished, Yasha said:

'You are sure this is true?'

'They saw the building with the instruments. They seemed sure of it.'

Susan said: 'It's the only thing that makes sense, isn't it? There had to be some explanation of the mutations.'

'I have seen no freak plants here,' Yasha said, 'in this valley.'

'That makes sense, too,' Susan said. 'The overhang would blanket the radiations.'

There was a silence. Yasha said, at last: 'Well, there is nothing we can do about it.'

His voice was calm, dismissive. It truly seemed less important here, Toni thought. But she was glad they did not know about her pregnancy; she decided she would ask Candie to help keep her secret. They would have to know eventually, but for the moment it could be kept.

She said: 'You came back here, then?' Yasha nodded. 'Before the storm?'

'Yes.'

'They will look for you here.'

'That was why we built ourselves a defence.'

'Not much of a one,' Toni said critically.

'We have throwing-stones,' Yasha said. 'And I have been trying to make a bow, to fire arrows.' He smiled ruefully. 'So far with little success. The vines are not strong enough.'

'They have a gun. And once inside the valley they could starve you out.'

'We have some food there, and a little water. You are right, though. But any kind of defence is better than none.'

Toni nodded. 'Yes.'

'And now that you are here, we are four, and they are only five. Not counting Sweeney.'

'I don't think there's any point in counting Sweeney,' Toni said. 'Either way.'

When Candie had recovered sufficiently they went to the small refuge behind the rampart. From there one had a good view of anyone climbing the opposite valley wall or swimming round the point into the bay. There was, as Yasha had said, food there – bananas, coconuts, oranges and a few avocadoes – and Candie and Toni were given some. Further up the valley, Susan explained, there was a patch which the typhoon had spared completely. When it was dusk, and one could be fairly sure there would be no invasion from the outside that day, Yasha would take a vine-sack up there to replenish stocks.

They talked peacefully and easily together as the afternoon declined. They did not discuss the installation on the top of

Proteus, nor the mutations, nor, for that matter, the others on the island. Toni realized that this should have seemed unnatural, but in fact it was not. There was a contentment about them which she could not have defined, but which was very real. There were some birds in this valley – presumably they too had found shelter – and their song was loud and lazy on the air as evening came on.

Candie had fallen asleep by the time Yasha went off for the fruit, and the two women talked in low voices so as not to disturb him. Susan said:

'You won't go back to Tony.'

It was more statement than question and it crystallized feelings in Toni which had previously been vague.

'No,' she said. 'That's over.'

'Do you feel sad?'

'No.' She thought about that. 'A little sad that I don't feel sad, perhaps.'

'I know what you mean.' Susan paused. 'When all this started, I was – mixed up with someone. That's over, too. Over for me, I mean. I think it was over long ago as far as he was concerned. It's strange.' She looked out across the rampart. 'I have the feeling this valley has something to do with it. It was like that the first time I was here. And more than ever now.'

'And Yasha?'

Susan smiled. 'Yes, perhaps and Yasha. But there's no hurry, no urgency. One can wait, as long as one has time.'

There was a silence. They were probably both, Toni thought, thinking the same thing: that there might not be time, that all kinds of unpleasantness might be pressing close. But there was no evasion in not talking about them; simply a shared refusal to sully the peace of this moment, this place. Thinking of the child again, Toni felt a wave of joy. This was happiness. She had not known it before.

Yasha came back with breadfruit as well as bananas and oranges but they decided they could not risk trying to make a fire.

Perhaps tomorrow they would find a place further up the valley, where the smoke would be less likely to betray them. They lay down together for the night, tired but at ease with each other and their surroundings. Candie seemed rather better than he had been: he went to sleep quickly and slept tranquilly. Toni herself was awake for some time after the others, it seemed, had gone off. She felt tired but self-enraptured by thoughts about the change in herself, the tiny burgeoning creature whose heart-beats matched her own. It was a long time before the reverie merged into sleep.

Nevertheless she was the first to wake in the morning, and into clear and active consciousness. The sun was not yet up but the sky was pale with dawn, the air cool and fresh, the first birds calling up the valley. Not disturbing the others, she got up and slipped away to the water's edge. The sea was considerably calmer: ordinary waves rolled in to break and bubble at her feet. She prepared to throw her clothes off and wade in for a swim, but before she did so she looked out across the level grey to the paler grey of the horizon. A silhouette broke the line, long and low, faintly wreathed in smoke, unmistakably Naval.

She called to the others, softly at first and then, as the full significance of it came home, shouting across the quiet sands.

The ship's boat was a rakish affair, shallow-drafted, fibre-glass tricked out with stainless steel, and she came right up on to the sand, her outboards smartly whipped up at the moment of impact. There was a lieutenant aboard and four ratings, in the uniform of the United States Navy. The lieutenant was a stocky gingery man with bright blue eyes and a skin that gave the appearance of sweating even now, with the sun not yet up. His manner, as he elicited information from them, showed more annoyance than sympathy. Yasha did the talking. When he had finished, the lieutenant said abruptly:

'This is a prohibited island, and so marked in all charts.'

'Yes,' Yasha said, 'we thought it might be.' The lieutenant looked at him sharply. 'But we did not see the charts.'

'Your skipper did.'

'Yes. You had better discuss that with him.'

'We will,' the lieutenant said grimly. 'We most certainly will.'

'If it's prohibited,' Susan said, 'you might have put a better guard over it.'

He looked at her with distaste. 'That was not considered necessary.'

'Not necessary! Never mind madmen like Sweeney. Anyone might have been cast away here – from a shipwreck, for instance. To find themselves trapped here and under radiation bombardment ...'

His gaze which had gone to the others flicked back to her.

'You know about the installation, then?'

'Yes. We know.'

'Have you damaged it in any way?'

Susan stared at him. 'Of all the inhuman ...'

'Has it been damaged?'

'No. Not as far as we know.'

The lieutenant allowed himself a slight smile. 'You have been in no danger.'

'The mutations,' she said, 'the freak animals ...'

'The results of radiation, but the source is not continuous. The experiment, as I understand it, consisted in drenching the island heavily with hard radiation, and then waiting to see the effects on plant and animal life over a period of some generations. It was felt important that the ecology should re-establish its own equilibrium.'

'But the instruments are still there.'

'I hope so. The purpose of our present mission is to make sure the station has not been damaged by the typhoon. They may be reactivated at some future time if an extension of the experiment is thought necessary. But they are not active now.'

Susan looked at him doubtfully. 'Some of us have been ill – we thought, possibly, radiation sickness.' She gestured towards Candie. 'He has been quite ill.'

The lieutenant leaned forward slightly and stared at Candie. 'Symptoms?'

'My arms and legs feel heavy all the time. And I get feverish attacks, spells of dizziness …'

'The Medical Officer will know more about it,' the lieutenant said, 'but it sounds like the early stages of elephantiasis. It's endemic in these islands.' He smiled faintly again. 'Nothing to worry about as long as you catch it early. We've got drugs to cure it.'

'But not radiation sickness?'

'No. There is no radiation.'

Toni said: 'Then any children we might have … ?'

For the first time his expression showed some sympathy. 'Will be quite all right. There is no cause for concern, ma'am. And I think now, if you will come aboard, we'll go round and pick up the rest of your party.'

Although no attempt was made to move quietly, their arrival in the clearing did not waken them. They lay sprawled in their drunken sleep. Bringing up the rear, Toni heard the shocked exclamations from those in front before she saw what sprawled with them, bloody and hideous, a mutilated caricature of humanity. She felt sick, and closed her eyes. There was a silence. No one seemed to want to break it, or to step forward into the clearing.

It was Yasha who said at last: 'Would it not be best … simply to go away, to leave them here?'

The lieutenant's voice said: 'We can't do that.' The voice hardened. 'No one can evade responsibility for his actions. That's what civilization is founded on. That's what sets man above the beasts.'

He stepped forward into the clearing, and his detachment followed him. Toni opened her eyes, but she could not look at what lay in the clearing. Instead she looked up. The cloud had re-formed on Proteus: it was lined with pink and gold by the rising sun.

ALSO PUBLISHED BY THE SYLE PRESS

by Sam Youd as John Christopher

with an Introduction by Robert Macfarlane

THE DEATH OF GRASS

The Chung-Li virus has devastated Asia, wiping out the rice crop and leaving riots and mass starvation in its wake. The rest of the world looks on with concern, though safe in the expectation that a counter-virus will be developed any day. Then Chung-Li mutates and spreads. Wheat, barley, oats, rye: no grass crop is safe, and global famine threatens.

In Britain, where green fields are fast turning brown, the Government lies to its citizens, devising secret plans to preserve the lives of a few at the expense of the many.

Getting wind of what's in store, John Custance and his family decide they must abandon their London home to head for the sanctuary of his brother's farm in a remote northern valley.

And so they begin the long trek across a country fast descending into barbarism, where the law of the gun prevails, and the civilized values they once took for granted become the price they must pay if they are to survive.

This edition available in the US only

ISBN: 978-1-911410-00-3

www.deathofgrass.com

by Sam Youd as John Christopher

The Caves of Night

Five people enter the Frohnberg caves, three men and two women. In the glare of the Austrian sunshine, the cool underground depths seem an attractive proposition – until the collapse of a cave wall blocks their return to the outside world. Faced with an unexplored warren of tunnels and caves, rivers and lakes, twisting and ramifying under the mountain range, they can only hope that there is an exit to be found on the other side.

For Cynthia, the journey through the dark labyrinths mirrors her own sense of guilt and confusion about the secret affair she has recently embarked upon. And whilst it is in some ways a comfort to share this possibly lethal ordeal with her lover Albrecht, only her husband Henry has the knowledge and experience that may lead them all back to safety.

But can even Henry's sang froid and expertise be enough, with the moment fast approaching when their food supplies will run out, and the batteries of their torches fail, leaving them to stumble blindly through the dark?

ISBN: 978-0-9927686-8-3

www.thesylepress.com/the-caves-of-night

by Sam Youd as John Christopher

THE WHITE VOYAGE

Dublin to Dieppe to Amsterdam. A routine trip for the cargo ship *Kreya*, her Danish crew and handful of passengers. Brief enough for undercurrents to remain below the surface and secrets to stay buried.

The portents, though, are ominous. 'There are three signs,' the spiritualist warned. 'The first is when the beast walks free. The second is when water breaks iron ... The third is when horses swim like fishes.'

Captain Olsen, a self-confessed connoisseur of human stupidity, has no patience with the irrational, and little interest in the messiness of relationships.

'I condemn no man or woman,' he declares, 'however savage and enormous their sins, as long as they do not touch the *Kreya*. But anything that touches the ship is different. In this small world, I am God. I judge, I punish, and I need not give my reasons.'

Olsen's philosophy is challenged in the extreme when, in mountainous seas, disaster strikes: the rudder smashed beyond repair, a mutiny, and the battered vessel adrift in the vast ocean, driven irrevocably northwards by wind and tide – until she comes to rest, at last, lodged in the great Arctic ice-pack.

ISBN: 978-0-9927686-4-5

www.thesylepress.com/the-white-voyage

by Sam Youd as John Christopher

THE POSSESSORS

When the storm rages and the avalanche cuts off power and phone lines, no one in the chalet is particularly bothered. There are kerosene lamps, a well-stocked bar and food supplies more than adequate to last them till the road to Nidenhaut can be opened up. They're on holiday after all, and once the weather clears they can carry on skiing.

They do not know, then, that deep within the Swiss Alps, something alien has stirred: an invasion so sly it can only be detected by principled reasoning.

The Possessors had a long memory … For aeons which were now uncountable their life had been bound up with the evanescent lives of the Possessed. Without them, they could not act or think, but through them they were the masters of this cold world.

ISBN: 978-1-911410-02-7

www.thesylepress.com/the-possessors

by Sam Youd as John Christopher

PENDULUM

*The sixties ... a foreign country: they did things differently then.
Or did they?*

An Englishman's home, supposedly, is his castle, and property
developer Rod Gawfrey was incensed when a gang of
hooligans gatecrashed his son's party, infiltrating the luxury
residence that was also home to his wife's parents and her
sister Jane.

He had no inkling then of the mayhem that was on its way, as
the nation's youth rose up in revolt, social order gave way to
anarchy, and he and his family were reduced to penury.

Jane hadn't seen it coming either, despite her professional and
more personal connection to Professor Walter Staunton, the
opportunist and lascivious academic bent on fomenting the
revolution.

A pendulum, though, once set in motion, must inevitably
swing back. And who would have guessed that Martin, Jane's
timid, God-fearing brother, would have a key role to play in
the vicious wave of righteous retribution that would next
sweep the land?

ISBN: 978-1-911410-04-1

www.thesylepress.com/pendulum

by Sam Youd

THE WINTER SWAN

In 1949, Sam Youd – who would later go on, as John Christopher, to write *The Death of Grass* and *The Tripods* – published his first novel. As he later said:

I knew first novels tended to be autobiographical and was determined to avoid that. So my main character was a woman, from a social milieu I only knew from books, and … [with] a story that progressed from grave to girlhood.

When Rosemary Hallam dies, what she longs for is the peace of non-existence. Instead, her disembodied spirit must travel back and back, through two world wars and the Depression to her Edwardian childhood, reliving her life through the eyes of her husbands, her sons and others less immune than she to the power of emotion. And the joys and the tragedies which had never quite touched her at the time now pose a real threat to the emotional aloofness she has always been strangely desperate to preserve.

'You remind me greatly of a swan, dear Mrs Hallam,' her elderly final suitor had declared, '… effortlessly graceful, and riding serenely over the troubling waves of the world as though they never existed.'

ISBN: 978-1-911410-06-5

www.thesylepress.com/the-winter-swan

by Sam Youd

Babel Itself

London in the late forties: strange shifting times in the aftermath of the war. A motley sample of humanity has washed up on the shores of the down-at-heel boarding house that is 36 Regency Gardens, their mutual proximity enforced by shared impoverishment.

Gentleman publisher Tennyson Glebe, no longer young, watches with mild interest as fellow residents go through the motions of seeking redemption, through politics, through art, through religion; the inconsequentiality of his present existence throwing the past into vivid relief.

And whilst Helen, as landlady, presides over the breakfast table, it is the unnaturally large hands of the diminutive Piers Marchant, Tennyson comes to realise, that seek to control the marionettes' strings – his own included.

Who was it, after all, who had decided that a séance or two might assuage the evening boredom before the nightly trip to the pub?

ISBN: 978-1-911410-08-9

www.thesylepress.com/babel-itself

by Sam Youd as Hilary Ford

SARNIA

Life holds no prospect of luxury or excitement after Sarnia's beloved mother dies: potential suitors vanish once they realise that marriage to the orphan will never bring a dowry. Yet her post as a lady clerk in a London banking house keeps the wolf from the door, and the admiration of her colleague, the worthy Michael, assures her if not of passion, then at least of affection.

Then the Jelains erupt into her humdrum routine, relatives she did not know she had, and whisk her away to the isle of Guernsey. At first she is enchanted by the exotic beauty of the island, by a life of balls and lavish entertainments where the officers of visiting regiments vie for her attention.

But Sarnia cannot quite feel at ease within this moneyed social hierarchy – especially in the unsettling presence of her cousin Edmund. And before long it becomes apparent that, beneath the glittering surface, lurk dark and menacing forces …

Her mother had scorned those of her sex who tamely submitted to male domination but, as the mystery of her heritage unfolds, Sarnia becomes all too painfully aware that the freedom she took for granted is slipping from her grasp.

ISBN: 978-0-9927686-0-7

www.thesylepress.com/sarnia

by Sam Youd as Hilary Ford

A BRIDE FOR BEDIVERE

'I cried the day my father died; but from joy.'

Jane's father had been nothing but a bully. His accidental death at the dockyard where he worked might have left the family in penury but it had also freed them from his drunken rages. He was scarcely cold in his grave, though, when another tyrant entered Jane's life.

Sir Donald Bedivere's offer to ease her mother's financial burden had but one condition: that Jane should leave her beloved home in Portsmouth and move to Cornwall as his adopted daughter.

To Sir Donald, Cornwall was King Arthur's country, and his magnificent home, Carmaliot, the place where Camelot once had stood. To Jane, for all its luxury it was a purgatory where her only friend was the lumbering Beast, with whom she roamed the moors.

Sir Donald had three sons, and Jane was quick to sum them up: John was pleasant enough, but indifferent to her. The burly, grinning Edgar she found loathsome. And Michael, on whom Sir Donald had pinned all his hopes, she disdained.

Sir Donald had plans for the Bedivere line – Jane wanted no part in them.

ISBN: 978-0-9927686-2-1

www.thesylepress.com/a-bride-for-bedivere

Made in the USA
Middletown, DE
14 February 2023

24842863R00158